Acclaim for Nam Le's

THE BOAT

"Le not only writes with an authority and poise rare even among longtime authors, but he also demonstrates an intuitive, gut-level ability to convey the psychological conflicts people experience when they find their own hopes and ambitions slamming up against familial expectations or the brute facts of history. . . . The opening story [is a] singular masterpiece." —*The New York Times*

"Tremendous, challenging and ambitious, worthy of the same shelf that holds *Dubliners* and *The Things They Carried*." —Charles D'Ambrosio

"Stunning. . . . Masterful. . . . Extraordinary. . . . These stories are so beautifully written and cross emotional barriers of time and place with such clear vision and strong command of language that we can only wonder with awe what Nam Le will offer us next." —*The Oregonian*

"Lyrical. . . . Powerful and assured. . . . Each tale a clean shot through the heart. [Le's] kaleidoscopic worldview . . . seamlessly blends cultural traditions, accents and landscapes that run from lush to barren." —*The Miami Herald*

"Captivating. . . . Heartrending. . . . A searing portrait of survival, love and sacrifice . . . revelatory and wise. . . . All of these stories break your heart in different ways, each as memorably as the others." —*The San Diego Union-Tribune*

NAM LE

THE BOAT

Nam Le was born in Vietnam and raised in Australia. He is the fiction editor of the *Harvard Review*. He splits his time between Australia and abroad.

www.namleonline.com

THE BOAT

NAM LE

Vintage Books
A Division of Random House, Inc.
New York

The Library of Congress has cataloged the Knopf edition as follows:
Le, Nam.
The boat / Nam Le. —1st ed.
p. cm.
I. Title.
PR9619.4.L398B63 2008
823'.92—dc22
2007037820

To—

Ta Thi Xuan Le, my mother
Le Huu Phuc, my father
and Truong and Victor, my brothers

Importunate along the dark
Horizon of immediacies
The flares of desperation rise.

—W. H. AUDEN

How strange that when the summons
came I always felt good.

—FRANK CONROY

Contents

THE BOAT

Love and Honor and Pity and Pride and Compassion and Sacrifice

MY FATHER ARRIVED ON A RAINY MORNING. I was dreaming about a poem, the dull *thluck thluck* of a typewriter's keys punching out the letters. It was a good poem—perhaps the best I'd ever written. When I woke up, he was standing outside my bedroom door, smiling ambiguously. He wore black trousers and a wet, wrinkled parachute jacket that looked like it had just been pulled out of a washing machine. Framed by the bedroom doorway, he appeared even smaller, gaunter, than I remembered. Still groggy with dream, I lifted my face toward the alarm clock.

"What time is it?"

"Hello, Son," he said in Vietnamese. "I knocked for a long time. Then the door just opened."

The fields are glass, I thought. Then tum-ti-ti, a dactyl, end line, then the words *excuse* and *alloy* in the line after. *Come on,* I thought.

"It's raining heavily," he said.

I frowned. The clock read 11:44. "I thought you weren't coming until this afternoon." It felt strange, after all this time, to be speaking Vietnamese again.

"They changed my flight in Los Angeles."

"Why didn't you ring?"

"I tried," he said equably. "No answer."

I twisted over the side of the bed and cracked open the window. The sound of rain filled the room—rain fell on the streets, on the roofs, on the tin shed across the parking lot like the distant detonations of firecrackers. Everything smelled of wet leaves.

"I turn the ringer off when I sleep," I said. "Sorry."

He continued smiling at me, significantly, as if waiting for an announcement.

"I was dreaming."

He used to wake me, when I was young, by standing over me and smacking my cheeks lightly. I hated it—the wetness, the sourness of his hands.

"Come on," he said, picking up a large Adidas duffel and a rolled bundle that looked like a sleeping bag. "A day lived, a sea of knowledge earned." He had a habit of speaking in Vietnamese proverbs. I had long since learned to ignore it.

I threw on a T-shirt and stretched my neck in front of the lone window. Through the rain, the sky was as gray and striated as graphite. *The fields are glass* . . . Like a shape in smoke, the poem blurred, then dissolved into this new, cold, strange reality: a wind-blown, rain-strafed parking lot; a dark room almost entirely taken up by my bed; the small body of my father dripping water onto hardwood floors.

I went to him, my legs goose-pimpled underneath my pajamas. He watched with pleasant indifference as my hand reached for his, shook it, then relieved his other hand of the bags. "You must be exhausted," I said.

He had flown from Sydney, Australia. Thirty-three hours all up—transiting in Auckland, Los Angeles, and Denver—before touching down in Iowa. I hadn't seen him in three years.

"You'll sleep in my room."

"Very fancy," he said, as he led me through my own apartment. "You even have a piano." He gave me an almost rueful smile. "I knew you'd never really quit." Something moved behind his face and I found myself back on a heightened stool with my fingers chasing the metronome, ahead and behind, trying to shut out the tutor's repeated sighing, his heavy brass ruler. I realized I was massaging my knuckles. My father patted the futon in my living room. "I'll sleep here."

"You'll sleep in my room, Ba." I watched him warily as he surveyed our surroundings, messy with books, papers, dirty plates, teacups, clothes—I'd intended to tidy up before going to the airport. "I work in this room anyway, and I work at night." As he moved into the kitchen, I grabbed the three-quarters-full bottle of Johnnie Walker from the second shelf of my bookcase and stashed it under the desk. I looked around. The desktop was gritty with cigarette ash. I threw some magazines over the roughest spots, then flipped one of them over because its cover bore a picture of Chairman Mao. I quickly gathered up the cigarette packs and sleeping pills and incense burners and dumped them all on a high shelf, behind my Kafka Vintage Classics.

At the kitchen swing door I remembered the photo of Linda beside the printer. Her glamour shot, I called it: hair windswept and eyes squinty, smiling at something out of frame. One of her ex-boyfriends had taken it at Lake MacBride. She looked happy. I snatched it and turned it facedown, covering it with scrap paper.

As I walked into the kitchen I thought, for a moment, that I'd left the fire escape open. I could hear rainwater gushing along gutters, down through the pipes. Then I saw my father at the sink, sleeves rolled up, sponge in hand, washing the month-old crusted mound of dishes. The smell was awful. "Ba," I frowned, "you don't need to do that."

His hands, hard and leathery, moved deftly in the sink.

"Ba," I said, halfheartedly.

"I'm almost finished." He looked up and smiled. "Have you eaten? Do you want me to make some lunch?"

"Thoi," I said, suddenly irritated. "You're exhausted. I'll go out and get us something."

I went back through the living room into my bedroom, picking up clothes and rubbish along the way.

"You don't have to worry about me," he called out. "You just do what you always do."

THE TRUTH WAS, he'd come at the worst possible time. I was in my last year at the Iowa Writers' Workshop; it was late November, and my final story for the semester was due in three days. I had a backlog of papers to grade and a heap of fellowship and job applications to draft and submit. It was no wonder I was drinking so much.

I'd told Linda only the previous night that he was coming. We were at her place. Her body was slippery with sweat and hard to hold. Her body smelled of her clothes. She turned me over, my face kissing the bedsheets, and then she was chopping my back with the edges of her hands. *Higher. Out a bit more.* She had trouble keeping a steady rhythm. "Softer," I told her. Moments later, I started laughing.

"What?"

The sheets were damp beneath my pressed face.

"What?"

"Softer," I said, "not *slower.*"

She slapped my back with the meat of her palms, hard—once, twice. I couldn't stop laughing. I squirmed over and caught her by the wrists. Hunched forward, she was blushing and beautiful. Her hair fell over her face; beneath its ash-blond hem all I could see were her open lips. She pressed down, into me, her shoulders kinking the long, lean curve from the back of her neck to the small of her back. "Stop it!" her lips said. She wrested her hands free. Her fingers beneath my waistband, violent, the scratch of her nails down my thighs, knees, ankles. I pointed my foot like a ballet dancer.

Afterward, I told her my father didn't know about her. She

said nothing. "We just don't talk about that kind of stuff," I explained. She looked like an actress who looked like my girl-friend. Staring at her face made me tired. I'd begun to feel this way more often around her. "He's only here for three days." Somewhere out of sight, a group of college boys hooted and yelled.

"I thought you didn't talk to him at all."

"He's my father."

"What's he want?"

I rolled toward her, onto my elbow. I tried to remember how much I'd told her about him. We'd been lying on the bed, the wind loud in the room—I remember that—and we were both tipsy. Ours could have been any two voices in the darkness. "It's only three days," I said.

The look on her face was strange, shut down. She considered me a long time. Then she got up and pulled on her clothes. "Just make sure you get your story done," she said.

I DRANK BEFORE I CAME HERE TOO. I drank when I was a student at university, and then when I was a lawyer—in my pre-vious life, as they say. There was a subterranean bar in a hotel next to my work, and every night I would wander down and slump on a barstool and pretend I didn't want the bartender to make small talk. He was only a bit older than me, and I came to envy his ease, his confidence that any given situation was merely temporary. I left exorbitant tips. After a while I was treated to battered shrimps and shepherd's pies on the house. My parents had already split by then, my father moving to Sydney, my mother into a government flat.

That's all I've ever done, traffic in words. Sometimes I still think about word counts the way a general must think about casualties. I'd been in Iowa more than a year—days passed in weeks, then months, more than a year of days—and I'd written only three and a half stories. About seventeen thousand words. When I was working at the law firm, I would have written that many words in a couple of weeks. And they would have been useful to someone.

Deadlines came, exhausting, and I forced myself up to meet them. Then, in the great spans of time between, I fell back to my vacant screen and my slowly sludging mind. I tried everything—writing in longhand, writing in my bed, in my bathtub. As this last deadline approached, I remembered a friend claiming he'd broken his writer's block by switching to a typewriter. You're free to write, he told me, once you know you can't delete what you've written. I bought an electric Smith Corona at an antique shop. It buzzed like a tropical aquarium when I plugged it in. It looked good on my desk. For inspiration, I read absurdly formal Victorian poetry and drank Scotch neat. How hard could it be? Things happened in this world all the time. All I had to do was record them. In the sky, two swarms of swallows converged, pulled apart, interwove again like veils drifting at crosscurrents. In line at the supermarket, a black woman leaned forward and kissed the handle of her shopping cart, her skin dark and glossy like the polished wood of a piano.

The week prior to my father's arrival, a friend chastised me for my persistent defeatism.

"Writer's block?" Under the streetlights, vapors of bourbon puffed out of his mouth. "How can you have writer's block? Just write a story about Vietnam."

We had just come from a party following a reading by the workshop's most recent success, a Chinese woman trying to immigrate to America who had written a book of short stories about Chinese characters in stages of immigration to America. The stories were subtle and good. The gossip was that she'd been offered a substantial six-figure contract for a two-book deal. It was meant to be an unspoken rule that such things were left unspoken. Of course, it was all anyone talked about.

"It's hot," a writing instructor told me at a bar. "Ethnic literature's hot. And important too."

A couple of visiting literary agents took a similar view: "There's a lot of polished writing around," one of them said. "You have to ask yourself, what makes me stand out?" She tag-teamed to her colleague, who answered slowly as though intoning a mantra, "Your *background* and *life experience.*"

Other friends were more forthright: "I'm sick of ethnic lit," one said. "It's full of descriptions of exotic food." Or: "You can't tell if the language is spare because the author intended it that way, or because he didn't have the vocab."

I was told about a friend of a friend, a Harvard graduate from Washington, D.C., who had posed in traditional Nigerian garb for his book-jacket photo. I pictured myself standing in a rice paddy, wearing a straw conical hat. Then I pictured my father in the same field, wearing his threadbare fatigues, young and hard-eyed.

"It's a license to bore," my friend said. We were drunk and walking our bikes because both of us, separately, had punctured our tires on the way to the party.

"The characters are always flat, generic. As long as a Chinese writer writes about *Chinese* people, or a Peruvian writer about *Peruvians,* or a Russian writer about *Russians* . . ." he said, as though reciting children's doggerel, then stopped, losing his train of thought. His mouth turned up into a doubtful grin. I could tell he was angry about something.

"Look," I said, pointing at a floodlit porch ahead of us. "Those guys have guns."

"As long as there's an interesting image or metaphor once in every *this* much text"—he held out his thumb and forefinger to indicate half a page, his bike wobbling all over the sidewalk. I nodded to him, and then I nodded to one of the guys on the porch, who nodded back. The other guy waved us through with his faux-wood air rifle. A car with its headlights on was idling in the driveway, and girls' voices emerged from inside, squealing, "Don't shoot! Don't shoot!"

"Faulkner, you know," my friend said over the squeals, "he said we should write about the old verities. Love and honor and pity and pride and compassion and sacrifice." A sudden sharp crack behind us, like the striking of a giant typewriter hammer, followed by some muffled shrieks. "I know I'm a bad person for saying this," my friend said, "but that's why I don't mind your work, Nam. Because you could just write about Vietnamese boat people all the time. Like in your third story."

He must have thought my head was bowed in modesty, but in fact I was figuring out whether I'd just been shot in the back of the thigh. I'd felt a distinct sting. The pellet might have ricocheted off something.

"You could *totally* exploit the Vietnamese thing. But *instead,* you choose to write about lesbian vampires and Colombian assassins, and Hiroshima orphans—and New York painters with hemorrhoids."

For a dreamlike moment I was taken aback. Cataloged like that, under the bourbon stink of his breath, my stories sank into unflattering relief. My leg was still stinging. I imagined sticking my hand down the back of my jeans, bringing it to my face under a streetlight, and finding it gory, blood-spattered. I imagined turning around, advancing wordlessly up the porch steps, and drop-kicking the two kids. I would tell my story into a microphone from a hospital bed. I would compose my story in a county cell. I would kill one of them, maybe accidentally, and never talk about it, ever, to anyone. There was no hole in my jeans.

"I'm probably a bad person," my friend said, stumbling beside his bike a few steps in front of me.

IF YOU ASK ME WHY I CAME TO IOWA, I would say that Iowa is beautiful in the way that any place is beautiful: if you treat it as the answer to a question you're asking yourself every day, just by being there.

That afternoon, as I was leaving the apartment for Linda's, my father called out my name from the bedroom.

I stopped outside the closed door. He was meant to be napping.

"Where are you going?" his voice said.

"For a walk," I replied.

"I'll walk with you."

It always struck me how everything seemed larger in scale on Summit Street: the double-storied houses, their smooth lawns sloping down to the sidewalks like golf greens; elm trees with high, thick branches—the sort of branches from which I imagined fathers suspending long-roped swings for daughters in white dresses. The leaves, once golden and red, were turning brown, dark orange. The rain had stopped. I don't know why, but we walked in the middle of the road, dark asphalt gleaming beneath the slick, pasted leaves like the back of a whale.

I asked him, "What do you want to do while you're here?"

His face was pale and fixed in a smile. "Don't worry about me," he said. "I can just meditate. Or read."

"There's a coffee shop downtown," I said. "And a Japanese restaurant." It sounded pathetic. It occurred to me that I knew nothing about what my father did all day.

He kept smiling, looking at the ground moving in front of his feet.

"I have to write," I said.

"You write."

And I could no longer read his smile. He had perfected it during our separation. It was a setting of the lips, sly, almost imperceptible, which I would probably have taken for a sign of senility
but for the keenness of his eyes.

"There's an art museum across the river," I said.

"Ah, take me there."

"The museum?"

"No," he said, looking sideways at me. "The river."

We turned back to Burlington Street and walked down the
hill to the river. He stopped halfway across the bridge. The water
below looked cold and black, slowing in sections as it succumbed
to the temperature. Behind us six lanes of cars skidded back and
forth across the wet grit of the road, the sound like the shredding
of wind.

"Have you heard from your mother?" He stood upright before
the railing, his head strangely small above the puffy down jacket
I had lent him.

"Every now and then."

He lapsed into formal Vietnamese: "How is the mother of
Nam?"

"She is good," I said—too loudly—trying to make myself
heard over the groans and clanks of a passing truck.

He was nodding. Behind him, the east bank of the river
glowed wanly in the afternoon light. "Come on," I said. We
crossed the bridge and walked to a nearby Dairy Queen. When
I came out, two coffees in my hands, my father had gone down
to the river's edge. Next to him, a bundled-up, bearded figure
stooped over a burning gasoline drum. Never had I seen anything like it in Iowa City.

"This is my son," my father said, once I had scrambled down
the wet bank. "The writer." I glanced quickly at him but his face
gave nothing away. He lifted a hot paper cup out of my hand.
"Would you like some coffee?"

"Thank you, no." The man stood still, watching his knotted hands, palms glowing orange above the rim of the drum. His voice was soft, his clothes heavy with his life. I smelled animals in him, and fuel, and rain.

"I read his story," my father went on in his lilting English, "about Vietnamese boat people." He gazed at the man, straight into his blank, rheumy eyes, then said, as though delivering a punch line, "*We* are Vietnamese boat people."

We stood there for a long time, the three of us, watching the flames. When I lifted my eyes it was dark.

"Do you have any money on you?" my father asked me in Vietnamese.

"Welcome to America," the man said through his beard. He didn't look up as I closed his fist around the damp bills.

MY FATHER WAS DRAWN TO WEAKNESS, even as he tolerated none in me. He was a soldier, he said once, as if that explained everything. With me, he was all proverbs and regulations. No personal phone calls. No female friends. No extracurricular reading. When I was in primary school, he made me draw up a daily ten-hour study timetable for the summer holidays, and punished me when I deviated from it. He knew how to cane me twenty times and leave only one black-red welt, like a brand mark across my buttocks. Afterward, as he rubbed Tiger Balm on the wound, I would cry in anger at myself for crying. Once, when my mother let slip that durian fruit made me vomit, he forced me to eat it in front of guests. *Doi an muoi cung ngon.* Hunger finds no fault with food. I learned to hate him with a straight face.

When I was fourteen, I discovered that he had been involved in a massacre. Later, I would come across photos and transcripts and books; but that night, at a family friend's party in suburban

Melbourne, it was just another story in a circle of drunken men. They sat cross-legged on newspapers around a large blue tarpaulin, getting smashed on cheap beer. It was that time of night when things started to break up against other things. Red faces, raised voices, spilled drinks. We arrived late and the men shuffled around, making room for my father.

"Thanh! Fuck your mother! What took you so long—scared, no? Sit down, sit down—"

"Give him five bottles." The speaker swung around ferociously. "We're letting you off easy, everyone here's had eight, nine already."

For the first time, my father let me stay. I sat on the perimeter of the circle, watching in fascination. A thicket of Vietnamese voices, cursing, toasting, braying about their children, making fun of one man who kept stuttering, "It has the power of f-f-five hundred horses!" Through it all my father laughed good-naturedly, his face so red with drink he looked sunburned. Bowl and chopsticks in his hands, he appeared somewhat childish squashed between two men trading war stories. I watched him as he picked sparingly at the enormous spread of dishes in the middle of the circle. The food was known as *do nhau:* alcohol food. Massive fatty oysters dipped in salt-pepper-lemon paste. Boiled sea snails the size of pool balls. Southern-style shredded chicken salad, soaked in vinegar and eaten with spotty brown rice crackers. Someone called out my father's name; he had set his chopsticks down and was speaking in a low voice:

"Heavens, the gunships came first, rockets and M6os. You remember that sound, no? Like you were deaf. We were hiding in the bunker underneath the temple, my mother and four sisters and Mrs. Tran, the baker, and some other people. You couldn't hear anything. Then the gunfire stopped and Mrs. Tran told my mother we had to go up to the street. If we stayed there, the Americans would think we were Viet Cong. 'I'm not going anywhere,' my mother said. 'They have grenades,' Mrs. Tran said. I was scared and excited. I had never seen an American before."

It took me a while to reconcile my father with the story he was telling. He caught my eye and held it a moment, as though he were sharing a secret with me. He was drunk.

"So we went up. Everywhere there was dust and smoke, and all you could hear was the sound of helicopters and M16s. Houses on fire. Then through the smoke I saw an American. I almost laughed. He wore his uniform so untidily—it was too big for him—and he had a beaded necklace and a baseball cap. He held an M16 over his shoulder like a spade. Heavens, he looked nothing like the Viet Cong, with their shirts buttoned up to their chins—and tucked in—even after crawling through mud tunnels all day."

He picked up his chopsticks and reached for the *tiet canh*—a specialty—mincemeat soaked in fresh congealed duck blood. Some of the other men were listening now, smiling knowingly. I saw his teeth, stained red, as he chewed through the rest of his words:

"They made us walk to the east side of the village. There were about ten of them, about fifty of us. Mrs. Tran was saying, 'No VC no VC.' They didn't hear her, not over the sound of machine guns and the M79 grenade launchers. Remember those? Only I heard her. I saw pieces of animals all over the paddy fields, a water buffalo with its side missing—like it was scooped out by a spoon. Then, through the smoke, I saw Grandpa Long bowing to a GI in the traditional greeting. I wanted to call out to him. His wife and daughter and granddaughters, My and Kim, stood shyly behind him. The GI stepped forward, tapped the top of his head with the rifle butt and then twirled the gun around and slid the bayonet into his throat. No one said anything. My mother tried to cover my eyes, but I saw him switch the fire selector on his gun from automatic to single-shot before he shot Grandma

Long. Then he and a friend pulled the daughter into a shack, the two little girls dragged along, clinging to her legs.

"They stopped us at the drainage ditch, near the bridge. There were bodies on the road, a baby with only the bottom half of its head, a monk, his robe turning pink. I saw two bodies with the ace of spades carved into the chests. I didn't understand it. My sisters didn't even cry. People were now shouting, 'No VC no VC,' but the Americans just frowned and spat and laughed. One of them said something, then some of them started pushing us into the ditch. It was half full of muddy water. My mother jumped in and lifted my sisters down, one by one. I remember looking up and seeing helicopters everywhere, some bigger than others, some higher up. They made us kneel in the water. They set up their guns on tripods. They made us stand up again. One of the Americans, a boy with a fat face, was crying and moaning softly as he reloaded his magazine. 'No VC no VC.' They didn't look at us. They made us turn back around. They made us kneel back down in the water. When they started shooting I felt my mother's body jumping on top of mine; it kept jumping for a long time, and then everywhere was the sound of helicopters, louder and louder like they were all coming down to land, and everything was dark and wet and warm and sweet."

The circle had gone quiet. My mother came out from the kitchen, squatted behind my father, and looped her arms around his neck. This was a minor breach of the rules. "Heavens," she said, "don't you men have anything better to talk about?"

After a short silence, someone snorted, saying loudly, "You win, Thanh. You really *did* have it bad!" and then everyone, including my father, burst out laughing. I joined in unsurely. They clinked glasses and made toasts using words I didn't understand.

Maybe he didn't tell it exactly that way. Maybe I'm filling in the gaps. But you're not under oath when writing a eulogy, and this is close enough. My father grew up in the province of Quang Ngai, in the village of Son My, in the hamlet of Tu Cung, later known to the Americans as My Lai. He was fourteen years old.

LATE THAT NIGHT, I plugged in the Smith Corona. It hummed with promise. I grabbed the bottle of Scotch from under the desk and poured myself a double. *Fuck it,* I thought. I had two and a half days left. I would write the ethnic story of my Vietnamese father. It was a good story. It was a fucking *great* story.

I fed in a sheet of blank paper. At the top of the page, I typed "ETHNIC STORY" in capital letters. I pushed the carriage return and scrolled down to the next line. The sound of helicopters in a dark sky. The keys hammered the page.

I WOKE UP LATE THE NEXT DAY. At the coffee shop, I sat with my typed pages and watched people come and go. They laughed and sat and sipped and talked and, listening to them, I was reminded again that I was in a small town in a foreign country.

I thought of my father in my dusky bedroom. He had kept the door closed as I left. I thought of how he had looked when I checked on him before going to bed: his body engulfed by blankets and his head so small among my pillows. He'd aged in those last three years. His skin glassy in the blue glow of dawn. He was here, now, with me, and already making the rest of my life seem unreal.

I read over what I had typed: thinking of him at that age, still a boy, and who he would become. At a nearby table, a guy held out one of his iPod earbuds and beckoned his date to come around and sit beside him. The door opened and a cold wind blew in. I tried to concentrate.

"Hey." It was Linda, wearing a large orange hiking jacket and bringing with her the crisp, bracing scent of all the places she had been. Her face was unmaking a smile. "What are you doing here?"

"Working on my story."

"Is your dad here?"

"No."

Her friends were waiting by the counter. She nodded to them, holding up one finger, then came behind me, resting her hands on my shoulders. "Is this it?" She leaned over me, her hair grazing my face, cold and silken against my cheek. She picked up a couple of pages and read them soundlessly. "I don't get it," she said, returning them to the table. "What are you doing?"

"What do you mean?"

"You never told me any of this."

I shrugged.

"Did he tell you this? Now he's talking to you?"

"Not really," I said.

"Not really?"

I turned around to face her. Her eyes reflected no light.

"You know what I think?" She looked back down at the pages. "I think you're making excuses for him."

"Excuses?"

"You're romanticizing his past," she went on quietly, "to make sense of the things you said he did to you."

"It's a story," I said. "What things did I say?"

"You said he abused you."

It was too much, these words, and what connected to them. I looked at her serious, beautifully lined face, her light-trapping eyes, and already I felt them taxing me. "I never said that."

She took a half step back. "Just tell me this," she said, her voice flattening. "You've never introduced him to any of your exes, right?" The question was tight on her face.

I didn't say anything and after a while she nodded, biting one corner of her upper lip. I knew that gesture. I knew, even then, that I was supposed to stand up, pull her orange-jacketed body toward mine, speak words into her ear; but all I could do was think about my father and his excuses. Those tattered bodies on top of him. The ten hours he'd waited, mud filling his lungs, until nightfall. I felt myself falling back into old habits.

She stepped forward and kissed the top of my head. It was one of her rules: not to walk away from an argument without some sign of affection. I didn't look at her. My mother liked to tell the story of how, when our family first arrived in Australia, we lived in a hostel on an outer-suburb street where the locals— whenever they met or parted—hugged and kissed each other warmly. How my father—baffled, charmed—had named it "the street of lovers."

I turned to the window: it was dark now, the evening settling thick and deep. A man and woman sat across from each other at a high table. The woman leaned in, smiling, her breasts squat on the wood, elbows forward, her hands mere inches away from the man's shirtfront. Throughout their conversation her teeth glinted. Behind them, a mother sat with her son. "I'm not playing," she murmured, flipping through her magazine.

"L," said the boy.

"I said I'm not playing."

HERE IS WHAT I BELIEVE: We forgive any sacrifice by our parents, so long as it is not made in our name. To my father there was no other name—only mine, and he had named me after the homeland he had given up. His sacrifice was complete and compelled him to everything that happened. To all that, I was inadequate.

At sixteen I left home. There was a girl, and crystal meth, and the possibility of greater loss than I had imagined possible. She embodied everything prohibited by my father and plainly worthwhile. Of course he was right about her: she taught me hurt—but promise too. We were two animals in the dark, hacking at one another, and never since have I felt that way—that sense of consecration. When my father found out my mother was supporting me, he gave her an ultimatum. She moved into a family friend's textile factory and learned to use an overlock machine and continued sending me money.

"Of course I want to live with him," she told me when I visited her, months later. "But I want you to come home too."

"Ba doesn't want that."

"You're his son," she said simply. "He wants you with him."

I laundered my school uniform and asked a friend to cut my hair and waited for school hours to finish before catching the train home. My father excused himself upon seeing me. When he returned to the living room he had changed his shirt and there was water in his hair. I felt sick and fully awake—as if all the previous months had been a single sleep and now my face was wet again, burning cold. The room smelled of peppermint. He asked me if I was well, and I told him I was, and then he asked me if my female friend was well, and at that moment I realized he was speaking to me not as a father—not as he would to his only son—but as he would speak to a friend, to anyone, and it undid me. I had learned what it was to attenuate my blood but that was nothing compared to this. I forced myself to look at him and I asked him to bring Ma back home.

"And Child?"

"Child will not take any more money from Ma."

"Come home," he said, finally. His voice was strangled, half swallowed.

Even then, my emotions operated like a system of levers and pulleys; just seeing him had set them irreversibly into motion. "No," I said. The word shot out of me.

"Come home, and Ma will come home, and Ba promises Child to never speak of any of this again." He looked away, smiling heavily, and took out a handkerchief. His forehead was moist with sweat. He had been buried alive in the warm, wet clinch of his family, crushed by their lives. I wanted to know how he climbed out of that pit. I wanted to know how there could ever be any correspondence between us. I wanted to know all this but an internal momentum moved me, further and further from him as time went on.

"The world is hard," he said. For a moment I was uncertain whether he was speaking in proverbs. He looked at me, his face a gleaming mask. "Just say yes, and we can forget everything. That's all. Just say it: Yes."

But I didn't say it. Not that day, nor the next, nor any day for almost a year. When I did, though, rehabilitated and fixed in new privacies, he was true to his word and never spoke of the matter. In fact, after I came back home he never spoke of anything much at all, and it was under this learned silence that the three of us—my father, my mother, and I, living again under a single roof—were conducted irreparably into our separate lives.

THE APARTMENT SMELLED of fried garlic and sesame oil when I returned. My father was sitting on the living room floor, on the special mattress he had brought over with him. It was made of white foam. He told me it was for his back. "There's some stir-fry in the kitchen."

"Thanks."

"I read your story this morning," he said, "while you were

still sleeping." Something in my stomach folded over. I hadn't thought to hide the pages. "There are mistakes in it."

"You read it?"

"There were mistakes in your last story too."

My last story. I remembered my mother's phone call at the time: my father, unemployed and living alone in Sydney, had started sending long emails to friends from his past—friends from thirty, forty years ago. I should talk to him more often, she'd said. I'd sent him my refugee story. He hadn't responded. Now, as I came out of the kitchen with a heaped plate of stir-fry, I tried to recall those sections where I'd been sloppy with research. Maybe the scene in Rach Gia—before they reached the boat. I scooped up a forkful of marinated tofu, cashews, and chickpeas. He'd gone shopping. "They're *stories*," I said, chewing casually. "Fiction."

He paused for a moment, then said, "Okay, Son."

For so long my diet had consisted of chips and noodles and pizzas I'd forgotten how much I missed home cooking. As I ate, he stretched on his white mat.

"How's your back?"

"I had a CAT scan," he said. "There's nerve fluid leaking between my vertebrae." He smiled his long-suffering smile, right leg twisted across his left hip. "I brought the scans to show you."

"Does it hurt, Ba?"

"It hurts." He chuckled briefly, as though the whole matter were a joke. "But what can I do? I can only accept it."

"Can't they operate?"

I felt myself losing interest. I was a bad son. He'd separated from my mother when I started law school and ever since then he'd brought up his back pains so often—always couched in Buddhist tenets of suffering and acceptance—that the cold, hard part of me suspected he was exaggerating, to solicit and then gently rebuke my concern. He did this. He'd forced me to take karate lessons until I was sixteen; then, during one of our final arguments, he came at me and I found myself in fighting stance. He had smiled at my horror. "That's right," he'd said. We were locked in all the intricate ways of guilt. It took all the time we had to realize that everything we faced, we faced for the other as well.

"I want to talk with you," I said.

"You grow old, your body breaks down," he said.

"No, I mean for the story."

"Talk?"

"Yes."

"About what?" He seemed amused.

"About my mistakes," I said.

IF YOU ASK ME WHY I CAME TO IOWA, I would say that I was a lawyer and I was no lawyer. Every twenty-four hours I woke up at the smoggiest time of morning and commuted—bus, tram, elevator, without saying a single word, wearing clothes that chafed and holding a flat white in a white cup—to my windowless office in the tallest, most glass-covered building in Melbourne. Time was broken down into six-minute units, friends allotted eight-unit lunch breaks. I hated what I was doing and I hated that I was good at it. Mostly, I hated knowing it was my job that made my father proud of me. When I told him I was quitting and going to Iowa to be a writer, he said, *"Trau buoc ghet trau an."* The captive buffalo hates the free buffalo. But by that time he had no more control over my life. I was twenty-five years old.

The thing is not to write what no one else could have written, but to write what only you could have written. I recently found this fragment in one of my old notebooks. The person who wrote that couldn't have known what would happen: how time can hold itself against you, how a voice hollows, how words you once loved can wither on the page.

"Why do you want to write this story?" my father asked me.

"It's a good story."

"But there are so many things you could write about."

"This is important, Ba. It's important that people know."

"You want their pity."

I didn't know whether it was a question. I was offended. "I want them to remember," I said.

He was silent for a long time. Then he said, "Only you'll remember. I'll remember. They will read and clap their hands and forget." For once, he was not smiling. "Sometimes it's better to forget, no?"

"I'll write it anyway," I said. It came back to me—how I'd felt at the typewriter the previous night. A thought leapt into my mind: "If I write a true story," I told my father, "I'll have a better chance of selling it."

He looked at me a while, searchingly, seeing something in my face as though for the first time. Finally he said, in a measured voice, "I'll tell you." For a moment he receded into thought. "But believe me, it's not something you'll be able to write."

"I'll write it anyway," I repeated.

Then he did something unexpected. His face opened up and he began to laugh, without self-pity or slyness, laughing in full-bodied breaths. I was shocked. I hadn't heard him laugh like this for as long as I could remember. Without fully knowing why, I started laughing too. His throat was humming in Vietnamese, "Yes . . . yes . . . yes," his eyes shining, smiling. "All right. All right. But tomorrow."

"But—"

"I need to think," he said. He shook his head, then said under his breath, "My son a writer. *Co thuc moi vuc duoc dao.*" How far does an empty stomach drag you?

"Mot nguoi lam quan, ca ho duoc nho," I retorted. A scholar is a blessing for all his relatives. He looked at me in surprise before laughing again and nodding vigorously. I'd been saving that one up for years.

AFTERNOON. We sat across from one another at the dining room table: I asked questions and took notes on a yellow legal pad; he talked. He talked about his childhood, his family. He talked about My Lai. At this point, he stopped.

"You won't offer your father some of that?"

"What?"

"Heavens, you think you can hide liquor of that quality?"

The afternoon light came through the window and held his body in a silver square, slowly sinking toward his feet, dimming, as he talked. I refilled our glasses. He talked above the peak-hour traffic on the streets, its rinse of noise; he talked deep into evening. When the phone rang the second time I unplugged it from the jack. He told me how he'd been conscripted into the South Vietnamese army.

"After what the Americans did? How could you fight on their side?"

"I had nothing but hate in me," he said, "but I had enough for everyone." He paused on the word *hate* like a father saying it before his infant child for the first time, trying the child's knowledge, testing what was inherent in the word and what learned.

He told me about the war. He told me about meeting my mother. The wedding. Then the fall of Saigon. 1975. He told me about his imprisonment in reeducation camp, the forced confessions, the indoctrinations, the starvations. The daily labor that ruined his back. The casual killings. He told me about the tiger-cage cells and connex boxes, the different names for different forms of torture: the honda, the airplane, the auto. "They tie you by your thumbs, one arm over the shoulder, the other pulled around the front of the body. Or they stretch out your legs and tie your middle fingers to your big toes—"

He showed me. A skinny old man in Tantric poses, he looked faintly preposterous. During the auto he flinched, then, a smile springing to his face, asked me to help him to his foam mattress. I waited impatiently for him to stretch it out. He asked me again to help. *Here, push here. A little harder.* Then he went on talking, sometimes in a low voice, sometimes grinning. Other times he would blink—furiously, perplexedly. In spite of his Buddhist protestations, I imagined him locked in rage, turned around and forced every day to rewitness these atrocities of his past, helpless to act. But that was only my imagination. I had nothing to prove that he was not empty of all that now.

He told me how, upon his release after three years' incarcera-tion, he organized our family's escape from Vietnam. This was 1979. He was twenty-five years old then, and my father.

When finally he fell asleep, his face warm from the Scotch, I watched him from the bedroom doorway. I was drunk. For a moment, watching him, I felt like I had drifted into dream too. For a moment I became my father, watching his sleeping son, reminded of what—for his son's sake—he had tried, unceasingly, to forget. A past larger than complaint, more perilous than mem-ory. I shook myself conscious and went to my desk. I read my notes through once, carefully, all forty-five pages. I reread the draft of my story from two nights earlier. Then I put them both aside and started typing, never looking at them again.

Dawn came so gradually I didn't notice—until the beeping of a garbage truck—that outside the air was metallic blue and the

ground was white. The top of the tin shed was white. The first
snow had fallen.

HE WASN'T IN THE APARTMENT when I woke up. There was
a note on the coffee table: *I am going for a walk. I have taken
your story to read.* I sat outside, on the fire escape, with a tum-
bler of Scotch, waiting for him. Against the cold, I drank my
whisky, letting it flow like a filament of warmth through my
body. I had slept for only three hours and was too tired to feel
anything but peace. The red geraniums on the landing of the
opposite building were frosted over. I spied through my neighbors' windows and saw exactly nothing.

He would read it, with his book-learned English, and he
would recognize himself in a new way. He would recognize me.
He would see how powerful was his experience, how valuable
his suffering—how I had made it speak for more than itself. He
would be pleased with me.

I finished the Scotch. It was eleven-thirty and the sky was
dark and gray-smeared. My story was due at midday. I put my
gloves on, treaded carefully down the fire escape, and untangled
my bike from the rack. He would be pleased with me. I rode
around the block, up and down Summit Street, looking for a sign
of my puffy jacket. The streets were empty. Most of the snow
had melted, but an icy film covered the roads and I rode slowly.
Eyes stinging and breath fogging in front of my mouth, I coasted
toward downtown, across the College Green, the grass frozen so
stiff it snapped beneath my bicycle wheels. Lights glowed dimly
from behind the curtained windows of houses. On Washington
Street, a sudden gust of wind ravaged the elm branches and
unfastened their leaves, floating them down thick and slow and
soundless.

I was halfway across the bridge when I saw him. I stopped. He was on the riverbank. I couldn't make out the face but it was he, short and small-headed in my bloated jacket. He stood with the tramp, both of them staring into the blazing gasoline drum. The smoke was thick, particulate. For a second I stopped breathing. I knew with sick certainty what he had done. The ashes, given body by the wind, floated away from me down the river. He patted the man on the shoulder, reached into his back pocket and slipped some money into those large, newly mittened hands. He started up the bank then, and saw me. I was so full of wanting I thought it would flood my heart. His hands were empty.

If I had known then what I knew later, I wouldn't have said the things I did. I wouldn't have told him he didn't understand— for clearly, he did. I wouldn't have told him that what he had done was unforgivable. That I wished he had never come, or that he was no father to me. But I hadn't known, and, as I waited, feeling the wind change, all I saw was a man coming toward me in a ridiculously oversized jacket, rubbing his black-sooted hands, stepping through the smoke with its flecks and flame-tinged eddies, who had destroyed himself, yet again, in my name. The river was behind him. The wind was full of acid. In the slow float of light I looked away, down at the river. On the brink of freezing, it gleamed in large, bulging blisters. The water, where it still moved, was black and braided. And it occurred to me then how it took hours, sometimes days, for the surface of a river to freeze over—to hold in its skin the perfect and crystalline world—and how that world could be shattered by a small stone dropped like a single syllable.

Cartagena

IN CARTAGENA, LUIS SAYS, the beach is gray at dawn. He points to the barrel of his G3 when he says this, *steel gray,* he says. He smiles. The sand is white, he says, this color, tapping his teeth. And when the sun comes up on your right, man, it is a slow-motion explosion like in the movies, a big kerosene flash and then the water is sparkling gray and orange and red. Luis is full of shit, of course, but he can talk and it is true that he is the only one of our *gallada* who has seen the Caribbean. Who has been to Cartagena.

And the girls? Eduardo asks.

Luis tosses back his greasy black hair. He knows we will wait for his answer. He is the oldest of us (except for Claudia, who doesn't count because she is a girl), and he has told this story many times with pleasure.

The girls, he says. He looks at me and it is proper, he is showing respect. Together we smirk at the immaturity of Eduardo.

No, says Claudia. The fishermen. Tell us the part—

The girls, Luis says, speaking over Claudia, they are the best in all of Colombia. They wear skirts up to here, like on MTV, and boots up to here, and it is not like the country, where the *autodefensas* will shoot them for it. They are taller and whiter and have beautiful teeth and can talk about real things. Nothing like here.

He pauses. Luis has grown a mustache that looks like it has been drawn on with wet charcoal, and now he strokes it with his thumb and finger. I remember a line from a movie.

With that mustache, I say, you look like a shit-eating faggot. Eduardo laughs happily. And it is you who would be shot for your long hair.

Luis ignores me. He says, speaking slowly, In Cartagena, everything is nothing like here.

We are five, including Claudia, and we are going downtown to do some business on behalf of Luis. Apart from me and Luis and Claudia and Eduardo, there is little Pedro, who walks behind the group with his hands in his torn pants pockets in order to fondle his testicles. It is not even funny anymore.

I have not seen any of them, except for Claudia, in the last four months. Claudia—the only one who knows where I have been staying—told me yesterday about this business. I did not want to come but she told me how strongly Luis had insisted.

They look younger than I remember. Only Pedro has grown— he looks like he has been seized by a fistful of hair and stretched up two inches. I wait for him to reach me and say to him, *Ay,* you are almost a man now!

Ask him if he has any hair on his *pipí,* says Eduardo.

Pedro keeps his hands in his pockets and does not react.

See, even now he is molesting it!

Come on, says Luis. He sounds distracted. Claudia is smiling to herself. I look away from her.

To do this business there would usually be more of us, but our old *gallada,* the core of it anyway, is three short. Carlos was shot in the throat outside the Parque del Poblado: it was night and he was selling *basuco* to the crackheads when the rich kids came in their yellow jeep and cleansed him. Salésio joined his elder brother in the local militia, where he sent back a photo of himself in a balaclava, holding an Uzi sub and a Beretta .45. You could see the shape of his stupid smile through the black cotton.

And then there is Hernando. I do not want to think about Hernando now.

We stop at the border of our barrio, in a dump at the bottom of a ridge. A thin ditch of water runs through the debris. Without a word, Pedro and Claudia take lookout positions. Luis and Eduardo straddle the sludge, one foot on either bank, and clear away the moldering cardboard and plastic junk. Soon they uncover the nylon three-seater that we stole, months ago, from a public bus. They tip it forward to reveal the large concrete tunnel into which the water runs. I stand sentinel as they crawl, one by one, into the hole.

This is one of our old *mocós*. Only the five of us know its location. It is a runoff from the main storm sewer, but smells like a sewage pipe. I am glad it is dark.

Over there, I say.

Eduardo and Pedro go where I point, navigating by the blue light of their cell phones. At a waist-high ledge they peel back a thick, water-resistant cover, and Pedro lets out a whoop, then muffles his mouth. The sound echoes against the wet concrete.

Luis grins. You come back after four months, he says, and already you think you are the dog's balls. He is grinning widely. These are yours?

On trust, I say.

Handheld grenades, he says, picking them up, weighing them in his palm like they are pieces of fruit. A new AR-15. And these?

Glock nine millimeters. You can throw away your thirty-eights now.

I heard the forty-fives are better.

They look like toy guns, Claudia murmurs from the darkness.

Well, Luis says to me, still grinning. Well, well. El Padre is a generous man.

Aside from Luis's G3, we take one of the Colts and the two pistols. As this is Luis's mission, I do not ask whether this is too much or too little firepower. Pedro is a child and will carry the bullet bag. He insists on bringing a couple of grenades. Just in case, he says.

In case what? jeers Eduardo. In case the target is hiding inside a FARC tank?

It is getting dark when we finally arrive in the correct neighborhood. We are on foreign turf and I am uneasy because it is the worst time of day to identify a target. I am also pissed off at Luis because he made a detour to check his emails. Luis is pissed off at me because I told him we could take a *chiva* bus and he replied, No, *puto,* they don't go that way, and just now a green one came by and almost ran us over on the narrow street. And we are all pissed off at Eduardo, who failed to dodge a pile of warm dog turd.

You sure you have done the recon? I ask Luis.

Fuck you, he says. Maybe I have no office job but I am no child.

And the target is not protected?

Listen to you and your fancy language, says Eduardo. Is the *target* not *protected*?

Under the darkening sky, everything melts into shapes of brown and gray. We pass buildings made of brick, of cement blocks, of wood and plastic. Faces of people merge back into the material of their houses. Street kids scavenge for food by the roadside, some of them inhaling the pale yellow *sacol* from supermarket bags—their eyes half-open and animal and unblinking. We pass unattended stalls, half-filled wheelbarrows, hot pillow joints, then there are no more houses and we reach an abandoned railway line running along the edge of a cliff. We cross the tracks and look down. The road dips steeply into a gorge jumbled full of bamboo poles and torn tarpaulin sheets and hundreds upon hundreds of boxes. It is our destination. The *tigurio:* the city of cardboard.

The few inhabitants we see do not interfere. We walk through dimly lit trenches, toward the northeast corner. Shadows of faces move behind candles and gas lamps. Luis lifts his fingers to his lips and points to a shack at the end of an alley. He creeps forward. Yellow gaslight glows from behind the gaps in the cardboard. Coming closer, I see a black man on his back chewing a sugared red donut. Luis goes in and grabs him by the hair and flips him onto his stomach. If it is the right person, Luis has done his recon excellently. The target looks older than all of us—even Claudia, who has sixteen years. His skin is a darker black than mine, and burnished with sweat in the gaslight. His mouth is still crusted with little sugar bits. Luis rests his boot on the side of the target's face as he reaches inside his pants to pull out the rifle. He frowns as the magazine gets stuck in the elastic of his waistband—this is a common hazard with the G3—a beginner's mistake. Eduardo has dropped to his knees, pinning the target's legs down.

Who is the son of a bitch now? Luis says. His voice is light and breathy as it is when he is excited.

You are, *puto,* squeaks the target. His lips strain to spit, and fail.

Claudia comes in and crouches down; there is not enough room to stand. We all sweat from the heat of the gas lamp. Luis succeeds at last in removing his rifle from his trousers and jams the barrel into the target's eye socket.

Do I kill him fast? he says. He is looking at me. Claudia and Eduardo are looking at me too. Pedro stands watch at the edge of the *tigurio.*

For a moment I am taken aback. Killing has never been the business of the *gallada,* unless things have changed with that too, in the four months I have been away. Maybe they are seeking to impress me, now that I have my office job. Or maybe that is why they asked me to come with them.

Do I kill him fast? Luis says again. His voice is tight—it sounds as though he is really asking for my answer.

What is his crime?

Luis falls silent. He lifts his gun and paces two steps this way, two steps the other way, stooped underneath the cardboard roof. The target twists his head up from the dirt and looks around for the first time. He sees Eduardo, who is holding his legs, and Claudia, and then Luis. He sees Luis's hand, trembling on the trigger guard.

He has many crimes, says Luis. But he called my mother the offspring of a dog.

I don't even know you, the target says. He swings around in my direction. And I am protected. Ask anyone.

I glance quickly at Luis, who opens his mouth.

The target follows my gaze and turns back toward Luis. When he speaks his voice is low and sly. What are you doing? he murmurs. His face is shiny in the gaslight. We both know you are no *sicario*.

Breathing hard, Luis grabs the G3 with both hands and jams the barrel into the target's mouth. I can hear the metal muzzle clatter against his teeth.

Ask him who is the offspring of a dog now, I say. I find myself thinking of four days ago, the calm face in front of my Glock. Ask if he will tell you that. Saliva starts to run from the target's mouth, quickly turning pink.

I will tell you, the target croaks out, whatever you want me to! He is not a tough anymore; no *soldado,* that is for certain. His words are slurred because his mouth is forced half open—it moves like the mouth of Claudia's demented mother. Please, he says.

Don't you get it? Luis shouts. The fringes of his hair drip with sweat.

From the ground, mouth ajar, the target shakes his head. I'm sorry, he groans.

Why are you sorry? I don't want you to say what I want you to say!

We all watch Luis.

I want you to *want* to say it.

Okay, man.

Okay?

Okay, man.

What are you going to do? He removes the gun from the target's mouth and presses it into his cheek.

I'm going to say what you want—

Luis's frown deepens.

I mean, I'm going to want to say it, I'm going to—

What are you? Luis breaks in.

It takes a second for the target to comprehend. I am the son of a dog, he says.

What kind of dog?

A dog. A bitch. A dirty, flea-bitten, whore of a bitch.

What else?

I am a dog that is ugly, that is an imbecile, that looks like a disease-ridden rat, that smells like shit . . .

You eat your own shit, too, don't you?

For a moment Luis sounds like a gangster in an American movie I recently saw in the city. His face even carries the same sneer.

Yes, yes. The target reaches for a piece of donut next to his face, rubs it into the dirt before stuffing it in his mouth. Claudia turns away. It is strange the things a girl will tolerate and will not.

From a distance comes the sound of ringing bells. I move to a gap in the cardboard to check with Pedro. After a moment he shakes his head and calls out in his high voice, Gasoline trucks.

Luis says, What else?

His mouth full of dirt, the target says, I am a dog that eats its own shit, and drinks its own piss, and, and—

But he cannot fully untangle his mess of words because at that moment Luis lifts his G3, flips it around and smashes the aluminum butt into the target's head. I think I hear a soft crack. For a brief moment Luis looks surprised, then he waves one finger from side to side in the manner of a parent scolding a child.

You are lucky, *puto,* he says, that my friends here are full of compassion. He spits on the ground next to the bleeding head. But they will not be so full next time.

You broke his head, says Claudia. He cannot hear you. She half-stands and shuffles over to the target—I think at first she is bending over to examine his wound—then she does something startling: she leans back and kicks him, hard, in the chest. Eduardo gets up from his knees and copies her. We know the target is still alive because his feet dance in response.

Luis gestures at the target with his G3, then says to me, Are you sure?

They all look at me. Their faces are flushed and full in the warm yellow light. It is strange, I think—their readiness to kill—for as far as I know, none of them has ever committed the act. This business was personal.

As we leave, Luis picks up a plastic bag that contains two donuts. The icing on them is green and yellow. For Pedro, he explains gruffly. He likes this sort of shit.

Outside it has turned into night. At the bus stop I ask Luis again what was the man's crime.

A shipment of *basuco,* he says. Or marijuana. I forget.

I thought you said a game of poker, says Eduardo.

Shut up, says Luis. Shut up, you fat punk.

MY NAME IS JUAN PABLO MERENDEZ, and I have been hiding at my mother's place for four days. People call me Ron because of the time when I was a child and, on a dare, finished a *medio* of Ron de Medellín and then another, and did not vomit.

I am a *sicario,* a hit man, an assassin. I have been a *sicario* for four months, although my agent, El Padre, says that in truth I am a *soldado,* fighting for a cause. It is no cause, however, but my own hands that have brought death to fourteen people for certain, and perhaps another two. For this El Padre offers me a safe house in the barrio, where I live alone, and pays me 800,000 pesos a month and another 300,000 for each hit. Of this at least 400,000 pesos a month goes to my mother, who prays to her God about my *delincuencia* but takes the money for her medicines and her clothes and her cable TV and asks no questions.

They call it an office job, as the *sicario* is waiting always by the phone. In Medellín, it is a prized thing to have an office job.

My agent is named Xavier—I do not know his last name, for everywhere he is known as El Padre. I have never met him. They say he is a large, light-skinned man with perhaps twenty-five years. They say he is the only agent in Medellín who is permitted a personal army. I am not sure who he works for, but it is clear from the pattern of hits he has ordered that he is connected with drugs.

El Padre has a powerful reputation. They say, when he had only six years, he was under the bed where the guerrillas came at night and killed his father, then raped his mother and stabbed her to death. The story goes that he memorized the killers' feet and their voices and their smell and tracked them down and made his revenge, one by one. The story goes that he allowed them each one final prayer and then, when they were only half-way finished, took his knife and opened their throats from behind. For this element of prayer they named him El Padre.

But the better story is that he was present, ten years ago, when his friend assassinated defenseman Escobar for the horrible sin of scoring a goal against his own country in the World Cup. This story goes that some time later he killed this friend over a spilled drink. It is something to murder a *sicario* of such reputation, but to do it over such a small failure of respect—an eyebrow revenge—that is a formidable thing. They say he now has hundreds of deaths to his name.

I have worked for El Padre for four months and have been a good *sicario,* a loyal *soldado,* never failing him until four days ago. Four days ago I was assigned a hit and did not make this hit. Of course, he is not interested in my reasons.

According to our usual practice, he called me on my cell phone the following day to confirm the hit.

Bueno, I said, getting up and walking outside so that my mother could not listen in. On the street I said to him, I could not find the target.

The phone line went quiet. You could not find the target, he said. His voice was soft, like he was recovering from a cold: Maybe the information was incorrect. Sometimes it is that way . . . the information is incorrect.

It had been a whole day and still I could not think of a better excuse.

I said, Maybe it is best to wait until Sunday. We both knew that Sunday is the best day to do the business as the target is usually at home.

You were ordered to do it yesterday.

I could not find the target, I lied again. Maybe he will be there on Sunday.

We have never met, have we, Ron?

No, sir.

You have been a good *soldado,* he said. I think it is time we met. This week, I think.

Yes, sir.

I will call you with the details.

Yes, sir.

I am no child, wet behind the ears. I have now fourteen years and two months. I know how things work. That there is not supposed to be contact between a *sicario* and his agent. I know that I have been summoned.

* * *

WHEN I RETURN FROM THE BUSINESS with Luis and the others, my mother is sitting in her dark room watching an American soap show. I quickly scan the street as I close the front door.

I switch a lamp on for her. In the yellow flood of light I see she is still wearing her makeup and her going-out clothes. For a moment I watch her as she watches the screen. She does not blink. The concentration of her face is calming.

Your friend called, she says, not turning her head from the TV. It is a large, forty-inch Sony model and was in almost new condition when Carlos sold it to us.

Claudia?

I wrote it all down, she says and gestures vaguely. On the screen a white woman with large lips is hugging her elbows and crying. I catch my mother's hand and make a show of kissing it gallantly, like I see in the old movies. It smells of fish and nail polish.

Oh *darling*! I say in high-voiced English. Come back to me for I am . . . *embarazada* . . . with your secret love child! I say this last part in Spanish so she will understand.

She shushes me and waves me away, then, as the commercials come on, she half turns and says, Do you think I should dye my hair more blonde?

Why do you want to, dear Mother?

I don't know, she says. Maybe it will make me look younger.

Younger? You already look young. In the streets, people do not think you are my mother. They think you are my sister. My mother has heard this before but still her face beams. I continue: They say, Is she your sister? And I say, Are you joking?

Tonto! she cries out. I go into the kitchen to get some *panela* from the large urn. You should learn from your friend Xavier, she calls out.

Xavier?

I feel a tightening in my stomach, like the tightening when you walk into a room with your weapon ready and the target is not there. Then I think, I am stupid to feel surprised.

He has nice manners on the phone. Who is this friend? He said you are lucky to have a mother such as me.

He said that.

I add milk to the *panela* and bring it out to her with some Saltina biscuits.

We need more candles, she says absently. They say there will be another blackout tonight.

What else did Xavier say? I ask, putting the tray down, but the commercials have ended and my mother is once again lost to her soap show.

I pick up the notepaper next to the phone. She has written down an address in her large, girlish writing. It means nothing to me. For a moment I consider telling her to turn off the TV and start packing once more, but already, I know, it is too late. My only hope is to meet with him tonight. I put the paper in my jacket, my heart beating *pá pá pá* from what I have just heard, and bend over the chair to kiss my mother's forehead.

Outside, I catch a bus to Aures. Claudia's house is the old cement one painted blue, halfway up the hill.

She turns from the large window when I arrive and says, *Buenas noches, guapo*. I am calmer now. The night air has cooled me. Claudia comes and lifts her hand to almost touch my face, then lets it drop. She knows I do not like to be touched around the head.

Let's go to the park, she says, like a question.

I nod. I am watching her. The window gap behind her is bigger than her whole body, and the dark openness is somehow beautiful; it is rare that any window in this city is not nailed up with grilles or latticework. Behind the window is a sheer drop of twenty meters into a marsh of mud and rocks and rubbish.

We walk up the hill together. The night air is cold and clean. All this time I am thinking about Claudia's window, and how it used to be filled with glass until one day her mother came home from the market, pulled the glass pane so far back the wrong way the hinges broke, climbed up onto the ledge and stood upright before throwing herself out. Even then, she only managed to ruin the right half of her body.

We arrive at the spot. It is dark. Ever since I showed it to Claudia she thinks of it as our spot, but in fact I prefer to go there without her. It is high, above the barrio, past the reach of the electricity cables, at the top of the hill where there are fields of yellow ichu grass and you can feel the wind from all four directions. Recently I have come here every day to sit in the long grass and sometimes drink or do the *basuco*. From this place I see the deep, narrow, long valley where the city of Medellín lies, cradled by mountains. The tall buildings rising out of the middle. I see the nameless streets, *carreras* running one way and *callés* the other. And in the evening I see the streetlights come on, running in gridded patterns until they reach the mountainsides where they race up and spread out until all the barrios that surround the city shimmer like constellations.

It is like that tonight, everything upside down. The stars are under us and above, a sky like dirt.

So you are really going to Cartagena? Claudia says.

Yes.

Why?

Why? To myself I think, To see the ocean. But I say, What did you want to talk to me about? I have important business tonight.

What business?

There is no reason not to tell her. I say, I am meeting with my agent.

So it is real, she says. You have been summoned.

I am silent. Everywhere around us is the whine of grasshoppers, and farther away the noise of people and machines sounds to me like the wash of the ocean. From far enough away everything sounds like the ocean.

There is a night bus to Tolú from the Terminal del Norte, says Claudia.

I shake my head.

I know about Hernando, she says. Everybody does.

What do you know?

She opens her mouth as if to speak, then stops. Then she says, The contract placed on him. By your agent.

You do not know everything, I say.

I watch Claudia's face carefully and it is hard, the face of a *soldado* with its thin cigarette mouth.

I must ask my agent for leave, I explain. Or he will find my mother.

Claudia pauses briefly. How is she?

My mother, I think, who I had assumed was safely hidden. She is glad I have been home, I say. Four whole days. I continue to watch Claudia. Excepting the business today, in the *tigurio*.

But she ignores me. Instead, she says, And you—how do you feel?

It is a question only a girl would ask.

Feel? I say.

She is right, though. Tonight, of all nights, I should feel something. If I think about it, then I am scared, yes, and sad, but it is as though that person who feels is someone other than me. In truth I sit here and I do not know what to feel. In truth I come up here to feel nothing.

The last time she asked me that was at Carlos's funeral, six months ago, at the Cemeterio Universal. It was the first death in our *gallada*. Everyone agreed he had died well. Then, too, I did not know what I felt standing before his grave. The hole was so small—he was never big, even though of us all he had the most hair on his legs and chest. My head was full of voices. One voice said, You should be crying, the other said, I want to, I want to, and behind both I could see myself, the fresh dirt on the mound, the bouquet of fake flowers, the statuettes of Marias and angels bobbing above the streets of headstones; I could hear the singing of birds and smell the plumeria and then feel the tears come, fake tears, watching my body and my hands so clearly as they moved, as through polished glass.

It is like that now; I am watching myself and it is like I am watching a different person.

You want to do some *basuco*? Claudia asks, reaching into her bag.

I have to go, I say to her.

Then I will come with you, she says.

CHICAS, THEY ARE A DISTRACTION from the important things, and as Luis says, sometimes to go between the legs of a *chica* is more dangerous than walking under a bridge in a strange barrio. As for Claudia, we used to go together, as far as that goes. I am fond of her but in truth I would not call her a friend. There is only one I would call my friend, and that one is Hernando.

Hernando used to be the head of our *gallada,* if such could be said, although nobody would have admitted it. (Especially not Luis, who had the same age.) There were more of us then, perhaps twelve, and Hernando organized the *mocós* and arranged with restaurants and market sellers for food in return for protection. The children he sent cleaning windshields, shining shoes, juggling machetes, minding cars, making sales. The older ones he organized to steal cigarettes, flowers, and gum for the children to sell. Only a few of us did the serious robbery. We worked only for ourselves. After my father's death, my mother and I struggled for money and it was Hernando who helped us survive: he took me into the *gallada* and taught me all the techniques—how to run the tag team, when to wear the private-school uniform, how to spot marks, such as those gringos who go to ATMs with laundry bags and conceal their bills in dirty socks. I learned quickly, and soon Hernando chose me to work with him on all the big scores.

When the others were not around, Hernado talked differently to me. Sometimes he liked to watch people going about their business, particularly in crowded places, at times when we were supposed to be doing recon. Once, in a plaza at noontime, he pointed to a farmer at a market stall, then a man at a construction site, and asked if I thought they were happy.

I don't know.

What about them?

I looked where he pointed.

They are probably happier, I said, half jokingly.

Pah! He spat on the parched grass. The suits, they are richer, yes. He turned back to the construction worker, lean and black-skinned and slow-moving in the heat. He thought for a moment, frowning all the while, then said, But to work with your hands, and to work with others—that is real work. He spat on the ground again. He had told me once that his father was a farmer in the west country—it was after I had told him about my own father, the details of his unforeseen death—but since then, the past had never been discussed between us.

It may not make a man happy, he said, but at least there is honor in it.

In that way, too, he was different. While most of the *gallada* was concerned with buying the new things, Hernando talked to me during those three years about happiness and honor—even about politics—about a future unconnected to money.

Then the day came, seven months ago, when we became

brothers. We were all playing football in a park on the edge of the city. Hernando was one of the better players and looked like a bronze statue in motion. Someone kicked the ball off the field. It went a long way, then stopped at the leg of a man sitting on a stationary motorcycle. The man got off his bike, removed his sunglasses, and kicked the ball—in the opposite direction—into the traffic away from the park.

Hernando had been chasing the ball. I had followed him because I wanted to speak in secret about a new strategy for the game.

What are you doing? Hernando called out to the man.

Hey, *puto*! the man said. Why aren't you working? Life isn't a bowl of cherries.

You should not have kicked our ball away, said Hernando.

I am doing you a favor. The man paused briefly, then swiveled to look over his shoulder. At that moment I realized he was there with another man, a uniformed policeman, also sitting on a motorbike.

Come here, the policeman said to Hernando. He was smiling. The first man began to smile too.

Hernando walked over without hesitating. He was wearing only pants and his sweating body looked large and powerful next to the shape of the sitting policeman. I watched and said nothing.

You would argue with a business leader in our community? the policeman said cheerfully. He unclipped his holster. Hernando did not move. Turn around, the policeman said. You will argue at the station.

I watched as the policeman handcuffed Hernando. Then I felt my arms being jerked behind my back—the other man had approached silently—and I felt the cold click of metal around my wrists. This man led me to his motorbike and sat me down behind him, facing backward, away from him. He smelled of alcohol.

As the motorbike started moving, I slouched into the man's back to keep my balance. I saw the park diminishing—everyone had vanished from the football game—but I could not see where we were going.

Hernando's bike was in front of ours so I could not see him either. The handcuffs cut into my wrists. Soon I realized we were going away from downtown Medellín. We were not going to any police station. We began to climb a hill leading us west, higher and higher, into steep slumland. Fear surged through my body: I twisted around, trying to locate Hernando, but the man growled and elbowed me on the side of my head. A voice sang out. We skidded onto a dirt road. The back tire kicked dust into my face and I coughed, my eyes still smarting. When the dust cleared I made out scrapwood shacks, a series of clothes lines, two women glancing up then down from a cooking fire—the power cables didn't run this high—then suddenly, as we swerved again, the city—far below—the vast concrete valley sealed in by a film of smog as flat and blue as a lake.

We turned away onto a narrow track. My breath now coming hot, fast. I could feel the man's sweat on the skin of my back, soaking through my shirt. Sunlight flared from corrugated tin roofs and plastic sheeting on the hillside below us. The ground grew thicker with olive-colored shrubs and banana trees.

The man said something but I could not hear it in the wind. At that moment I realized there were no more houses anywhere in sight. The motorbike slowed.

Jump! someone yelled. It was Hernando. Automatically I leaned to the side of the bike. I tried to jump but my pants got caught in the chain. Then the bike pitched onto its right side and I began to roll down the grassy hill, my hands cuffed behind me. I heard a couple of gunshots. I kept rolling until the ground leveled off. My head felt like it had been stabbed at the back. Moments later I felt someone's boots roll me onto my stomach. I waited for the shot. All I could smell was earth, and grass, and it smelled richer than I had ever smelled anything before. I waited. But the gunshot did not come, and then I felt someone unlock and remove my handcuffs. Hernando helped me to my feet. Blood leaked from his right armpit. He led me up the hill to where my captor, the businessman, lay under the bike, one leg bent so far back the wrong way the foot almost touched the hip. Hernando handed me a gun.

It is his, he said.

And the policeman? I asked.

Your corrupted friend is dead, Hernando said sternly to the man, as though it were he who had asked the question.

The man groaned. The flesh around his mouth had gone loose. I did not know then—as I do now—that this was a sign of fear.

You must do this, said Hernando. He looked at me like a brother. He said, Ron, you must do this so we are in it together.

I took the gun, which felt unexpectedly warm and heavy in my hand, and which gave off a smell like a match being lit in a dark room. I pointed it at the man's head. His sunglasses were broken and bent around his ear and the fragments shone in the afternoon light. I aimed at the blackness in the middle of his ear and shot.

After a while, I turned my back to the man's face and tried to lift the motorbike from his broken lower body. I felt filled with a tremendous lightness, as if every breath I took was expanding inside me. Then I remembered something.

The policeman. How did you—

Hernando let out a short, burp-sounding laugh. He bent his knees as though about to sit down on an invisible chair, then tipped onto his ass. He seemed suddenly drunk.

The stupid *puto* stopped, he said, because the handcuffs were uncomfortable against his back. But he would not turn me around to face the same way as him—he said he did not want a

faggot rubbing up behind him. Hernando burped again. So he
handcuffed my hands in front. At the top of the hill, I stopped
him like this.

Hernando tilted his head backward and lifted his arms up,
high up, arching them over his head. I saw the gashes in his right
armpit that the policeman's fingernails must have made when
the cuffs looped over his face and under his throat.

I watched him and he laughed again. Inside, the light air filled
me like *sacol*. Help me lift this, I said. But he did not look at the
bike. He remained sitting on the grass, half naked, embracing his
legs tightly.

For me too, he said. That was my first time too. He frowned,
looking straight ahead. His face was as white as a plastic bag.
Then a change came over it as though he was going to be
sick. Then his face changed again and he smiled, but now the
smile only affected his mouth.

Finally, I lifted the bike and rested it on its side stand.
We have to go, I said. You ride behind me.

He nodded. I helped him to his feet and onto the motorbike.
All the way down the hill he gripped me tightly, like a *chica* on
her first ride.

AFTER THAT, OF COURSE, more things changed than just the
fact that Hernando and I became friends. You do not kill a
policeman and business leader and expect the streets to owe you
protection.

El Padre approached me—through a *nero* whom I knew but
did not know to be employed by El Padre—and told me he
would protect me. He would take me off the streets, like he took
other kids off the onion farms, but he would raise me above these
farm kids: I would be given an office job. There was strength in
me, he said on the telephone. I could go back to my own barrio,

where, with my new status, I would be safe. We are similar, he said. We are both *soldados,* we do what needs to be done, and we have both lost our fathers to the conflict of Colombia. He said, I will be your benefactor.

Hernando, meanwhile, had disappeared from the *gallada.* His reputation had increased as a consequence of killing the policeman, and we all assumed he was hiding. Then several weeks later, someone reported seeing him at one of the gringo-led programs in the city that are known to combat violence and drugs and poverty by staging plays in public parks.

I tracked him down and told him about my new job and said that I could ask my agent to give him an office job as well, or at the least, employ him as a *soldado.* What is this shit? I said, grinning. I gestured at his windowless, white-plastered room, crammed with stacks of cardboard and paper. The room smelled strongly of bleach. Hernando sat behind a scratched steel desk and behind him was a poster depicting a gun with a melted barrel, and underneath, the words: THIS MAKES YOU A MAN?

Forget all this, I said. You can start again. My agent will get you a stainless police record.

Hernando looked at me for a long time. Then he told me he was happy to see me. He had cropped his hair and it changed his face, making his features seem somehow tired, muted. Finally he said, So now you have an office job. What is it like?

I told him about everything: the salary, the bonuses, the weapons. The respect from the barrio. He listened carefully. Then he leaned back in his chair and closed his eyes. I sat down, watching him, wondering what he did in this room every day. He looked older.

But what is it like? he said at last.

I realized he was asking about the killing. At that point, I had not yet received my first assignment and the question irritated me. It is easy, I said.

Who is your agent?

I told him.

He paused again.

What?

You must listen to me, Ron. The man you know as El Padre is a dangerous man.

I laughed, thinking he was joking.

Listen to me.

Of course he is dangerous. He is a legend.

Yes, said Hernando, speaking slowly. And even so, in the game, he is a small player. Which makes him even more dangerous for you. He leaned suddenly forward, the steel desk wobbling under his weight. Listen, Ron, you must stop. You must quit your office job.

You are being funny, no?

I was embarrassed for him. What had the *nero* said who had found him? That Hernando, looking like a peasant, had instructed him to return to school or he would surely end up the victim of the never-ending culture of violence—at which the *nero* had applauded and told Hernando to return to his new faggot friends. I had hidden my uneasiness. No one in the *gallada* would have dared to talk to Hernando in that manner before.

This is what your gringo friends tell you? I asked.

I do not need a gringo to see with my eyes. He looked away from me. But they are right about some things. About El Padre, for instance, who is a dog of the drug lords. He is a man who kills the innocent to protect the rich.

They are not innocent, I said quickly. He is cleaning the streets of the very people you denounce. I caught myself at the last moment from saying "I." His words affected me. I calmed my breathing. You say this when you do not even know him.

He came to me too, Hernando said.

Neither of us spoke for a while. His clothes were faded and worn, his left shoe ripped at the toe. I became conscious of my Nike shoes, my Adidas Squadra jersey with its mesh panels.

It is dangerous for you to say this shit in public.

Hernando said softly, as though to himself, No one should have to do what you do. He stood up and walked around the desk.

They pay you? Where you work, this program?

Hernando smiled. His smile was heavy at the corners of his mouth. I am happy here, he said.

I can help you. I have made almost one million pesos already.

You are like a brother to me, he said simply, and I want to see you safe. He frowned, trying to follow a thought with words. We cannot help each other, Ron. Maybe it is too late. But maybe you can still help your own family.

Maybe you should leave the city, I said.

He smiled again, then leaned forward to embrace me. Maybe, he said.

The next week I used a proxy to buy a house in the barrio next to El Poblado, and moved my mother there in secret. I did not speak to Hernando again until four days ago, when I was given the order by El Padre to assassinate him.

WHEN WE WERE STILL LIVING at the old place, and I had nine years and my mother twenty-four, it rained for a week and another two days. School was canceled—the rain so heavy the roads were waist-high with mud, people trapped in their houses. On the tenth day the rain stopped and it felt like a holiday. People wandered outdoors, as though for the first time, and the sun was warm against their skin and the grass and the trees deeper in their color and the faces of strangers flushed like ripe fruit. During this time a militia set up roadblocks along the Avenida Oriental and hijacked a public bus at the exit to our barrio. They raped two of the women and killed my father, then dumped his body and his guitar outside the back alley of my school. The papers said some of the hijackers were police agents.

They broke his guitar? my mother asked when the uniformed men came, their shirts wet at the armpits and their leather shoes splashed with mud. Of course by that time we already knew.

Why? one of them asked. Would you like it? He looked surprised. Maybe—

He stopped talking at his partner's look.

That evening it rained again, heavily, the air a mix of gray and green before the night came down. A couple of neighbors visited—my mother exchanged soft words with them at the front door—then afterward no one else came. All night she did not speak and I did not know what to think. She sat on the brown carpet in the main room, in the dark, with my father's notepapers and sheet music. The gaslight from the kitchen made her face seem misshapen. For hours I sat on my parents' bed with the door open, watching her arranging the papers in careful piles, calmed by how her fingers moved individual pieces from pile to pile, without pause, as though following some special sequence. I watched her fingers and her strange face, and I watched the rain leaking from the thatched kitchen ceiling behind her, and I waited for her to tell me what would happen to us.

He had been a musician, a teacher at an elementary school. His death had been a mistake—everyone told us this. What no one told us was that he, too, had made a mistake: to challenge his attackers—to even draw attention to himself—when he had only his mouth and his hands for protection. What no one told us was that in this city no death is entirely a mistake.

The rain did not stop for two days. My mother stayed cross-legged on the carpet, which, in the rain-dimmed light, changed color to dull orange. She wore the same gray dress and did not eat. On the third morning, a car with mounted speakers drove past and announced that Andrés Pastrana Arango had won the presidential election. I remembered that my father liked to call him the hippie candidate. I took some money from my mother's purse and went out into the street to buy some food. I played football with some kids.

That night, when I put two mangoes and a bag of boiled water in front of her, my mother saw me again. She told me to sit by her. We sat in silence. Then, in the dark, she leaned toward me and kissed whatever part of my body was closest to her, the outside of my knee, she kissed it twice, then two more times. And then she spoke my name, Juan Pablo, she said, and I looked at her and she said, You must say nothing of it, and think nothing, for you are a man now. I said, Mother? but her only answer was my name, spoken again like a chant, *Juan Pablo, Juan Pablo, Juan Pablo.*

THERE ARE BLACKOUTS EVERY MONTH in the barrios, sometimes for days in a row. As Claudia and I enter the barrio where El Padre's headquarters is based, the entire mountainside stops humming and everything turns black. In the sudden dark, ghosts of light dance at the edge of my vision like memories, trapped at the back of my eyes. There are no stars. Gradually the glow of city rises over the black line of mountains, and beneath the clouds the effect is one of torchlight smothered by gray blankets.

We continue up the hill in the half darkness. Dim lights begin to shine onto the street from candles placed in windows. At last I see a high lookout on the hill that must be my destination: two youths stand outside the gate holding mini Uzi submachine guns. Even from this distance I can see that they are nine millimeter with twenty-five-round clips. The house is two-storied, with a balcony on the second floor overlooking the hill. Another guard patrols the balcony. The shadow of yet another glides and starts behind dimly lit windows. On the perimeter, the outer wall is topped by shards of glass of different shapes and colors, and shimmers in the candlelight.

From the midst of the slum, the house rises like a palace.

Stay here, I say to Claudia.

To my surprise, she does not argue. I will wait here, she says, and then pulls back into the shadows of an alley.

At the gate, I say my name and am searched roughly, professionally, and then escorted to the house by one of the guards. He opens the front door, gestures for me to enter, and returns to the gate. Inside it is dark, and the air is heavy, as in one of those houses where the windows have been left closed through the heat of the day. It smells as though someone has been smoking a spliff laced with cocaine.

You are Ron, a female voice sounds out from the corner, where a triangle of light slants down at an angle. I see someone coming down some stairs, her pointy boots first, her tight jeans, and then her bare stomach and then her tank-top breasts and then her face and her tied-up hair, all white and amber in the light. She is extremely beautiful.

Yes.

Xavier is waiting for you, she says. She comes directly to me and takes my hand. Her touch is warm and smooth, and the tips of her fingers lightly trace a circle on my palm. Here is a *chica,* I think, who would fuck me as soon as slit my throat.

Upstairs, El Padre is sitting at a large wooden desk. Behind him are bay windows overlooking the balcony. The room is filled with candles—candles placed on every flat surface, in every window, like in a basilica. I glance around, almost expecting to see a statue of a crucifixion. It is ten o'clock at night and El Padre is wearing a suit with an open-necked shirt. Even sitting, he is tall and broad at the shoulders, and, consistent with the rumors, his complexion is light, but mainly I notice his hair, which is braided into cornrows. I find this surprising. There is oil in his hair—it holds each individual braid as tight as a cable—and the oil glistens in the candlelight.

Sit down, he says.

The wooden planks creak under my weight as I walk to the chair in front of the desk. He is looking through some papers. Aside from his hair, he looks like he could be any businessman leaving the office at the end of the day. His features seem somehow strange to me—then I realize that even though his skin is fair, he has the wide nose and thick lips of a black man. His eyes, also, are black. I watch the play of candlelight on El Padre's braids, on his fair skin, on his slow-moving hands. He gathers up a pile of papers and taps them on the table to align them, then pulls a pen from his breast pocket and signs the top sheet with a gesture that makes plain his disgust. He puts the pen away. Then he looks up at me with cold, snake eyes.

So we meet, he says.

Yes.

His eyes flick to something behind me. I remember from when I first walked in that there are two others in the room: the *chica* and another guard who carries a rifle and has a joint in his mouth. El Padre looks at me again.

You know, Ron, you will never become an agent. His voice is soft.

Because I'm too dark?

Because you think you are smarter than your superiors.

I do not say anything.

You were given an assignment and you refused to carry it out.

I did not find the target, I say quietly.

He pauses. A good *soldado* does not choose which orders to obey from his *general,* does he?

No.

He swivels around on his chair, leans back and speaks out through the bay windows as though addressing the night. I am your *general,* he says. I must look after an entire army. If two women fight, I shave their heads. If somebody cheats me, I shoot them in the hand. If a *soldado* fails me, or betrays me . . . what choice do I have?

I watch as a gecko runs along the top frame of the window. It stops, testing the night air with its tongue. El Padre turns back around to me and frowns.

You have been getting high on the *sacol,* he says.

I recognize the insult. I do not do that stuff anymore, I say. It is for children.

The heat from the candles on the desk, the scent of wax, the smells of marijuana and cocaine from the guard's spliff—all combine and condense in my head.

You disobeyed me, he says—I who have been your benefactor— and decided instead to spare your friend.

I do not say anything.

Do you know what your friend has been saying? For the first time El Padre raises his voice. Do you know what ears listen to those kinds of words? Do you know what it costs to quiet those words? You pull on the hand that feeds you.

I remain silent.

Worse, you make me lose face. Respect.

You can send other *sicarios* for him, I hear myself say.

When you have already told him to run?

I told you I could not find him.

I have already sent Zeno, he says.

I do not know Zeno. But I hear he is good.

Yes, Zeno is good. His thick lips purse together, then part. Already he has achieved his mission. Two days ago.

I feel my mouth pool with cold spit. I remember I am sitting before a snake. I remember that Hernando is skilled in the ways of leaving the city unseen. And that he has had four days.

Yes?

I do not lie, he says, as though reading my thoughts. In fact, Zeno told me this himself when I visited him earlier today. In the Hospital San Vicente de Paul. He looks at me intently with his dark empty eyes. Then he says, Where he was admitted for a severe fracture of the skull.

Once again, I feel myself sliding out of my own body.

This is peculiar, El Padre goes on, because Zeno said Hernando did not resist. An easy hit. So his injuries must have been caused afterward. But of course you do not know anything of this?

It is not easy for me to contain my surprise. I am looking at El Padre but what I see is the black body underneath the cardboard roof, the red donut crumbs and the sugar on his lips. My mind races like a fast-rewinding movie. So they all knew, I think— Luis and Claudia and Eduardo. I should not have gone into hiding. But I had to go into hiding—to give him time to escape. Above all this I think of Claudia, who knew, who knew where I was hiding, and who had made a choice not to tell me. I realize El Padre is still waiting for me to speak.

If you do not trust in my ability, I say, I can go away. My voice sounds like a series of echoes inside my head. You can take my salary for this month as compensation.

That is generous of you, Ron. Perhaps I will return the favor and give it to your mother.

He has not taken his eyes from me. I say to him, I am a *soldado*. You said this. There is no reason to involve my mother.

We look at each other. On the desk between us a thick candle sputters in a sudden draft, but neither of us blinks. His eyes are black puddles.

A bell rings in the outside darkness. I cannot hold my eyes to his—I look away. Everywhere I look are the flames of candles. It is truly like the inside of a church, I think, although I cannot remember having been inside one for years. My head feels humid. I look at El Padre again and realize I no longer know the words to any prayers. Hail Mary, full of grace, I think, but after that my mind is as dark as an empty barrel. I wonder if the stories are true. I wonder where he conceals the knife. I wonder if he will ask me to turn my back to him, or if he will come to stand behind me.

HERNANDO WAS READING THE NEWSPAPER over an evening meal as I watched from my concealed position, behind a thick shrub, in his backyard. Four days ago. My Glock loaded and ready. I watched him for a long time before coming in. When he saw me his face was grave with surprise, his eyes blinking down and up from the gun. Then he stood to embrace me.

They sent you? he asked quietly.

I nodded.

And?

He looked at me, calmly, as though I were a brother he had grown up with every day of his life. He looked at me as though he already knew what I would say. I wondered whether he knew better than me what I had been thinking as I stood outside in his yard, underneath the warm, polished leaves, testing the trigger in the half dark.

I told you, I said. I told you.

He smiled. My fingers tightened around the Glock. I looked at his forehead. Then, as though following a separate will, my hand lowered the gun to the table, let go of it.

Run.

I was not sure if I said it aloud or merely thought it.

His smile froze. Run?

He will send others. You must go. Now.

What of you?

I did not know. I had never thought it would happen this way. My mind was still clear—as it was whenever I did the business—but before the broad calm of Hernando's look I could feel the clarity slipping away.

He asked, Are you sure? After a while he frowned, then said abruptly: Come with me.

He nodded, as if it had been I who had made the suggestion, then nodded again, more vigorously, saying to himself, Yes, yes. But where? Far away. The coast. North is better. Cartagena. Come with me to Cartagena. We will be fishermen. He laughed aloud. After all this! he said.

Cartagena?

Yes, he said. Why not? He spoke playfully now, as if we were kids again, as if we were in one of our *mocós* and bragging to each other about our day's score.

I cannot go, I said.

I will not go without you, he said. When I brought my eyes to his I realized he was serious.

Even then, I understood the consequences. He was my brother but I owed him nothing—he knew that. I had not seen him for three months. He knew I had come in from the streets and—like them—had promised nothing, was incapable of betrayal. He laughed, and as I watched him laughing, his face made childlike in the act, I suddenly saw a glimpse of the old Hernando and in that moment I realized how completely he had left that person behind. I remembered him tall and bronze-skinned, then handing me the gun on the hill, then weak-kneed and pale, and now as I watched him his face was again new. It was unlike any of the faces I had seen in their last moments—always too tight or too loose—his was settled somehow, clear of weakness, the face of a *soldado* ready to die—for what, I did not understand—but whatever it was, I knew then it was not mine to impede. I would let him go. I thought of El Padre. I thought of my mother, and of Claudia. I thought of Cartagena and won-dered how many times a person could start over. After a while I started laughing as well.

Yes, he said again. Yes, yes. He paused, his face sly: Claudia likes Cartagena.

Fishermen, I said.

Yes, he nodded, grinning widely. Do you remember how Luis described it?

I brought my hand to my mouth, tapped my teeth with my fingernail. This sent Hernando into a renewed fit of laughter. We were like two drunken schoolgirls. Do I remember? I said. Only after the fortieth time.

AFTER A LONG SILENCE, El Padre sighs, his breath fluttering the candle flames on his desk, then smiles with his mouth and says:

You are right. You have been a good *soldado.*

I do not say anything. He leans back in his large chair and clasps his hands behind his neck. Even the darkness of his armpits somehow suggests violence. Hail Mary, full of grace . . .

When I was your age, he says—even younger—I too had to eliminate my friends. He pauses. His voice has changed; it is softer now, damper. I did not mark your friend as a hit, he says. But I chose you to make the hit.

I bow my head, not knowing what to say. I remind myself that, of course, I already knew this. I think of the World Cup story, and wonder distantly if El Padre's face looked then as it does now: like a gangster in an American music video.

He continues speaking. As he speaks, it seems that his words harden into deep noises. Afterward, he says—he is saying—afterward, I learned to not care so much about the death—only the details. Death is just a transaction. A string of consequences.

I nod. I am becoming heavier. His words are weighing me down. My body is a rock in this chair.

Take me, for example, El Padre says, looking at me carefully. If I die, do you know how many deaths will follow? He tells me the number. I do not know whether he is saying it with pride or sorrow or disbelief.

But part of me is capable of thinking that this is an extraordinary thing. That one life can hold so many others up. That the other lives can be ignorant of this. It reminds me of a game of wooden blocks I used to play with my parents, where the push of a single piece could bring the whole tower crashing down.

El Padre watches me and I watch him back, and when the realization comes through the hot swamp of my mind it comes with no satisfaction. You are no Hernando, a voice says in my head, and at that moment I know it to be true. Then another voice says, You are no El Padre. And as it speaks I watch him— this man sitting in front of me with a head of gleaming cornrows, in this warm atrium of candles—I watch him, in control, alive, and absolutely alone in a power he cannot share.

I understand, I say.

You have been a good *soldado,* he repeats. He takes a deep breath. You understand that you cannot continue in your job, however?

Yes.

And I will require the weapons back.

Of course.

I will send Damita to tell your friend who waits in the alley. She knows where they are?

I pause. Hail Mary. Then I say, I must tell my friend myself or she will not go.

He watches me impassively.

The weapons are at our *mocó,* I add.

He thinks, and then nods. Then go with Damita, he says. To the alley—no farther. And come back afterward for a drink.

In the front yard outside, before we reach the gate, Damita says, He likes you.

I laugh shortly, the first time tonight. There is something about the coolness of the air that brings me back closer to myself. It is almost over, I tell myself.

No, he does, she says. I can tell. He always acts that way, the first time. She gives me a sidelong look. Her face is the kind they put on the cover of shiny magazines. The first time I met him, *ay!* I heard the same speech! *If two women fight, I shave their heads,* she mimics, then laughs, a quick darting laugh that makes me imagine sparks from a fire racing into a night sky.

She stops at the gate to have a cigarette with one of the guards. Stand where I can see you, she says, waving to me like a schoolgirl stepping down from a bus.

At first I cannot find Claudia, then I hear her harsh whisper from the opposite alley.

Just come out, I say. They know you're here.

She comes as far as the corner, her forehead and kneecaps glowing white under the streetlights, and I walk to meet her there. She frowns—it makes her face look angry.

He is letting you go?

I don't know, I say.

She begins to cry—and I realize it is the first time I have ever seen her cry. Not even after her mother tried to kill herself did I see Claudia's face like this. It is all soft.

Hernando is dead, I say. I have to force myself to say it rather than ask it.

I know.

Hearing her say it severs something deep within me. For a moment it is as though I have lost contact with myself. I force myself to concentrate. In that case, I say, tell Luis I thank him. For organizing the business today.

She nods.

He knew that you would want revenge, she says. But he did not want to tell you about Hernando's death, if you were in hiding, and did not already know, and there was no need . . .

She trails off, seeing where that leads. Everyone knew, I think again. But I do not feel bitter at all.

El Padre knows you are here, I repeat. He wants you to go to our *moco* and bring back the guns.

I do not want to look at her crying face. I look into the half dark behind her, make out the contours of a ditch, the banks of rubbish packed hard as rock. I think I see the face of a child appear behind a candle, and then disappear. The sky feels like it is sinking closer and closer to earth.

My mother, I say.

Don't worry about that, she says. I will take her away.

A strange look crosses her face and her narrow shoulders lurch toward me. Her teeth scrape across my lips. I feel embarrassed. I try to kiss her back but I have difficulty controlling my mouth. Her lips are on my ear. She is saying something. She is saying something but I cannot hear her, and when I try to listen I cannot remember what her voice sounds like. I am pulled back into myself.

She is saying, Take it. She presses it into my hand, guides it into my pocket. It is hard and cold and shaped like an apple. It is one of Pedro's grenades. I do not dare to look down.

How do you feel? she asks me for the second time tonight. She asks it with a small laugh.

I do not know what to say. Can I say, My body feels like it is all water? Can I say, Perhaps, perhaps I am glad?

The revenge killings will not finish for a few weeks, I say.

She nods again. You are scared.

Her left hand is still wrapped around mine and it is trembling. This, I think, from Claudia, who has the steadiest hands I know. I look at her and then, in her eyes, I see a window, framed by her mother's body, and I find myself thinking about how easy it seemed for her mother to jump to a death she did not want that badly.

Yes, I lie to her. Yes, I am scared.

I look back toward the house and it is clear from Damita's posture that she has finished her cigarette, is bored with the guards, is cold and is waiting for me. The house, with its candlelights, looks somehow sacred under the gray clouds, and the moon, which has come out beneath them, looks like a huge yellow magnet.

My fingers rub against the cold metal in my pocket. I have to go, I say.

Claudia embraces me again, her fingertips digging into the gaps between my back ribs. She is breathing shallowly now. Tell him you will never come back. Tell him he can trust you. She says it quietly but there is enormous pressure behind her words.

Yes, I say. But first you must go get the guns.

She will not let go of me.

I hate this place, she says, wiping her eyes on my shoulder. We will leave together. Your mother too.

My mother, I say.

I look up at the house, shimmering high on the black hill before us. Claudia clings to me. Her body is warmer than usual. From the gate, Damita looks in our direction and I step back, away from Claudia, seeing her now as though from a growing distance. She is small, and soft, and alone, and I force myself to look away from her.

You must get the guns, I say.

He will let you go.

She has gathered her voice with effort. I smile into the night.

He will let me go, I say after her.

At the front door Damita loops her arm around my elbow and leads me inside. This time the guards do not search me. As we walk up the stairs, Damita's hip bumps against mine and her bare stomach shifts and lengthens in the angled light. El Padre is behind the bay windows, standing outside on the balcony. He gestures for me to join him.

From the balcony, the brightness of the candlelit house makes the hillside seem even blacker. We stand there in silence—El Padre and I, and a guard motionless against the far railing. As my eyes adjust, I can make out hazy lagoons of light in the distance.

El Padre makes a quick gesture with one hand. I spin around: another guard holding a submachine gun is jogging toward me. I fumble against the leathery skin of the grenade in my pocket and maneuver it between my fingers: the pin.

Better than *basuco,* says El Padre. He continues to look out over the hill. It is only when the guard is next to me that I realize he is holding out a spliff. El Padre takes it from him, takes a long drag, then holds it out to me.

I nod—I am unable to speak—and unclench my fingers from the pin of the grenade. When I draw in the smoke it rushes deeper and deeper, without seeming to stop, into the cavities of my body.

Much cleaner, no?

He smiles now: a charming host. In the deflected light, I notice for the first time a flabbiness in his cheeks. His braided hair looks wet. We stand on the balcony and look out over the blacked-out barrio. There are valleys out there, and swells, and rises, all unseen by our eyes. The night air gives off traces of wood smoke, sewage. In the immediate candlelight, the glass on top of the walls glimmers hints of every color, and it is beautiful. For a moment I imagine the house is a ship floating on the silent ocean, high in the wind. This thought calms me, which is strange, for I have never seen the ocean—and I am reminded of evenings when I have stood in the cobbled yard outside my mother's back window, watching her asleep with her makeup on, or taking her medicine with *aguardiente* when she thinks no one sees, or coming out of the glowing bathroom with her hands in her hair, a towel and a quick unthinking motion. It calms me, watching her like this.

El Padre says something. His words splinter endlessly down the dark well of my thoughts. *Vámonos,* he is saying. *Vámonos,* I need something to warm my stomach.

I look at his smiling face, the black moons of his eyes.

Come on, he says. I have a special room for drinking. We will wait for your friend there.

The two guards on the balcony do not move.

We will toast your farewell, says El Padre. I hear you like to drink. He begins to walk indoors. Where will you go? Have you decided?

I don't know, I say. Maybe Cartagena.

Cartagena, he repeats. Then he beckons, and the two guards fall into line behind me. Cartagena, I think, where Hernando waits for me. Even now, at the last, we are connected. I can feel Claudia's teeth, her dry lips against my mouth. I rotate the grenade in my pocket—Hail Mary, I think—my palms slippery with sweat—and finally, when my thumb finds traction on the safety lever, I thread my middle finger through the pin and pull it out, hard. It falls free. El Padre looks back at me and smiles.

So, he asks, have you ever been there?

Gripping the lever tightly, I follow my benefactor into the house. A third guard opens a door from the main office and goes in ahead. No candlelight shines from inside. El Padre goes next and I go after him, as though deep into the throat of a cave, the two guards unfailingly behind me. The smell of Damita's perfume is strong in the darkness. Somewhere in front of me, El Padre's voice asks again about Cartagena, and this time I say, No, and as I say it, my thumb wet and unsteady on the lever, the memory returns to me, the picture as I have imagined it so many times in the past. Luis is sitting on the old colonial wall and looking out toward the ocean. As the sun rises, he says, you can see ten black lines leading into the steel gray water, each line maybe twenty meters apart, and as the water turns orange, then red, you can see that each line is made up of small black shapes and that they are moving away from the water, together, all in harmony, and then as the sun rises higher on your right you can see that each black shape is a man, there are hundreds of them, and they are hauling one enormous fishing net in from the ocean, slowly, step by step.

Meeting Elise

SHE'S COMING TODAY. It's 11:40 a.m. and I can feel my ass again. I get into a kneeling position in the bathtub then slowly stand up, one trembly, lard-like leg at a time. Water runs down my chest, over my creased stomach, coalesces on my creased balls. With my right hand I reach down and squeeze them, sponge-like, until what remains in my fist is a shriveled sac of skin. My ass is burning. My head was doing okay for a while there. I flick the soggy cigarette in my other hand into the bath-water, grab the tube of lidocaine and smear some of that sweet stuff onto my rosebud.

You're a dirty old man, Olivia used to say, speaking generally, smiling that toothy, canine-sharp smile she reserved for me. It made me horny and she knew it. We used to spend half our time here, sitting in this long, deep tub, spying on the street below. She liked to watch strangers. I liked watching her. I almost demolished this apartment so we could both get our perve on. It took a binder full of expert appraisals and zoning permits before I was allowed to knock out the wall, put in a steel frame and glass-brick the whole thing back up.

It gets me a bit loose-headed, all this reminiscing. I climb out of the bathtub and take off my sunglasses. It's not so bright out-side, not today. Some days it gets so I can barely even see the street, its lines and depths—cars, buildings, people—everything looks so bleached out. But not today. I light up another cigarette, avoid the mirror, ignore a wolf whistle from outside and half lope, for the dozenth time that morning, to my computer screen. I quickly scroll down through her website bio: Elise Kozlov, cello prodigy, noted for her precocious facility of technique, her inventive fingering for passagework, her grace of phrasing, etc., etc. There's a mention of me too: Henry Luff, "well-regarded neofigurative painter"—as well as her mother, credited as "raising" her in Russia. Selected by Elena Dernova for the St. Petersburg conservatory at age five; member of Anatoly Nikitin's celebrated Cello Ensemble at age twelve; world's youngest owner of a Guadagnini. Then there it is: the solitary statement that popped up only a few days ago: "Delighted to announce her engagement to Jason Sharps."

I leave off, walk into my walk-in wardrobe. It hurts less when I take small, shuffling steps. *Get your clothes on and get working.* Olivia liked to say that too. But the thought of picking up a paintbrush right now makes me jittery. The order of the day, then:

First, get dressed. Something swanky for the concert, a penguin suit, probably. It's Carnegie Hall. No counting on time to go home to change after our late lunch. I run my fingers along the plastic-wrapped shoulders of my tuxedo rack: full dress, half-tailcoat, black tie, white tie . . . finally I pick out a classic number and truss myself up. There I am in the mirror. Craggy, sure— heavy in the lips and nose—but not altogether undistinguished.

Just as I'm leaving I feel the compulsion—one last time—to see what she looks like. The computer blinks the photo on. Long black hair; impatient, deep-set eyes. She's mine in the strictest, most accidental sense. She's beautiful. She looks nothing like me.

I'M TAKING MY CLOTHES OFF AGAIN. This time for my gastroenterologist, Eric IIingess, whose patient list includes the likes of Ed Koch and Art Garfunkel—and who charges accordingly. I was lucky to get this appointment just before the long weekend.

"I may as well admit it," I tell him. "I'm nervous as hell."

"It's a natural response."

He leans back in his chair, wearing a suit that looks stitched together from carpet samples, watching me as I try to undo my bow tie. Rabbit chasing the fox. Oddly, Hingess seems more nervous than me, sniffing and jerking his eyebrows like a conductor rehearsing a piece in his head.

"This is a big day for me."

"Here," he says, handing me a pill and a plastic cup. After a moment he sighs: "Valium. To relax you."

I swallow the pill. "Yeah, I'm meeting my daughter today. First time in seventeen years."

"Goodness," he says absently. "How old is she?"

"Eighteen."

The metal disk of his stethoscope against my chest is as cold as an ice cube and I imagine it melting, trickling down onto my gut, Olivia's squinting eyes above it and her tongue retracing its route. I follow the lines her tongue chooses. I shiver. The doctor's saying something.

"Your trousers too," he's saying. His eyebrows contort operatically. Then he sneezes. Two, three times: wet, clotty sneezes. "I'm sorry," he says. "What were you saying?"

"Hold on," I tell him. "I thought we went through all this last time." I try to stare him down. The effort is fruitless, though, in light of my last visit: me passing him stool samples, him digging around inside my asshole with his lubed, latexed, incredibly knuckled finger. It felt like he was feeding a knotted rope into my gut.

He's still watching me. I take off my patent leather shoes, unwrap my satin cummerbund, slide down my black pleated trousers and roll miserably onto the examination table. He doesn't even show the token modesty to look away. Instead, he starts talking. He talks about fecal occults and flexible sigmoids and adeno-something polyps and asks me if I've read the pamphlet he gave me.

"Yeah," I lie. "But I thought I just had piles."

"Hemorrhoids, yes. They certainly cause some blood in the stool. Today we're testing farther up."

He stops talking to sneeze again. I turn away from him, wince as he grazes the hard lump outside my rosebud, then a sharper pain, then a real humdinger:

Elise—my daughter, my baby girl—just a bloody, scraggly mess between my wife's harness-hung legs. Hideous under the man-made lights. Then a lump of flesh, stewing in sickness, pulling every possible contagion out of the air and into her body. The pain burns. Weeks and months she lay, first in the incubator, then the cot, under the watchful eyes of her mother. Her mother, who watched me as closely as her. Elise inherited her seriousness. Even before she could speak she'd look at me, unblinking, bringing me down to an accusable level, her eyes deep with understanding. I hadn't wanted her and she knew it. My lower body floods with water. It feels warm and wrong. Something's yanked out of me and my eyes tear up.

We're done, I realize. From the pain, my ass must look like black pudding. I start pulling up my underwear when I hear Hingess's voice, "Hold on there." I look over my shoulder. He's wheeling something toward me—a laptop—attached to about ten feet of evil-looking black rubber hosing.

"That was just the enema," he says, "to prep you. This is the sigmoidoscope."

"You're not going to—"

"Only two feet of it."

"I want a smoke," I say. My face is salty, sopping with sweat.

I eye the hosing. Easily as thick as my thumb—probably thicker.

He frowns. Then he purses his lips and says, "All right. It'll help you breathe."

It hurts too much to sit up so, slouched on my side, I fumble in the bunched pant pockets around my ankles for a cigarette. I light it.

"Will you mind if I ask someone to assist?"

"What?"

"A medical student. I want to demonstrate the procedure."

And then she's there, white-smocked, clipboard in hand, hair tied back in a bun. From sideways she's hot in a birdlike way, and I wonder reflexively if the doctor here has slipped it to her. She studies me with a detachment that verges on impudence. No way she's just some schmuck med student. It's Park Avenue—someone must have called in a favor. She acts like she sees this every day: a sweat-drenched man, naked save for his white wing-tip formal shirt, blood leaking from his ass, lying in a fetal position, shakily smoking a cigarette. Her coolness feels familiar to me.

The two of them start doctor-talking. I'm ordered to shift onto my left side. Someone lifts my right buttock, then from the locus of my rosebud the cold-hot pain flares again through the grid of my body. I can't breathe. It's okay, the doctor says. Slowly, breathe slowly through my mouth. Then he talks to Birdgirl, quick-fire, every word punctuated by a twist in my guts. The hosing goes in so deep it feels like part of it might snap off, stay trapped in there. My wobbling fingers drop the cigarette. I arch my head to look at the laptop screen, for some sign that it's worth it, that it'll be over soon, but all I see are smudges of gray and white. Large, hob-knuckled fingers pointing to them.

Then silence. The doctor and his sidekick are studying something on the screen. They mutter, speaking in Latin and percentages. I rest my eyes. On the website photo she's got her mother's mouth. It doesn't smile.

"It's a big deal," Birdgirl says in a casual voice. When I turn to look I see it's Olivia; she's running her hands in small circles on her white smock, shaking her head at my thickness. "Of course it's a big deal. The Mayakovsky String Quartet. Carnegie Hall. Eighteen years old."

"She's getting married," I say. "To her manager."

"It's a big deal. It's serious."

"He's English."

"It's serious."

I agree with her—I'm nodding full of agreement when a putrid smell jogs me awake. Old anchovies and drain-clogged vegetables. The doctor, an inch from my face. My eyes heave into focus.

"Henry. You all right?"

Without asking permission I pull up my crinkled pants, cram my shirt into them and haul myself upright with only a slight moan. My feet dangle, toes stretched down, trying to hook my shoes. She doesn't usually come so close, so clear. The doctor confers with Birdgirl in a low tone. Then he turns to me.

"You have a number of adenomatous polyps in your colon."

"It's not your fault, Doc," I joke automatically. I grope again for my shoes.

"Most polyps are benign and the sigmoidoscope can remove them. However, the size and number of adenomatous polyps I have observed means we will have to carry out further tests."

"It's serious," Birdgirl murmurs. The doctor glances at her and she frowns, blushing.

At this point I catch on. They're not talking about my hemorrhoids. I zip up my pants.

"Tests? For what?"

He shows me pictures he's saved on the laptop. The polyps, he explains, are superfluous bits of tissue, generally shaped like mushrooms. There, he points, and there. I study the grainy images, trying, pretending to see. Then I see: the colony of little mushrooms in my colon. He's only inspected one third of it. He will perform biopsies through a colonoscope, he tells me, during a full colonic examination. He has awful breath. He will use a scythe-like wire to harvest my mushrooms, but there is a chance that malignant cells have already metastasized into my blood-stream or lymph system. I'm having trouble getting past the mushrooms. Birdgirl looks down, nods thoughtfully.

"Give it to me straight," I say.

Hingess is one of the most expensive gastro men in town and this is why I pay him: for his straight-shooting, no-holds-barred, expert opinion: "You will very likely develop colorectal cancer," he says, "if you haven't done so already."

I'm a painter. A good one, by most accounts. I look for the angles, the things that lend complexion, the joke in things. My doctor's mouth smells like a fish has flipped inside and died. I'm sweating in my penguin suit, my asshole burning from all the wrong-way traffic. There's a girl in the room who I'd jump if I could stand up, but even if I did—get this—her face wouldn't budge from the same mix of tenderness and pity holding it together now.

I'm looking, waiting, but I can't find it. It doesn't exist. There is no joke.

IT WAS JACOB APELMAN'S DOING that I met Olivia eigh-teen years ago, when I was unhappily married to a terminally passive-aggressive wife, father to a chronically ailing baby daughter, and caretaker of a career that made my domestic life seem idyllic. I'd been with him a few years—he wasn't yet the hotshot he is now, of course—and maybe I wasn't his most gracious artist. In any case, when a life-study model canceled at the last minute, Apelman kept mum (he said later he was afraid I'd take it personally) and found a girl to replace her. He didn't tell me she was seventeen years old, had never modeled before, had been plucked like an apple from Washington Square.

The girl had a boyish haircut and a botany textbook. Immediately she took charge. Without a word, she let her clothes fall to the floor and stepped out of them, as though from a pool of water. My studio—the top floor of an old box factory in Gowanus—faced westward, and as the day wrung itself into evening the sunlight streaked across the river and through my tall, rust-flecked windows, stenciling light and shadows across the room. A chintzy coral effect. The girl ignored the chair, sat on the cement, naked, on a reef of light. She sat so her knees touched, her feet splayed apart to create a triangle of dark space. I was taken aback by the perfect fluke of the composition. Then, cool as you like, she picked up her book and said: *I'm ready.*

For years after that day, I'd continue to be amazed by the ability of her body to hold light. Even at the end—when she was flat and wooden under the hospice sheets. I'd watch her endlessly: following her body across each foot and nook of my studio; outside, walking through Central Park, lying down, the sun caught in her skin—or in bathtubs, watching how the water refracted the light on her face. I'd paint. It felt like cheating. Even after she moved in—after my wife and daughter left—she posed for me almost daily. Then, when she was tired of being watched, she'd lick a fingertip as though to turn a page but the finger would drop below her book and dangle over her groin. This didn't mean anything special, of course. If she smiled, though— not any old stretch but a smile broad enough to reveal her chipped canines—that was it, my cue, the first infallible move in our formula of sex. Always enough—there and then—to make me happy.

OLD APELMAN BEAMS WHEN HE SEES ME. "The big day!" he cries out, before marching across the polished floorboards of his gallery, dodging sculptures made of wire and rubber bands, to give me a hug. Apelman's a sucker for all that man-to-man contact stuff. Right now, though, I'm a convert. I can't get enough: I'm nestling my chin against his beard when he shoves me away, pats me hard on the back a couple of times and says, "You smell like the main floor at Bloomingdale's."

It's true—I smell good. Mixed with sweat, the half ounce of French cologne I splashed on this morning seems to have brought forth a chemical pungency.

"And hey, buddy, did I see you *power walking* just now?"

I realize, after a while, he's talking about my squirmy, gimpish gait. A new aerobic regime, I tell him. We joke around about black-tie marathons and cardiac arrests—who'll finish first—but my heart's not in it. My mind's jammed. I know why I'm here—I'm ripe for Apelman's pep—and honestly, I'm trying to follow him as he jabbers away, but in my head I'm still inside her matchbox apartment, sharing a bathtub so small we both sit chin to knee; I'm watching her eat, sloppily, lips smeared with mango juice, sweet with the nectar of plums. I never thought it would be me: the painter who falls for his nude model. *I love that,* she says. What? *When you look at me too long.* Then she smiles. I drag her toward me, fend her off. Through it all, she loves hitting me. Her lips turn martial. Afterward we fall apart, marks on our bodies, smelling of fruit and mineral spirits, soap and charcoal. *You're a dirty old man,* she says, giving me her best dirty young girl look, steering my cigaretted hand to her lips. I leave, each time, with new bruises.

No, I think to myself, no, get with it. Stay with the program.

"How's business?" I ask.

Apelman's looking at me funny. I take another drag. Maybe he'd been hot for her. Maybe not. He'd never married. After a prolonged period of sulking and half-veiled threats on my part, they'd both denied it.

"Better," Apelman says slowly, "if my biggest name would give me something to sell."

"Freud's up to eight months now. Per painting."

"He's a perfectionist."

"I'm a perfectionist."

"Well," he says, "that explains why you've got nothing to give me."

We both grin. We're a regular riot together.

"Listen," I say. Then I stop—I realize I've got no idea what to tell him. "Actually. I've been meaning to talk—"

He motions me toward the back office. "Hey," he says, "forget it, buddy. That's not why I asked you here." He rests his hand on my tux shoulder. "Take all the time," he says.

But I know what he's thinking. I glance at the walls as I dodder behind him: splashes of chalky-colored oilsticks on linen and vinyl, photogravures and woodcut prints—all pulled off with the impatient skill and insolence of youth. They're good. Clamoring at his door. He always had a good eye, Apelman. He's thinking of my last exhibition—when was it?—more than a year ago now: those obsessive portraits of Olivia, black-layered and liquid, how I'd worried the same lines—trying to keep in the light— before it was shut off for good. The tube running out of her mouth, two plastic offshoots from her nose and the bright green wires that led to the bright blue box pumping breath in and out of her. Disney colors.

"How are your eyes?" Apelman asks.

I blink, looking for a place to throw my cigarette butt. A few months ago, my eyes joined in on my body's general strike. Some condition that made them more sensitive to light. An ironic inca- pacity. Everywhere I looked, everything looked brighter—then dimmer in a bright way through my sunglasses—like the color was drained out, like I was seeing everything at twilight. Any- way, my ophthalmologist, Andrew Werner, ran some tests and found nothing physically wrong.

"It comes and goes," I say.

"We're getting old." He peers quickly through the glass parti- tion into the gallery. A young couple is walking in. "So, have you talked to Elise?"

"Not since last week."

"Where are you taking her?"

"Picholine. Her fiancé too."

"The manager?"

"Yeah." I snort. "The Leech."

The young couple drag their feet as they move, heads sway- ing and slanting, through the gallery. Grad students, proba- bly. As they get close to the back office, I see them glance in, eyeballing my outfit. The girl starts whispering to the boy behind a magazine. I stare back and they scurry out. The boy tries to affect a relaxed amble but he's irrelevant; there's something about that girl—I watch as she darts across the street—how, past all the glass-fronted galleries, the low brick chop shops and warehouses, she walks without moving her hips, how the cute little beret holds down her hair against the Hudson wind . . .

"Still got it," Apelman chuckles. Then, "Hey, buddy—hey, you okay?"

I shrug. He reaches into his coat pocket, leans across the office desk and hands me a white, ironed handkerchief. I'm not sure if I'm supposed to blow my nose into it. For a moment I want to

tell him about the diagnosis. I can't. It's clogged there somewhere, blocked by a little mushroom in my throat, maybe more
than one, maybe deeper.

"It's a big deal," he says gently. "You're meeting your daughter for the first time in—for the first time, really."

I nod.

"She's an adult now," he goes on. "She's making her own
decisions. A new life. And she's decided she wants you to be part
of it."

It's pathetic how okay this guy can make me feel. With his
smooth talking and chic Chelsea gallery I don't get how he's
managed to stay unhitched.

"Henry, I'm going to tell you something." He sets his mouth
in a tight line in the middle of his beard. I know this look. I'm
about to be *advised*. And what's more—I want it. I *crave* it.
"I know you've been having a hard time of it," he says. "I
know you miss Olivia. I miss her too. You're angry." Only Apelman could pull this off, this primped wording, this deadpan
goodness. He goes on in this vein—nothing I haven't heard
before—his eyes so earnest he looks like a cross between a TV
evangélist and a cow. He only wants what's best for me, he says,
and in that precise moment I realize it's true. He's the only one.
At last he stops, breathes, waits for me to catch up to him, then
says, "Just don't let your anger get away from you. You know how
you are. And another thing: Elise is not her mother. Remember that."

Her mother. I realize I'm wincing. It's the one thing I could
hold against him and he knows it. All those years he stayed in
touch with my ex-wife—the witch—after she kidnapped Elise,
exiled her to Russia—all that time I was cut off from my own
daughter until it was too late, then much too late. The poisoning
complete. He didn't deny it. He'd as much as admitted that my
letters wouldn't get through. Nothing in, nothing out. In seven-

teen years I'd heard from them precisely three times. The first
time, four years in, when her mother hit me up for $520,000.

"It's a Guadagnini," Apelman had explained. "Made in 1752,
by an Italian master."

"Half a million bucks? For a *cello*?"

"Nothing like this has come on the market for years. Helen's
right. It's a good deal."

"She's five years old, for God's sake!"

"And already accepted, personally, by Elena Dernova—"

"No one even told me," I broke in, "that she was learning the
cello."

Apelman waited for me to calm down. Then he told me I was
right: she was too young yet, her body too small. But I could
afford it, he said. He kept his tone careful, urgent. It was in my
hands, he said, to have it ready for her—for when she was ready.
He'd given me the same look then as he's giving me now. Almost
under his breath, he added, "You should hear her play."

So it came to pass that Apelman, consummate networker,
faithful go-betweener, brokered the international deal to buy
my little girl a cello half again as tall as her and fifty times as
old. Nine years of nothing later, I received a handwritten invitation to attend her debut in Russia. She was playing the Rococo
Variations with the St. Petersburg Philharmonic. A big deal
(only fourteen years old!). The invitation came in the post—not
through Apelman. No return address. At the top of the page,
in her neat teenage cursive, she'd written "Father." Both Apelman and Olivia urged me to go—I booked my tickets—then at
the last minute Apelman, gray-faced, handed me another letter.
From the witch: "Under no circumstances . . ." etc., etc. She would
cancel the concert if it came to it. She'd somehow spooked out
the whole scheme. I canceled my tickets.

"*That* means laying off the Leech," Apelman says, permitting
himself a smile. He leans forward and punches me on the shoul-

der. It's like I'm one of those enormous bell carillons and the single clapper of his fist sets off a whole chorus of emotional peals and chimes within me. He might be everyone's friend, Apelman, but he's my only friend. He looks me in the eye. Then he says what I've been thinking ever since I picked up the phone and heard her voice a week ago—no—honestly—ever since I saw her last, blanket-wrapped and pillow-sized and hot with fever on my apartment stoop—"Family is family. You might only have one shot at it."

A MESS. I'M A MESS. Things are a little off upstairs, I know that. That was always a lark to Olivia—now she *is* the lark. Banging around in my belfry. My ass is back to its old pyrotechnic tricks. On top of that, I'm sore all over. It's all the reflection. Seeing Apelman hasn't helped. The past's a cold body of water for me and nowadays my bones ache after even a quick dip.

He's right, though. I'm sitting in the private wine room at Picholine trying to pull myself together. My daughter hasn't arrived. Our table's the only one there—I called in a favor. The sound of the restaurant wafts through the hallway—low voices, laughs, the tinkling of glasses—the place, recently renovated, seems a lot cheerier than I remember. An odious young man is attending me. He's got so much gel in his slicked hair it pulls his face back tight. Traversing the harried catwalk of the front room I noticed him eyeballing my outfit; I'm at one of the most over-priced joints in town and still this kid-waiter makes me feel overdressed.

For starters, I order the crab salad with the grapefruit gelée, the spiced squab pastrami and the sea-urchin panna cotta. Then I remember Apelman's advice. The Leech might take offense if I don't wait—Brits being sensitive about things like that. How sensitive are they, though, to punctuality? I bark at the waiter and cancel the order. He smiles as though I've just made his day. For a second I'm worried his face might crack.

Half an hour later, I tell him to check the restaurant, both rooms.

"Under what name?"

"Kozlov," I tell him. Her mother's maiden name. When he comes back I tell him, "Or Sharps. Jason Sharps."

I hear a rowdy burst of laughter from the main room. When Gel-head trots in again, I tell him I've changed my mind. I'll order a bottle of red wine. I'm in a wine room, for God's sake! As I drink the room shrinks around me. It feels damp now, and smells—it smells like the inside of a janitor's closet. It smells of sickness, of dripping fluids, of saturated tissues. Forty minutes late. Fifty.

My body feels alien to me. I don't know it at all, I want nothing to do with it, I disown it. There's something inside me and *it's* dying—not me. So this is how it feels. Betrayed by your own body. I'd thought she lived most of her life on the surface of her skin but she'd found a way to get beneath, my Olivia. She'd discovered the flesh was hollow. I flew into a jealous rage. She left me. I begged her to come back. Who picks up a smack habit in their thirties? I thought. After fifteen, sixteen years together— wanting for nothing. Well, wanting for something, obviously. She blamed her body and so did I. She quit time and time again and then, at last, the time came when she didn't need to quit anymore.

More than an hour late. I signal for a second bottle. I know Gel-head's smirking behind his mask. I want to smash it in. I've been getting like this lately: irate at people I don't know.

"Would you like to reorder any appetizers, sir?"

No, he's a good kid. Just doing his job. I shake my head, lean over to squeeze his arm—give him some man-to-man contact—

but he skips back, bumping against the wire mesh screen of a bookcase-like cabinet. The dust-rimmed clinking of a hundred bottles fills the room. He freezes, gapes at me—untrained to deal with the moment—then scuttles out.

Don't get me wrong, I like kids—Olivia was thirty years younger than me. I even wanted to have some with her. The problem is there are just too many of them. You can't throw a brick on this island without concussing one. I wish I had more restraint. But I can't help but hate how they look at me, how they don't look at me, I hate their interchangeable bodies, their mass-rehearsed attitudes, their cars that look like boxes, like baseball caps, like artificial enlargements, their loud advertising, their beeps and clicks and trings, I hate how they speak words as though they're chewing them, how they assume the business of the world revolves around them—how they're right—and how everywhere this cult of youth, this pedomorphic dumbing-down, has whored beauty—duped, drugged, damaged, pixelated it and everywhere turned it to plastic.

I'm almost done with my second bottle. All this alcohol will do wonders for my piles. Ninety minutes. Gel-head comes back in and delightedly hands me a cordless phone.

"Henry?"

As with her call last week, I feel as though I've stumbled upon the middle of something. Her voice is slow, sleepy, warm with music. Nothing like her mother's. I'm surprised, anew, by its power over me.

"We're really sorry. We've been trying you at home all afternoon."

I'm untrained to deal with this; I say nothing. After a long pause she says:

"We're sorry. We can't make it to lunch. We hope you haven't been waiting."

"I've been waiting ninety minutes."

The line goes muffled and the sotto voce whispering starts. In the background I can hear the vague strains of a string instrument warming up.

"I'm really sorry. It's just, with the concert—"

More hushed coaching. I look around, as though to ground myself outside her voice. Candles have been cleverly hidden in secret niches and the room glows and twinkles the colors of wine: ruby, amethyst, burgundy, bronze . . .

"We thought maybe it's best to leave this to another time."

"You don't want me to come?"

"Henry."

She can't hang up. I can't let her. I look around. How did I end up in this flinking dungeon?

"I don't mind paying. If it's money—"

"The show's sold out," she says quickly.

"Just a drink, then. I'm close by."

"Henry, I'm not sure I'm ready." I recognize the tone instantly. It belongs to the witch. I know I should stop but I can't.

"Tomorrow. There's a place in the East Village. No, the West Village. We'll have breakfast."

I hear activity on the far end of the phone line, then a muted thud, then an English-accented voice:

"Elise doesn't want to talk to you right now."

"Fuck you," I say playfully.

"Well, that's that," he says.

"I'm sorry. I'm sorry. I'm a bit emotional."

"There's no need for that language."

He's right, I think. The Leech is right. I try to remember what Apelman told me.

"Family is family."

This shuts him up. So I say it again. It doesn't come out quite right the second time.

"You're drunk," he says.

"Hey, genius. Genius—can you put my daughter back on?"

"You're in no state to talk with her." There's a scuffing sound, which I recognize as the universal prelude to hanging up.

"Hey!" Clear air. I frantically search for something to say. "I've got cancer. Tell her that. Press release for you, Mr. Manager: C-A-N-C-E-R. Of the ass. Got that?"

"I've had about enough—"

"Hey! Wait!" I'm screwing this up but I know there's something I can say, something perfect, something that will smooth over the past, pucker open the future. What would Apelman say? It's always been like this. It's always been me who's had to ask forgiveness.

"I'm hanging up."

"And a lot of money," I blurt out. "You know that, right, Leechy? Half a million bucks for a cello, right? There's plenty more where that came from. I bet you'd like to manage that, wouldn't you, once I'm gone? Leechy boy? Hey?"

He hangs up.

I WISH I HAD MORE RESTRAINT. I wish they'd taught it at school, or even before that, when I was still learning things. I shouldn't have quaffed those two 1989 Bordeaux. Let myself attempt full sentences on the phone afterward. At the least, I should've restrained myself from waiting so patiently, so long, for the two of them. Mostly, I wish I had the restraint to stop myself from doing what I'm about to do.

I throw a wad of cash on the table—Gel-head's lucky day— then go back and count it, peel back a few notes. No sense in losing one's head. Hobble through the twisty, curiously grungy hallway, through the mauve-colored, chandeliered restaurant, dodging cheese carts and briefcases, then outside. The sky's overcast. I opt for walking, give myself time to sober up. Cool down. I limp through the southern chunk of Central Park, a tuxedoed booze-breathed cripple among the mass of tourists, families and couples. Children look at me strangely. Everyone else looks away. It's crowded as hell. Then I remember—Columbus Day weekend.

I'm not sure I'm ready. What did she mean? Ready for what? To see me? Or for the concert? I shouldn't have pestered her hours before her big performance. But did that mean she'd be ready after the concert, though? Maybe she meant she wasn't ready for marriage to the Leech. A coded message. I shamble under the elms, past the hackberries and maples, lindens and ashes, deep in thought. When we came here Olivia had always insisted on teaching me the names of things. By the pond a group of amateur photographers click away at the asters. I decide to go the long way, double back later. I shuffle painfully through the crowd. Then, at the line of horse-drawn carriages, I stop, my body burning, let myself think it. She wasn't ready to see me at all. Maybe she'd never be ready.

I don't realize until I'm a little ways down Fifth. It's the height of fall. I turn around. Central Park is in bloom, spastic with color—red, orange, green, yellow, purple, brown, gold. The asters have broken out into their annual parade of white, lavender, red, and pink. My head knows this but my eyes missed it—my poor eyes didn't see it.

I hang my head, trudge west along Fifty-seventh. Finally I get to Carnegie Hall. *Focus,* I tell myself. I convince the man at the box office that I'm Elise Kozlov's father. This makes me feel grubby and proud at once. Of course it's important, I tell him. He tells me where they're rehearsing, doing sound checks or something. I follow the sound to the parquet entrance of the main auditorium, push the door open and see her immediately, the black-gray smudge of four smudges on the distant stage, the one with the instrument between her legs. The one made small by her instrument. I move closer. She's just a girl in a dress that barely covers her knees. She looks like the girl in the website photo. Her face under the heavy lighting so young, yet so stern. Even the way she holds the cello is stern. I see it all clearly now.

And she's beautiful without me. I hate the young for that too. That they're assured in their beauty, in the way that only animals are assured—unmussed by the thought of death.

At the end of the piece she looks up and sees me. I'm in the half dark nearly a hundred yards away but she looks straight at me. No startlement, no gasp, no hand-to-mouth dramatics. It's me who's too stunned to do anything. Looking directly at me, she says something—her lips move—and I try desperately to decipher her words, to puzzle out a fitting response. By that point a young man in jeans and a black T-shirt glides out of the wings and down the aisle. Without touching me once, he escorts me outside the auditorium.

"Are you Sharps?"

He shakes his head. Then he looks up at me curiously. "Hey, sir, are you all right?"

"Tell her I want to see her. Just for a second."

"Sorry?"

"Elise. Tell Elise—her father's here to see her." Her lips in my head, the lines of them, merging into one another. Her eyes. "Tell her . . . he says he's sorry."

"Wait here."

As soon as he leaves, I slip back into the auditorium. Stand in the shadows. Then I see them onstage. The Leech attaching himself. He's a gangly, womanly-shouldered redhead. She's kissing him, her face upturned. I resent the grace of it, and the want. She's on tiptoes and both her arms are lifted up to his ears. He doesn't stoop at all to meet her lips. I feel my stomach in my throat, breath hot and thick through my nostrils. Apelman's voice in my head like an advertising jingle. I creak the heavy door open and slink back outside.

Minutes later the door opens again and Black T-shirt hands me a note. His face is insouciant now, verging on rude. By this time I don't care. My heart is hopping. I was wrong. I remembered—she looked *straight at me*. She wants to see me, she knows it's inevitable. I wait until he's gone before I unfold the note:

> *Henry,*
>   *I don't want to see you. Please meet Jason backstage after the concert (show this note) to discuss a payment plan for the Guadagnini.*

FIRST, DRAW A BATH. Outside, light thinning into the color of piss. Everything looks like the color of piss. Peel off my jacket, shirt, pants, throw them into a corner where they squat, stiffened from starch and sweat, malevolent. Lidocaine my bloated, inflamed rosebud. Lower it—*aaaaarggh*—into the steaming hot bath. Then something I haven't done for almost a year: try to sketch. My fingers jiggling. I keep them out of the water, clinching a stick of charcoal, meek above the wet-splotched pad.

Apelman doesn't know I haven't done this at all since Olivia died. Sketched or painted. He doesn't know, either, that I've been seeing her everywhere. Today, though, I saw my daughter. And she saw me. Maybe for the last time. Why am I drawing? Apelman would love the idea: painter turns to art to redeem suffering. Sometimes, if the hand moves, the mind can rest. But not this time. I'm drawing to grab hold of her. If the hurt's all I have left of her, I want to keep it, keep it alive—hurting—because right now I think I need everything I have.

It was her handwriting. Unchanged in four years. She called me by my name.

It starts drizzling outside. The room darkens. Water condenses and runs down the full length of the windows, spills over the curved limestone caps. There's an exhaustion in the quality of the light. On the street, leaves catch moisture, gleam like the scales of dead fish. The gutters go black and wet.

A dot. Another dot. A line between them. I remember the last face I drew. Believe it or not, she, Olivia, was the only one. My single dalliance—through five years of matrimonial, blue-balled freeze-out. She was my risk. When my wife found out about her and blew the country, dangling our daughter from her broom, Olivia told me, "You've made your choice. Don't keep on choosing. Not every day you're with me."

Young women fuck like they're running out of time. It's like they know something. When her time ran out, I sat there, weeks, sketching her. Wondering if she could hear me, sense me, through her coma; if, when she slept, she completed a thought with each breath. An old man and a beautiful, serious young girl. I wondered how long she'd known about the diagnosis. I wondered whether—if *I'd* known—it would have made a difference. But all I had known was her perfect hunger, the painful playing out of her imperfect satisfaction.

At the hospice, I frightened away her visitors: mostly young people holding tight-bunched, crinkle-wrapped flowers, fuzzy toys, heart-shaped balloons. They came with nothing to say, stretching their lips as though smiling to me. They leaned over her machine-lived body with their face piercings and earplugs and iPods and cell phones and I wanted to rip all their things off, throw them away, and show them—*show* them—if they wanted so badly to plug the sockets of their bodies—what it was to be fixed upon that bed.

Only Apelman stayed, sitting by me as they pumped cocktail after cocktail into her polluted veins, her self-savaging body, watching me as I watched her . . .

The drizzle turns to rain. Outside the glass wall, the last of the color is sucked out of the air. The streets are filthy with debris and the wind picks up papers, plastic wrappers, dead leaves— tosses them on its invisible surf. Holding my hands up, I immerse my head in the bathwater. Suddenly the plumbing of the whole building comes alive, like the massive groaning of the earth itself. I can hear the rain drumming on every exposed surface. Olivia taught me that trick.

I sit up, look out through the glass. I like the rain, how it makes monochrome of things. Even its own noise. People pass by, faces darkened under black umbrellas. Feet mutely slapping shallow puddles. Some caught unprepared: rushing arms crossed, heads bowed, as though shouldering their way out of an emergency room. Others slow down, look up, faces spotted with raindrops, mouths agape, pretending they're actually enjoying it. Chumps.

The drawing takes shape. She's looking at me and her mouth is open. Her hair so dark it looks wet. My wife's sitting on a suit-case crying. They'll be staying, she says, at her friend's place in Bushwick. In her carriage, Elise is asleep, features clouding in dream. She lets out a slight gargle as I pick her up. "Don't," my wife says through her sniffling, "she's sick." I put her back down and tuck her in. It's a relief; she's the only thing that can make my hands feel graceless. Now I see the perfect little beads of sweat on her forehead. Her body giving off warmth like a hot-water bottle. I think about kissing her but don't want to scratch her awake with my whiskers. To the dramatic sounds of my wife's surfacing, strangled sobs, I duck my head and go upstairs. Leaving them on the front stoop. Not knowing that the taxi that comes will take them not to a friend's place in Bushwick but to JFK. Not knowing that it will smuggle my daughter seventeen years away from me. But all that night—night after night—my dreams are filled with the image of her doll-small body on the stoop, burning, fevered with her father's sin.

I try to capture her eyes on the page. In my head—my mind's eye—they're stern, accusing. But then it was either-or, either-or, and knowing what I knew, feeling what I felt, how could she have expected me to choose differently? How much does a moment carry? Across a gap of seventeen years, now she shows me shame again? Blood made hard and broken to bits. On the stage, her eyes were so clear and deep and large and true. The light from them—if she had turned them fully on me—could have made even a dirty old man like me look new again.

I throw down the pad and charcoal, stand up, clean as a corpse. Olivia always got a kick out of that, standing naked in full view of passersby on the street. Apelman's right. Family is family. I look at the floor, at the drawing, her gray-sketched face made bleary by spots of bathwater. As I climb out of the bath I feel warmth dribbling down my legs. I look down and see it—for the first time—blood—in the water: suspended, its pink wisps shifting like the petals of a flower.

Here's what I'll do: Look at myself in the mirror. My face stark white, a shock of bone and skin and hair. My teeth yellow, carious. The valves of my body corroded. *Get your clothes on and get working.* The order of the day: Get dressed—she's coming today.

Something swanky, maybe the white-tie suit. The satin peak lapel, besom pockets, with the white piqué vest. I pad my underwear with Kleenex to catch the blood. Outside, it's still raining— I skate the sidewalk, finding my way by the light of office buildings. The streets vacant, dark as a lung. When the wind is up it sounds like the trees talk to each other above the noise of a crowd.

I'm late. The performance has already started. In fact, it's almost over. The ticket clerk repeats this before he trots out his supervisor. I tell them who I am. There's a buzzing in my head— the sound of a fluorescent tube—as we argue, and then, finally, I have it in my hands—my ticket.

Side balcony. The signs leading up and up. The carpet is red-plaided and oil-darkened and feels like freshly mown grass—each step sinking in a bit. My footsteps leave damp craters. Music, all the while, audible from behind the neoclassically reliefed walls, floating to me as though from a distant boat. The stairs get steeper. I imagine I can hear it, her centuries-old cello. By the time I reach the top my legs feel weak, hollowed out, flush with hot bathwater and whiskey. My cummerbund is up underneath my nipples, my collar like wet cardboard, every seam in my shirt stamping itself into my skin. Sweat spurting out of every furrow.

"Sir," the gilt-brocaded usher begins, but I stare him down. I recover my breath. Then, slowly, I lean open the heavy door. The sound sudden, heart-flooding. She's onstage, the four of them forming an almost closed circle: playing as though only to each other.

The people in my row half rise, half brace, anything to avoid touching me as I sidle to my seat. My ass smarts when I sit down. There's a buttress blocking half of my face. I imagine the Leech in the front row, the hatchet silhouette of his head, his gangly legs all stretched out. It doesn't matter, though—I can still hear her, the sound of her cello, full, sonorous, rising through my body and slowly transmuting the pain into warmth, the carry of it through the auditorium, and it's as though my body is without substance and I'm dissolving into the sound she scratches out of her contraption of wood and steel and hair. The concert hall the space inside my skull.

Rain and sweat puddle the floor at my feet. It's getting hot. The music goes on in its slow, gorgeous, devastating burn. When I lean over for a better view my neighbor recoils, initiating a long sequence of public sighing. Now I see her, my Elise. Her head remains still: her bowing neat, precise. Her hair gleams burn-white and black under the spotlight—she's floating out there on a skiff of light—my daughter, my baby girl. A severe beauty all the way through her. My heart hitches underneath its tight cummerbund. I see her. She has everything she needs. She has wrung all my weaknesses out of her strong, straight body.

Get up. I get up. Light in myself, brittle—unable to hear, hold, any more—I breast, woozily, the row of half-risen knees. On the hallway stairs the applause starts up. It sounds like rain. Then, amazingly, there are shouts, stamping feet. I leave the building and go outside—into the brindled rain, the rain become iridescent—into the steel-lamp night. Above the world's dead weight. It's raining outside. I catch my breath and watch as the crowd comes out. She's coming out. She'll be out any second now.

Then I see her—in the walk of a young boy, in the languor of a twenty-year-old—uncommon economy for someone so young— no, there—at fifty, on a billboard, heartbreakingly beautiful and advertising the power of business solutions. Eyes gray, smile gas-blue. A deeper run of colors in her cheekbones. No, no—the darkness, through rain, is deceptive. The crowd empties out of the theater like a last exhalation. I count her as she passes.

It's raining. There she is. Stooped and somehow swanlike, waiting under the corner streetlight. The light drawn into her skin, soaking it, making it refulgent in the black mine of city. A serious young girl. Wind splaying her dark hair. No, I never had a shot—not really. Move, out of breath, toward that shore of light. Catch her and she'll smile, teeth showing—draw it for me—this matter of memory, word by word. Dirty old man. Wait up, Olivia, I'm coming. I see you now! Are you ready? Wait up for me!

Halflead Bay

IT WAS SHAPING UP TO BE A good summer for Jamie. Exams were over. School was out in a couple of weeks—the holidays stretching before him, wide and flat and blue. On top of that he was a hero. Sort of. At assembly that morning, the principal had paused after his name and the school had broken into spontaneous cheering and clapping. Jamie was onstage with the rest of the first eighteen. He could barely make out the faces beneath him—the lights turned off on account of the heat—but what he remembered were voices swelling out of the large, dim hall as though out from one of his daydreams. You couldn't buy that feeling. Still, his dad. Seated in the front row with the other guests of honor—unimpressed as ever. His smile as stiff as his suit.

"C'arn, Halfies!" the principal called out. He opened his arms. From the back of the hall students started stomping their feet.

Jamie had scored the winning goal in last week's semifinal. For the first time in five years, Halflead Bay High had a real crack at reclaiming the pennant. All his school years Jamie couldn't recall even having a conversation with Alan Leyland, the principal, but now Leyland turned around from the podium and half bowed to him. Everyone looked at the two of them. Then the cry was taken up—*Halfies! C'arn, Halfies!*—even teachers, parents, joining in—Jamie still and rapt in the hot roar until he arrived, again, at his dad's face. The uneasy grin. Of course. The stomping, chanting, Leyland's theatrical attitude: a faint film of mockery slid over it all. Jamie pushed it aside. His dad was wrong, he thought. He was wrong, and anything was possible.

ALISON FISCHER APPROACHED HIM AT RECESS.

"Leyland was licking your arse," she said.

He clutched up from the drinking fountain, mouth brimming water, swallowed. "Hi," he said. The word came out in a burp and left a wet trail down his chest.

"Hi yourself."

She stood with her head cocked to one side, hip to the other. Her school dress was stretched so tight it bit into her thigh. He wiped his mouth, looked around. Alison Fischer. It was a morning of firsts.

"Leyland couldn't be stuffed about footy."

"What?"

"He's thinking about enrollments," Jamie said. He tried to remember how his mum had put it. "He just wants the pennant to sucker new parents."

"Shove over," Alison ordered. She bent down to the nozzle and pursed her mouth in a glossy O. Her top button was undone—sprung open as though by heat—and he could see the inside line of her breasts. The stripe of sweat gleaming between them.

She said, "I've seen you down at the wharf." Her lips bright wet.

"I'm working there these holidays."

"Nah, the jetty, I mean. Fishing. With that surfie mate of yours."

"Cale?"

He looked around again. Most of the kids had stayed indoors for recess; others were lying in shade, as still as snakes, under the casuarinas. It was too hot for sport. Off in the paddocks a knot of boys poked at something on the ground. Alison switched hips and smiled patiently at him.

"That was your dad in there, right?"

"My dad?" He laughed weakly.

"With the tie."

This was how it happened: these girls, they did it for kicks, daring each other to go up to random blokes and act interested. He'd seen it before. A gaggle of them—Alison their leader—sitting apart from everyone else, watching on; they sealed off even their amusement, coughing it around their circle like a wet scrap. Tammie, Kate, Laura—all the rest of them, faces mocked up—they were bored with everything and totally up themselves and every boy at Halflead wanted them.

"He didn't even come to the game."

"*My* parents," she said, "after *that* game." Her smile went lopsided. "I reckon they'd adopt you."

He pretended to wave away a fly, looked around again. None of them were in sight. No Dory either. The sound of a piano started up from somewhere—each note hung—tin-flat, percussive—then evaporated in the heat. So she wanted to talk about the game. No way they'd mess with him, not after last weekend. That assembly. She was alone. She was smiling at him as though she didn't belong to somebody else.

"That'd make you my sister."

"We couldn't have that, right?"

Whoever was at the piano was a beginner, trying out a new scale: slow, stop-start. Jamie felt himself trapped between the notes, inside the heavy spaces where nothing moved. He realized his whole body was sweating. So she'd talk about his dad—himself sweating in that funereal suit, several sizes too small for him, cuffs up past his wrists—and he'd let her. Applause in his ears. That wry, skeptical smirk.

"So you reckon we can beat Maroomba?"

"I'm there heaps," he said. His voice came out rougher than he'd intended. "The jetty, I mean."

"What?"

"Don't be such a bloody snob. Say hi next time."

"And then what?"

"What are you after?"

"Alison!" a voice called from the school building. Everyone started moving back inside. The sound of the piano petered out, blaring moments later as passing hands bashed its keys.

She leaned toward him. That band of sweat between her breasts—he wanted to bring his mouth to it and lick it up. He wanted her to giggle, push him away, tell him it tickled. Her smile seemed different now.

"I can teach you how to squid," he said.

"Fuck," she said in a low voice, "you're a fast worker, aren't you?"

He didn't say anything.

"Who would've guessed it. Loose Ball Jamie—that's what they call you, right?"

His face flushed. Someone shouted her name again. The school grounds were almost empty now but he had the overwhelming feeling of being watched. Every window in the building blazed with reflected light.

He inclined his head in the classroom's general direction. "We should—"

"So is that what I am? A loose ball?" Her voice went weird, slightly off-pitched: " 'Just come down to the jetty and say hi?' "

The sweat on her collarbones, too, burned white in the sun. The back of her hip-cocked arm. That was the problem with Alison Fischer: you never knew which part of her to look at.

He looked at her face. She was grinning crookedly, her mouth still wet.

DORY'S GIRL—SHE WAS DORY'S GIRL—but then who knew how serious that was? Jamie had liked her forever. And not just in the way everyone talked, in the change rooms, about chicks at school: Laura Brescia, who wore a G-string under her school uniform; Tammie K, who gave Nick a head job and then gave Jimmy one as well so he wouldn't dob about Nick to her big-smoke boyfriend. She was gagging but kept going, Jimmy crowed. He mimed it: gripping her long hair, kneading it into her scalp. No—Alison was more than that. She ran with that crowd but kept herself apart, reserving herself, everyone knew, for the thrall of the big city. Where her family—and their money—were from. Where everyone assumed she'd head once accepted into the university there next year. Until this morning, Jamie would never even have thought to lob his hopes that high.

Still. Dory Townsend. You'd have to be a lunatic.

THEY LIVED, THE FOUR OF THEM, on a spur overlooking the sea. Their house must have been one of the most elevated in town. His parents had bought it twenty years ago, back when Halflead Bay was little more than a petrol station and stop-over to and from the city. According to Jamie's mum, that was how they'd first met: she was filling up the tank of her rented car when his dad's crew traipsed up from the wharf and into the pub. He was the one who walked without moving his hands. Hungry, worn out from her day in an adverse office—she worked, then, as a forensic accountant—she'd decided to go in too, for a counter meal. Two months later—her own car fully loaded, her career resolutely behind her—she returned to seek out the man who'd seemed, all that evening, to stand for a world of simpler details: a big sky, a sustaining sea, a chance to do work whose usefulness a child could understand.

At first they stayed with his dad's folks on the southern prom. A family of fishermen. Then, when they got married, they moved up the hill. Before the advent of all the developers and holiday-homers, the winemakers and tourists. Back then, Jamie's dad said, you could buy property for next to nothing: the town was dying, hemorrhaging people and industry first as the bay was overfished, then again when Maroomba poached its port traffic. Only the few hardy locals stayed behind. For the next fifteen years his parents had lived exactly how they'd dreamed, his dad skippering one of the town's few remaining trawlers, his mum working on her landscapes—seascapes, really—low, bleached blocks of color settling on a horizontal line. Sky and sea. It was why she'd picked this place. She needed to live in sight of the ocean as much as his dad needed to be on it.

Then, five years ago—the diagnosis. MS. The devastating run of relapses. Despite his wife's protests, Jamie's dad sold his stake in the trawler—started working in the home workshop, knocking out shop fittings, furniture. Jamie and Michael kept going to school. Everyone carried on—working through, around, the illness—as though every moment wasn't actually a dare. As though every word wasn't a word more, every act a further act of waiting.

MICHAEL WAS STANDING at the mouth of the driveway. His body bleared in the heat haze above the bitumen. Coming closer, Jamie felt a spark of affection toward him and almost called out his name.

"Dad wants us," Michael said first. He didn't look up from his Game Boy.

"I'm gonna head down the jetty." He hesitated, watching Michael's thumbs wagging on the gray console. "You can come if you like."

"They're fighting."

"So?"

"I just told you, they're fighting." His voice was too deep for a ten-year-old.

Jamie stopped himself laughing. "Mum okay?" He peered up the slope. The house was barely visible from the road, blotted out by foliage: ironwoods, kurrajongs, ghost gums bursting up through the brush. The garden was wild. As he started up the driveway, everything described itself as though to Alison: overhanging branches, knee-high grass, yellowed in places by warped, gutted objects—miscarriages of his mum's interest. Sprockets of leaves. Green everywhere plaited with brightly colored spikelets and bracts. There was his bedroom, the shedlike bungalow. Once his mum's studio, it still gave off an aftersmell of turpentine—faint as something leaked by a body in the dark and dried by morning. And there, a stone's throw away at the top of the driveway, was their double-storied house: a worn weatherboard that seemed choked by bushes and creepers, by the old white veranda that buckled all around it. What would she make of it?

He went round back and into the workshop. The lamps—they must have made it ten degrees hotter indoors. His dad was bent over a long, slightly curved piece of wood, one end wrapped in tape like a boxer's fist.

"I'm almost done," his dad said. His shirt clung wetly all the way down his back, right down to the apron string. "Figured it out. Front struts were too heavy, that's why it wouldn't rock." Using vise-grip pliers, he clamped down on the taped end with his left hand. With his right he started planing the length of the wood. The top half of the chair—the seat and back—lay tipped forward on the table before him.

"I'm going down the jetty," said Jamie.

"Storm's coming."

"Yeah?"

"Day or two. I need you to bring in your mum's stuff first."

"Okay."

"Make sure you look everywhere. Her stuff's everywhere."

"Okay."

"Hang on," his dad said. He put down his tools and turned around. His face and neck—except for two white trapezoids behind his goggles—were plastered in sawdust. It cracked around his mouth when he smiled. "You should've heard them cheering this morning," he said. "For your brother."

Jamie was confused, then heard Michael's voice: "What'd they say?" His brother stepped around him into the workshop.

Their father aimed a roughhouse swat at Michael's hair, then wiped his own brow with the back of his gloves, leaving a wavy orange smear. "Sounds like we missed a big game. But we'll make it next week." He nodded at Michael, the smile still tight and dry on his face. Was he taking the piss? "Biggest game of all, right?"

"We're gonna get slaughtered," said Michael.

"Shut up," said Jamie.

Michael shied away, out of his reach. "Everyone says so."

"Boys."

"Okay," said Jamie. "I'll move the stuff to the shed." He kicked some dust at Michael. "Come on."

"Hang on." His dad took off his gloves, then his safety goggles. Sawdust swirled in the lamplight. "I need you boys to do something for me," he said. "For your mum."

He went to the sink. Using the heel of his palm, he pushed

open the tap, then washed his hands under the water violently, absorbedly, the old habit of a fisherman scrubbing off a day's stink. He threw water on his face.

"I got an offer on the house," he said.

Neither of them said anything.

"It wouldn't be till January. But they need our go-ahead by Friday." After a moment, he reached behind himself and untied his apron, looped it over his head. "We talked about this." He glanced at Jamie, "I know you got that dock job these holidays. Shouldn't clash, though."

Michael said, "I don't wanna move."

Jamie corked him just beneath the shoulder. He felt his knuckle meet bone: that one would bruise.

"Don't," said Michael.

"Don't be such a little dickhead then."

Their dad frowned at them, blinking water, rust-colored, out of his eyes. Michael massaged his arm and muttered, "That was a good one."

"But Mum wants to stay here," said Jamie. He was thinking about Alison.

"Last month," said his dad, "when me and your mum went to Maroomba." He inhaled noisily, the sawdust jiggling on air currents in front of his face. "We talked about this," he repeated. "Everything's in Maroomba. All the facilities. Your mum—right now—she needs to be there."

"What's that mean, 'right now'?"

His dad sighed. "Come on, Jamie."

Earlier that year he'd seen his mum naked, slouched back, knees spread, in the bathtub and his dad kneeling over her, holding a sponge. The water was foamless and he saw everything—most of her body the color of the water except for two large dark nipples, her pubic hair. Dark spots wrinkling under the liquid skin. That time, her eyes were closed.

"I need you boys to talk to her. Tell her you don't mind. Moving, I mean."

"She doesn't want to, but."

"Not if you boys keep acting like this. Like you don't want to either." He ran his hands through his hair, orange sweating down his forehead.

Her body a ghostly rippling film of her body. Ever since the diagnosis she'd been separating, bit by bit, from her own body. His dad hadn't even fully turned around from the tub. *Come on, Jamie*—he'd said that then too.

"What'd the doctors say?" Jamie asked at last. He remembered, before they'd left for Maroomba a few weeks ago, his mum's familiar protests—she was okay, she didn't need to go, not this time.

"Jesus—what's so bloody complicated about it, son?" His dad was blinking hard now, as if to bully his eyes into some new clarity. "You can't just do what I tell you?"

Michael, still caressing his arm, didn't look up.

His dad went to the sink and washed his face again. A stool beside him was stacked high with creased linen and he used a corner of the top sheet to towel off. His face in his hands, he said, "You know what she's like."

"Sorry," said Jamie. His voice sounded too loud. "I'll talk to her."

After a few moments, his dad nodded. "So you going down the jetty."

"Probably the flats first."

"Sandworm?"

"Yeah."

"We need to let the buyers know by Friday."

"I know."

By then—Friday—the sheets would be washed, hanging from lines that zigzagged across the backyard. They'd fill with light and puff themselves up like curtains. She'd be upstairs, on her reclining couch, looking the other way. Out toward the water.

"You know what she's like," his dad repeated.

HE'D FALLEN OFF THE JETTY ONCE. He was with a group of mates, chucking rocks at the moored boats. Longest throw won, loser was a poofter. His turn: one moment he was doing a run-up and the next he was dead—what death must be like—a thrown switch, a fizzling of the senses, the sound sucked out of things. Your eyes a dark cold green hurt.

He'd come into his mum's studio and offered her his head.

"This is what I mean," she said in her clear voice. His dad was by the window, leaning heavily with crossed arms over the top of an easel, a sandwich in one hand. Underneath him a canvas was set and stretched and primed—this was years ago, when she would work on several paintings at the same time.

"I better go, Maggie, I'm late. What happened?"

Jamie looked up. His dad's forearms seemed as dense as the wood they rested on, scored with scabs, sun lesions. He stuffed the last of the sandwich into his mouth and came closer.

"You okay, son?"

His mum poured Dettol on the wound, rubbed it in with her sleeve. The thin, toxic fluid leaked down Jamie's face and into his mouth. In his spit, still, the gagging memory of seawater.

His mum slapped her palm against his dad's cheek as he was leaving, pulled it in for a kiss. "Of course he is," she said.

At first she kept it to herself. There may have been minor episodes but Jamie and Michael were both at school, their dad out on the trawler all day. She worked alone. Her city life a lifting impression. By that time she was beginning to make a name for herself painting with big steel spatulas, smearing and scraping her compositions over broad canvases. She mixed her own paint. The house and studio and yard were cluttered with the junk of her labor: glass panes and book dust jackets used as makeshift palettes, improvised seashell slabs as mullers. Every window she passed was thrown open—for ages afterward she'd come across sketches and enigmatic notes to herself crammed between books, weighted down under tins of pigment powder, turps and binding oils. Even before the diagnosis, her work— and it was heavy work—seemed driven by mania.

As if she knew. As if before it all, she already understood how it would happen: one moment you were bunching up the full strength of your body for a throw and the next you lost your purchase on everything, you'd slipped on squid guts and woke up drowning in paint, your body a hurt, disobedient in paper-thin sleeves. After all, what was to say it shouldn't hurt?—to feel, or move; to push a hand or eye across a plane? If your body endured for no real reason, what was to say you should feel anything at all?

SEAGULLS, HUNDREDS OF THEM, wheeled and skirled over- head. Jamie lay down on his back and followed the light-dark speccks against the sunlight, tuning out Cale's voice.

"Easy, big man," Cale was saying. "Easy." He was talking to Michael, his speech already slurry with pot.

"The backpackers too."

"Nah, big man, they're not the enemy," said Cale. "Them and the blackfellas, they just mind their own business. They're all right by me. It's the holiday-homers, those rich wankers. And the local bogans."

"Yeah."

"And the Asians, hey," Cale added.

The line tweaked under Jamie's fingertips. He sat upright, fumbled with the rod, but already he could tell the tension had slipped out of it. Seaweed, probably. He sucked down a couple of deep breaths to ease the head rush.

"Some of them are okay," mumbled Michael. "At school." He was playing with a scuffed cricket ball, sending it into elaborate spins from right hand to left.

Cale turned his attention to Jamie. "Monster bite, hey?"

Jamie couldn't remember how they'd become mates. Cale had blown into town a couple of terms ago and started hanging around the beach. Just another shaggy-blond layabout in his twenties. One day he ran up the jetty and helped Jamie gaff a big banjo. They clubbed it dead and Cale held it up under the gills, both of them gape-mouthed, then introduced himself: he was from out west, a surf-chaser: he'd surfed off the coast of Tassie, in Hawaii, around the Horn in South Africa. That leather topaz-studded necklace had been souvenired from his girlfriend's body, wiped out in Europe. He'd glazed his eyes, letting that sink in. Sure, he'd teach Jamie to longboard.

"You're stoned."

Cale nodded, almost shyly, then his face sank into its usual easy, thick-lipped smile. "Those Israelis, man. Always farkin stashed." He teetered up in his red boardshorts and reeled in his line. After prolonged examination, he set a fresh worm on the hook.

"You seen them?" he asked Jamie. "Out near the heads?"

"The Israelis?"

"The Asians, you dimwit."

"What about them?"

"The reef. That's where they poach now."

He had, of course, from a distance. Everyone had. Sliding in and out of rubber dinghies, slick-faced—indistinct even about town where they banded together, laughing in low lilts. An impudence in their laughter. And why not? thought Jamie. They pretty much ran the fishing racket in town now—they'd bought out the fish plant when it was going belly-up years ago. He vaguely recalled being dragged to those rowdy town meetings— all the tirades against those money-grubbing Chinks—his parents arguing on the way home.

"Makes sense," Jamie said. "Hundred bucks a kilo."

Michael looked up. "A hundred bucks?"

"That's right, big man. Flog it off to posh restaurants, don't they? And those restaurants, they flog it off to posh wankers— for ten times that much."

"Ten times easy," said Jamie.

"Farkin abalone." Cale grinned. "A month's pay, hey?"

Jamie's parents, finally, had agreed to his getting a job over the break. He'd have cash of his own. He'd be able to buy things. He was starting at the fish plant, where Cale worked as well, but secretly he hoped to get a spot on a commercial boat before too long. He was his dad's son, after all.

Michael started whistling, then stopped. Jamie lay down on his back. The wooden planks seared his skin for a second, then eased their heat throughout his body. He closed his eyes: a dark orange glow, shadowed fitfully by gulls. He felt, in his bones, the slap of Michael's cricket ball against his palm. Muzzy with warmth, he allowed himself to relive that morning's assembly: the gale of applause . . . Alison . . . but each time, at that point, his mind looped back around. He found himself thinking about Dory. That huge, mean body—the man's face on top of it. He'd been held back a couple of years. He'd been full forward for Halflead four years running. From the sudden silence, the irregular scuffing of feet, Jamie could tell Michael had tossed the ball high into the air. He pictured it arcing slowly up, out—over the water. The dangerous thought came; he brushed around it, then he let it in: What if they—Alison and Dory—weren't together anymore? When was the last time, anyway, anyone had seen them together? Michael caught the ball. Then, against the planking . . . *thump* . . . *thump* . . . each bounce a mottling shape in the sunglow.

"Cut it out," Jamie murmured.

The bouncing stopped. Cale wet his lips loudly. Water lapped against the pylons.

"So," said Cale. "What the fark."

Jamie remained quietly on his back.

"Look who's in a good mood lately." He said it accusingly. "Alison Fischer. She got anything to do with it?"

"What?"

"Yeah yeah." His mouth made more slopping noises. "What a shifty cunt. You, I mean."

Jamie sat up, opened his eyes—the world bursting yellow and vivid—and gestured his head toward Michael. His brother's shape crouched over the tackle box.

"Sorry." Cale lowered his voice. "He's always around so I forget."

"What'd you hear?"

"Nothing." He smirked. "She's a bit alright—that's all." He licked two fingers and held them curled upward, then glanced dramatically at Michael. "Remember Stevo . . . Stefan? That Danish show pony? He reckons he got a finger in—you know. After that school play in April."

Jamie rolled over onto his stomach. He hadn't expected word to come round so quickly. Who was where, with who, how far they got—a town like this spread gossip like the clap. Cale, despite being older, hung out a lot with high-schoolers—couldn't hack being out of the loop. He was looser-lipped than any girl. But it'd only been a couple of hours since Alison had come up to Jamie . . . and—he kept reminding himself—nothing had happened.

Cale paused. " 'Course Dory never found out . . . that time."

"Shut up."

Of course what Cale meant was: Remember those other times? Jamie remembered. The whole town remembered. There was an element of community ritual in remembering all the things Dory was known or suspected to have done. The worst, of course, being the to-do with the Chinese poacher. Never cleared up. He was only twenty but he stood in as the town's hard man. And Alison—the girl with the silver spoon, the girl with the reputation—was known to give him plenty of reason for it.

"So?" said Cale.

"You don't know shit."

Cale nodded in satisfaction. "Ahh," he said. "If only you truly believed that."

Jamie laid one eye up against a crack between two timbers, felt the old, beaten wood on his face. If he could choose a place— if it could be all his—this was it. Strange how trying to think and trying to forget amounted to the same thing here. Cale was still talking about Alison. The sound of his voice familiar, pointless, in keeping with the complaint of the mooring lines, the metal creakings from the wharf's gantry crane across the bay. He was talking about Alison and Jamie wasn't listening but then something dislodged itself from the craw of his memory and the incident was undammed, clear and natural as breathing: Last summer—sun-white day—Jamie crabbing on the flats when word was sprinted down from town: *Fight.* The thrill in his blood as he raced up the main street. Kids streaking in from every direction, breathlessly swapping accounts on the way: Dory—him and some bloke—Vance Wilhelm, that was his name— who'd been spending time with Alison. Sirens started up to the south just as Jamie veered into the main carpark. Through the mayhem he took in the whole scene at once: a black jeep, its windshield smashed, keeled back at an odd uphill slope; people limping off, nursing arms; the flash of a blood-slagged face. He was about to scatter as well when he saw, on a grassy strip, two bodies asprawl one another—elbows bloody, pebbled with glass—one finally shunting its knee into the other's back, wrenching the head up into an armlock. The face looked full at Jamie. It was to Lester—Dory's best friend. *Jamie,* it gasped, *get him off me.*

"Hey, Romeo," Cale called out.

Always he returned to this. *Get him off me.* And—weak in the legs—he'd frozen. A heavy shape barreled across his vision and lifted the body clean off Lester and drove it hard into the ground. Trapped beneath Dory's weight, it gave out an odd creaking sound. Jamie circled around for a last look, saw Dory holding down the head, then saw the stranger's face—it could only have been Wilhelm—his mouth agape and crammed over a steel sprinkler head, cheeks streaming and shuddering. His face a picture of drowning. Lester staggered to his feet and glared at Jamie, then Dory looked up at him too. Lester made to speak but Dory stopped him. His arms still bearing down on Wilhelm's head, he'd said: *You're rubbish.*

But that was a year ago. Now, things were different. He was a hero now.

"Hey, Jamie, wake up." Cale's voice sounded as though it had risen a meter.

"Hmm."

"Your girlfriend's here."

"Piss off."

Bit by bit his thoughts tailed off; he began to feel the knurled wood jutting into his hip bone. His back roasting. He gazed down. Small schools of baitfish inflected the clear water. Old squidding lines and sinkers caught on the crossplanks, bearded with kelp.

"Nothing you wanna say to her?"

Jamie reached behind himself and pulled down his boardshorts, flapping one bum cheek open and shut: "Piss . . . off."

Michael sniggered.

"Piss . . . off . . . Cale . . . y."

"Any luck?"

A girl's voice—he spun over, shielded his eyes. It couldn't be. She was standing at the head of the jetty with Tammie, both decked out in their netball gear. Alison still wearing a bib that spelled "GA"—goal attack—in large lettering. Cale, next to him, cracking up.

"Nope," reported Michael. "No fish."

"What'd I say?" said Cale.

"You're a fuckwit," said Jamie.

"I'm a fuckwit? Whose knickers are down?"

Even Michael couldn't conceal his smile. Tammie laughed, a squeezed sound like the yapping of a small dog. She was playing with her camisole straps, studying him.

"You told me to come," said Alison.

He got up, face burning. He felt suddenly naked in front of them. Even though everyone, all summer, went around in just their boardies, he felt naked. "We're actually heading back," he said, gesturing to Michael. Why had he said that?

"Cool," said Alison. "C'arn, then." She turned to address Cale: "There's a party on Thursday. Slogger Tom's place—you should come too."

"What's in it for me?"

For a second Jamie was thrilled by his friend's boldness, then he felt strangely uneasy.

"You're Cale, right?"

"Yep," he said, grinning broadly.

But Alison didn't fall for his act. Her voice turned clerical, polished: "This is Tammie." Tammie smiled dutifully. She was hot alright, thought Jamie, but when she smiled there was something puddled about her face.

Cale said, "So *this* is Tammie."

———

The whole way, Michael walked in front of them, lugging the gear in one hand and his cricket ball in the other. He kept his head bowed and never looked back. By some instinct he led them on a roundabout route—avoiding the foreshore, the main street with its drab, dusty stretch of shops—and cut across the edge of the tidal flats. The afternoon was cooling fast.

Still plenty of people around.

When they reached the asphalt Alison touched her hand to the back of Jamie's elbow. She crossed the road and started hiking up the scrubby slope. Jamie watched his brother trudge the other way, up the road to their house. Then, without a word, he followed Alison. The ground beneath them skiddy with shell grit. As they climbed, the sun absorbed itself into her body: calves, hamstrings, the belt of skin above her skirt, the backs of her golden arms. The glaring nylon letters on her bib. She scuffed through the saltbush and mulga, kicking up little plumes of dust, and he stepped hypnotically into them.

They reached the clearing. At the center of the bluff—on its highest table of land—was the old stone courthouse, long ago ruined. It was arched with white, oxidized columns, reared against a low sky. The seaward wall had been torn away by the weather, creating the impression of a great stage overlooking the ocean.

Alison led him around the jagged masonry and leaned against a wall, bouncing on her heels.

"What's the saddest place you know," she said, "this is mine."

He didn't speak. Baffled by her question. Still catching up to the fact of being there, alone, with her. Then he said, "Why?"

Before her sickness, his mum had often dragged him here in the dark of first morning. She liked painting the sea before sunlight came up and flattened the water. He'd cart her stuff along the ridge, trying to stay awake, and she'd talk, sometimes to him, sometimes to herself. She'd always been fascinated by the courthouse's history. How, more than a hundred years ago, the town council, flush with fishing money, had commissioned a series of public buildings—of which the courthouse was to be the first—and how, a week after the naming ceremony, a storm had rolled in and ripped it apart. According to the legend, the chief benefactor, after whom the courthouse was named, had packed his wife and five children into a skiff the very next day and rowed them out to sea—never to be seen again. The story appealed equally to his mum's senses of the romantic and the absurd. The town had abandoned its building program, closed off all the access roads. Too many bad omens all round. As she laughed to herself he'd see the courthouse ahead, floaty and blue-glowing—hinting at a past that seemed, at that hour, still very much present.

"Have you ever . . ." Alison began. "Nah, that's stupid."

Below them sunlight lay over the whole bay. The sea breathed against the lip of the pale shore. Back from the water's edge, flats and dunes encircling it, the town glinted like a single eye.

"What?"

"Nah."

He looked around, listened. So exposed up here. The wind loud and brackish. He made out somewhere nearby the clickety sound of skateboarders, the high-pitched drone of jet skis out on the water. Human voices skimming like mozzies across its surface.

He turned away from the sea and pointed out his family's house on the adjoining spur, along the winding saddle.

"That's you guys?" she asked.

"My mum used to come here to paint."

She let it pass. She said, "Your brother looks like you," then, noting his lack of enthusiasm, went on, "You'd think you'd get an awesome view from up here—of all places, right?" It came out in a single quick exhalation: "But you look and you look and everything's just shithouse." Skating her hands down the side of her pleated skirt: "Your friend, Cale, is he always high?"

"He's a good bloke."

She didn't seem happy with that.

"His girlfriend died in Europe," he added lamely.

"Europe?" Her voice twisted up.

"Yeah, he's been everywhere. Hawaii and Africa and everywhere, before he came here."

She chortled. "Why would anyone come here?"

Now she'd stopped bouncing, now she was brushing her hands together. Both of her hands were within reach.

"I mean," she said, "there's not even fish here anymore."

With other girls, it was just the next thing—hands, neck, pash, fingers under their tops. But with her, for him, nothing was next.

"C'arn, then," she said softly.

She eased forward and leaned her body into his bare chest. Her smile lopsided, bigger and bigger. Then her mouth sprang open and then they were kissing. He was kissing Alison Fischer. There was a mineral tizz on her tongue, the smell of wet rock. He lifted his hand to her hair.

"Ugh." She stepped back, soles crunching on broken glass. "It stinks in here." She skipped over to the opposite wall, standing beneath a deep, high crevice that might once have held a window. The wind even choppier in that corner.

"Animals come here for shelter," he said. Who'd told him that? The musty smell seemed familiar.

"Well, they stink."

She kissed him again. He felt the start of a hard-on, pressing through the mesh lining of his shorts—then quickly wilting. Maybe thinking about it. Maybe thinking about Dory. An awful lag behind this happening and the idea of it. She lifted her bib and wiped her mouth.

"Okay, then," she said.

"Sorry."

Wordlessly they looked out of the broken wall over the bay. The sun full in the sky. There was a blue kite on the wind and far below, way out on the ocean coast, the black half bodies of surfers, ducking into early-breaking waves or standing, slewing across the tall steep faces until they dropped into white slag. Every ride ended in failure. He'd never noticed this before.

"I'm not scared, you know."

He didn't say anything.

"Me and him aren't really together."

"Who, Dory?" He tried to sound nonchalant.

"Everyone just assumes." She smiled into the open, blustery air. "So how well do you know him? Are you guys, like, friends?"

"Dory?"

"No, the fucking postman. Yes, Dory."

"I mean," Jamie said carefully, "we play on the same team. He's a good ruck." He paused for a moment. "A good bloke."

"A good bloke," she mimicked.

He fell silent. The water of the bay seemed, if possible, to bulge. In that light it seemed as though the courthouse was tilting, about to slide into the ocean.

"See that?"

The kite hung in the high wind, still and full. Then a slip of color again. Way out a ship coughed up black smoke ever more feebly. He realized she was looking off to one side—past the dunes, past the old rock pier, even—to the low, wet lines of swale behind. Deep where it was dark, shallow where pooled with light.

"That's where he lives," she said. "With his uncle."

"Good fishing out there." Immediately, the rock pier imagined itself into his mind. Black and slick, lathered with surf. He'd managed, for so long, not to think about it.

"Their place, though—you wouldn't believe."

But it, too, was clear to him: one of those fibro, tin-roofed affairs, a single naked bulb shearing light through planked windows. He'd seen it from the boat. Stray dogs ganging outside.

"How much cash you got on you?" she asked abruptly.

"Cash?"

She stepped out from the stone recess and a breeze snapped up a fistful of her hair, suspended it above her head.

"We could go to the bottle shop," she said.

He thought frantically for a moment. "What about ID? Do you have—I know, we could get Cale's ID."

But she was already somewhere else in her head. It struck him she was bored with him. Without warning she came over and leaned into his shoulder and, slowly collapsing her knees, traced her upper lip—inch by inch—all the way down to the tips of his fingers. He stood there inside the stone walls, suffused in sun, shock-still, the hot tension through his body almost painful. What happened now?

"It's you!" She crinkled up her nose. "You! You stink of fish."

His cheeks flared red. "Shit," he said. He brought up his fingers and smelled them. Bait. "You're right. Shit, sorry."

She hopped back with a childlike little scowl. He struggled for an excuse and she watched him, letting him struggle, saying nothing. Finally he slinked off. Now she was saying something but he was too busy with shame to take in her final words. The easterly gusted up. Then, at the edge of the granite ruin, he forced himself to turn around.

"There's tonight," she called into the wind's low howl.

"What?" He cupped his ear.

"Thursday night," she was saying. "See you Thursday night."

HIS MUM WAS DYING and seemed torn between ignoring it and rushing toward it. She wanted to meet it in the middle of many arrangements. After the first relapse—the scans, the taps, the tests—she sank back into her work, her only concession to the diagnosis being a switch from spatulas to paintbrushes. She spent even more time outdoors, painting, gardening. She was always a physical gardener: sporting Blundstone boots and a singlet, gloves up to her elbows and her ginger hair scrunched back with anything at hand—a rubber band, a torn strip from a plastic bag. She was indefatigable. If asked, she'd say it was just like pins and needles. What was the phrase people used?—she refused to become her illness. She beat it back.

Then, two years ago, the second major relapse. She claimed, afterward, that she didn't remember any of it. But she'd seen him. They'd seen each other. She'd lain on her side, the easel also knocked on its side. It was as though she'd been dancing with it and they'd tripped over together. Her face was compressed against the floor, strands of hair streaked diagonally across it, captured as though in a thrash of passion. Everywhere there was bright cerulean blue paint, the entire floor slick and sky-colored, a centimeter deep, leaching into her arms, her scissored legs, her smock and boots. Her palms were vivid orange.

"Mum," he said.

But she couldn't speak. The blue paint coated her lips—through it he saw the tip of her blue tongue—it matted her hair, enclosed her right eye like a face mask. That eye was open. It didn't blink. You could see. It was nightmare in her head.

"Mum?"

Never—it'd never been this serious. Once before, he'd come upon her slumped on the kitchen lino. Just dizzy, she'd said. She'd made him promise not to tell Dad. He knelt, now, watching her. He put out his hand but it seemed incapable of touching anything. Her eye roved, jerkily, like a puppet's, around the room—to him—away—to him again. She was frozen in the middle of her mangled sidestroke, the paint frothing in front of her mouth. Slowly it hardened into a lighter blue paste. He felt as if he were breathing it as well. Then the footsteps, the bottomed-out growl of his dad's voice—what happened, how long, how long—*how long*—the dark form crouching down, standing up, crouching down again and cutting off her hair, the crunch of the scissors, then stripping her up, limb by limb, out of the dry blue muck. A long pause.

Come on, Jamie.

Once, he'd seen her in front of the bathroom mirror. She was plunging a bone-gray comb again and again into her hair, as though punishing it. Arms trembling. She caught his eye in the mirror and smiled. Here, she said, holding it out. Help me.

He washed the sand off his feet at the outside tap. When he came into the living room she shifted in her reclining couch, in his direction. She looked shrunken, he thought, diluted somehow. The red of her hair slowly ashing.

"I could see you," she said, "at the courthouse." A mischief in her voice, even through its slow woolliness.

He kissed her on the right side of her face. Then he stuck his head out her window, dodging the potted plants and flowers and trailing philodendrons. She wasn't lying. There was a clear view the whole way.

"It was nothing," he said.

"Didn't look like nothing."

"I was fishing with Michael."

"Yes, I know. He came home an hour ago."

An electric saw revved up from the workshop downstairs. Despite himself, Jamie started smiling. Silly with the memory of kissing Alison. He recalled his dad's instructions.

"How're you feeling, Mum?"

"You're avoiding the question. Do you like this girl?"

"Yeah."

No other answer occurred to him. Her illness had had the effect of completely opening up their conversation.

"And she likes you?"

He hesitated. Summoning back the smell of her, the smell on your hands after scaling a wet chain-link fence. He smiled again. Then he remembered her reaction when she smelled his fingers. "I dunno," he said. "It's more complicated than that."

"One more reason for us to stay here." The right side of her mouth edged upward; automatically he gauged the bearings behind the effort. Too much. During the worst spells, her face lost most of its sensation. "Yes," she went on, "I know why you're here."

"Dad said to tell you—"

"Tell your father," she said, "he can stop having his secret meetings." Her breath was coming out serrated now, in little huffs, and he realized she was trying to clear her throat. "Tell him to tell those bankers, and real estate agents, and all those others . . ."

She stopped. He wasn't used to seeing her this bad. Speechless—almost entirely immobilized. Not so long ago she'd have never run short of a few choice words for real estate agents. The scum of the earth, she called them. Nor would she have been able to get out of her chair—any chair—fast enough. But she'd already been a couple of weeks in this one. She'd missed his semifinal in this one.

He shook his head. "I'm with Dad," he said. "We'll go to Maroomba and come back when you're better."

"Live with the enemy? You kids."

"They need to know by Friday, Mum."

She attempted another half smile. "Look at you now," she said. She scrutinized him for some time, then turned back toward her window. She said, "It's more complicated than that."

He left the house. Partway down the drive he saw Michael sit-

ting on the bungalow steps. Jamie went over to him and yanked
out his earphones.

"Hang out in your own room, will you?"

Michael shrugged.

"Go tell Mum you wanna move to Maroomba."

"What? I don't, but."

"I don't care. Go tell her."

Michael slouched up from the concrete steps, sheaves of
hair—he cut it himself, using kitchen scissors—hanging over his
brow. He was too skinny and his arms too long and every part of
him that bent was knobbly. No way they looked alike.

"I hate Maroomba, they're all posh there."

"Would you rather move to the city?"

Michael jerked his head up. "Do you think she'll get better if we
go?" At one point his voice dipped into a lower register and sounded
like their dad's. The earphones still buzzing around his neck.

Jamie tsked impatiently. "Why else would we go?"

"Cale said he'd teach me how to surf."

"Cale won't teach you shit." He instantly felt bad for saying
this. "Look, it's not till next year anyway."

Michael put his hands in his pocket.

"Go," said Jamie.

Michael pursed his lips as though readying to whistle.

"Go!"

"Lester saw us. Before—with Alison." He glanced up ques-
tioningly. "Just past the service station."

For a moment Jamie felt booted outside himself. His voice
spacey in his skull. He heard himself say, "So what? Stop following
me around."

Michael shrugged again. "I saw him, and he saw us," he said.

Jamie came at him and punched and pushed him against the
doorjamb. "You better shut up."

"Sorry," Michael cried out.

"I mean it."

"I'm sorry I'm sorry."

At teatime, Michael ate by himself in the kitchen. Sulking in front of some TV show. Jamie joined his parents, who'd already started, in the living room. As soon as he walked in he could tell they'd been fighting. His mum sat facing the window under her striped blanket and his dad was angled opposite, feeding her. They ate in silence. A light breeze rumpled the curtains. Jamie watched the dull green of eucalyptus leaves bleed into the darkening sky. His mum started coughing.

"Are you okay?" his dad asked.

Once she'd fetched her breath she said, "Jamie."

"Yeah, Mum."

"You know what no one ever asks me?"

His dad stared straight ahead, over her shoulder. "Ask her," he said.

"What, Mum?"

"Everyone always asks me if I'm okay. No one ever asks me if I'm happy."

The sound from the kitchen TV faded, then amped into the voice-over for a commercial. His dad put down his plate and left the room.

She'd already made her instructions clear. She wasn't timid about these things. She didn't want a machine breathing for her, nor her body grafted into a computer. She didn't want any hoo-hah. She wanted to be cremated and then planted in the soil under the waratahs. Part of this was slyness—they'd be more likely to keep the property. She wanted this, and she wanted his dad to buy back his stake in the trawler. Jamie remembered their conversations, after her second relapse, about moving. Money. Dim voices and lamplit silences. One night he was in the driveway and glimpsed a slice of his dad's face through their bedroom window. It was hard and tear-smudged and sneering with hurt. Then he saw a dark shape flit in front of the window in the next room. Michael. Both of them, sons, watching their parents. One handful, his mum said, she wanted brought to the bluff, where she watched the storms come in, and she wanted it scattered—she said the word cheekily—into the ocean.

She was in fine form when his dad came back in. Teasing Jamie about incredible views at the courthouse.

"Jamie was up there today," she explained.

"Got some free time, has he?"

"That reminds me," she said. "Your holiday job, Jamie—when you get a chance, go talk to John Thompson at the wharf. Word is he's got a spot on his boat."

His dad made as though to say something, but didn't.

"Tell him I sent you. He might even start you straightaway."

"The final's coming up," his dad broke in. "Can't it wait till after then?"

"Fishing and football." She let out a dramatic sigh. "That's all this town cares about."

The room lightened, loudened, as Michael barged in from the kitchen. His expression anxious. "Thirty percent chance of thunderstorms tomorrow," he said. "But higher on the weekend."

His mum looked at him intently. She said, "Thank you, sweetie."

"I'll have your rocking chair done by then," said his dad.

It was dusk outside now—the window a square of black, brooding colors. Waratah shrubs lifting their scent of honey into the room. Hundreds of kilometers away the ocean streamed into itself, careening its mass over and over, sucking even the clouds down.

"Shall we open a bottle?" his mum asked.

"You sure, Maggie?"

"Let's open a bottle."

* * *

THE NIGHT WAS WINDY. Clouds hung low and fat, lit up by the massive bonfire in the backyard. People were feeding it anything they could toss a couple of meters: furniture, textbooks, beer cans and bottles, even their clothes. Farther back from the fire the darkness was crumbed with cigarette ends, glowing, fading, each time seemingly in different spots. People might have been dancing out there.

Cale quickly ditched him for some surfie mates—the bloke could trace a sniff of mull through a dust storm.

"Hey, Jamie!"

Someone lifted a bottle to his mouth. Jamie hurled his head to the sky.

"Jesus," he said, coughing, laughing as a hand thumped his back. He spun around and saw Billy Johnson—left half-forward flank, an ordinary player, but one of those blokes everyone got along with.

"Hell's that?"

"Bourbon, I think," Billy said, teeth gleaming widely.

"Fuck you," said Jamie.

"Stole it from my sister's room." He held it out like a handshake. "Have some more."

Jamie took another swig. The burning rushed through him, mixing with the fumes from the fire. He felt deeply awake.

"Thanks," he said. "Thanks a lot, man."

"Ready for the game next week?"

He tossed the bottle back to Billy. "What game?" he jeered.

By midnight, the party was peaking. She hadn't arrived. He sat in a tight pack with the other Halflead High kids, drowsing in their cheap deodorant. Norsca and Brut and Old Spice. They had the next day off—curriculum day—and everyone was going balls out. They drank. They drank and talked about the upcoming game. Jamie watched the bonfire, gusts of wind playing havoc with the smoke, people gliding in and out of its thrown light.

Cale rocked up, off his face. He started making toasts—to footy, to cunt, to mates, to getting fucked with your mates—each word swerving in the smoke-dark wind. At one stage he threw himself to the ground. Everyone watched as he did a strange, simian dance across the lawn.

Jamie drank. The wind moved through the tall purple grass, sifting the light of an arriving car's high beam. Like the wind was made of light. Next to him one of those UV bug lights thrumming purple above a pit of carnage: skeletal legs, carapaces, wings.

Cale held something up: "Got it!"

Then he saw her. Trying to light a cigarette, her face in the brief flare of a struck match. White skirt and a boob tube. She looked somehow smaller-figured in the night. On an instinct she turned and met his gaze and then, bold as you like, started walking up to the group. Tammie and Laura close in behind her.

He looked away.

"Got a light?"

But she was talking to Cale, the twenty-dollar bill flapping between his fingers. Billy rifling through his pockets, striking, restriking the wheel of his lighter, hands cupped, body swiveling to shield the flame.

The girls waited and then walked off, giggling.

Cale whispered to him: "So?"

But he couldn't speak. His head teemed. It was late and he sensed all around, in the shadows, mouths straining against each other as though to breach, to break through to a clear feeling.

"So what?"

"So you gonna score with her?"

"What, are you stupid too?"

She was waiting out front. Cross-legged on the trunk of an old

Holden, cornered by a chaotic blockade of cars and bikes. Someone next to her in the darkness. As he came closer, he saw that it was Tammie: she flicked down a cigarette, whispered something into Alison's ear before leaving. Under the cloud-strained moonlight Alison's skirt was hitched up past her gleaming thighs. Her two legs interlocked.

"You look different," she said.

"You too," he replied. He wasn't lying. Closer up, the light wasn't kind to her face. Makeup moved like a tight gauzy screen on top of her skin.

"Most of these things," she said, "no one even talks to me."

He nodded. Laughter spilled from the backyard. Then the smash of a breaking bottle. He spun around.

"Dory's not here tonight," she said.

He deflected it, the cold edge held up to his warm drunken cocoon. From the house came the rising scud of voices. Then the wind shifted. They were alone again.

"He hates these high school parties."

He said, deliberately, "You can talk to me."

She looked at him without smiling. "You're funny," she said. "But seriously, all me and him do is talk. How his uncle's gonna get an abalone license one day. How he's got friends in Fisheries. Remember that time with the Chinese poacher?"

The chill came back, darting through every fissure in him. He remembered. The young woman's body they found in the swale—within shouting distance of where Dory lived with his uncle. Its blank, salt-soused face. The cops at school, pulling Dory, and later Lester, out of the classroom. After they were released from questioning, Lester had pantomimed the whole thing in the school paddocks. Jamie was too far away to hear anything, but saw the circle of boys reshape itself as Lester knelt down—he was Dory now, straddling the woman's body. Punching the ground like a piston. Dory himself standing aside, watching on without a word.

Alison soured her face. "His uncle—he's a nasty piece of work."

She quickly looked behind her, then swung back around. His heart pounding his skull as she considered him. He took a long breath.

"So are you and Dory together or not?"

She bounced her shoulders. "Honestly, sometimes I wonder if he's a poofter. Seriously, Tammie cracked on to him once, the slut. And, you know."

"Yeah?"

"You know. He didn't do anything."

"He didn't do anything."

"I even asked, but you know him. Won't talk to save his life."

Her conversation was like surface chop, trapped in the same current, backing over itself. It made him seasick. He realized she hadn't answered his question. He was about to ask again when he heard her name being called out. The front door of the house banged open and a figure surfaced from the red rectangular glow, coming straight at them, trailing a small wake of commotion.

"Fuck," Alison muttered.

"*A*—lison." A singsong tug, stretching out the first syllable.

His stomach rose up thick and rancid. He swallowed, breathed it down. Here it came. "Who is it?" he asked, as if he didn't know—as if asking were proof he didn't care. Always there were the rules, plying, pressing in around you.

"Alison?" The voice affected surprise now. Two black shapes— then another two—their shadows scrambling ahead of them across the yard. One by one the faces came into sight. "Dory's been worried about you."

"Fuck you, Les," said Alison evenly.

In response Lester dipped his head and lifted his bottle above it. Then he turned and leered to the person who'd accompanied him out: a tall, lanky mullet-head who'd dropped out of school last year.

A few steps back Tammie tottered against Cale. They seemed engrossed in their own windy drama. Both held their beers out in front of them like candles.

"I'll pass that along," Lester said.

"Sure," said Alison, "once you pop his cock out of your mouth."

Lester's tall mate started snickering. "Slut," said Lester. He was unfazed. "You think you're top shit now? After one fluke goal?"

In a single moment Jamie realized that Lester was talking to him and that Alison was watching. He prepared himself to say something. The words, however, snagged deep inside him.

"We'll see you at training on Monday," Lester went on. "He's gonna fuck you up." He shook his head in amazement. "You're fucked." He turned to Alison: "Remember your old loverboy, Wilhelm?"

Alison stayed quiet. Her face stern, narrowed, like she was trying to light a cigarette. Cale took a step forward. "Come on, man." He sounded unsure—and unsure who he was talking to. Lester's mullet-headed friend watched him steadily.

"Fucked," repeated Lester.

What should he say? He felt sickened by his words—hollow, soggy-sounding—before they even came out. He said, "Whatever, mate."

Lester laughed. "So fucked."

And it was true: each iteration struck Jamie with its truth, drained his body cold. The sick dread soaking and the worst was how familiar it felt. Too late to turn back. You'd think it was too much for one person but no, he'd already made room for it. He was rubbish.

Alison watched, then nodded. "Let's go, Jamie."

"See you Monday," Lester sang out. "Have a good weekend!"
She led him off.

For a while they walked without speaking. There was a shape
to the silence between them: unfolding, contracting in the night.
At the end of the street Alison reached out her hand. He held it
desperately but there was no exhilaration in it. He wondered if
she could feel that it wasn't his hand at all—that it wasn't he
who was connected to it. They ducked under a fence and then
his knees gave way beneath him.

"Sand," she said.

They skirted the edge of a caravan park. Light and music
wafted over from the lots, carrying the day-old scent of sun-
screen, charred barbecues. Early summer tourists. Finally they
reached a shoulder of cliff. There was a steep drop-off behind it,
and, behind that, the bay.

"You wanna keep walking?" she asked.

"Okay," he said. A strange formality had arisen between them.

"You know a spot? I'll follow you."

He continued on the same track. Along the headland, abstracted
from any thought of direction, through the mulga scrub, and
paddocks of wild grass, and fields stubbled up to burn marks
delineated by dark trees. Maybe he could just keep walking. Just
not stop. And what if he did? Would he want her to follow him?
The wind was sharp, and salty, and then there was water on it.

"It's cold," said Alison. She hugged her bare arms. "Where are
we going?"

He was dazed, for a moment, by the trespass of her voice.
He looked out. In the high moon the water was sequined with
light. Muted flashes from the freighters past the heads. Beyond
that, stars. But directly beneath him—that, there, was the real
shocker. The black stub in the black bay. He'd brought them
right to the rock pier.

"You wanna go down there?" Her tone was a little impatient.

"It's gonna rain."

"C'arn," she said. "It'll rain up here too."

She swayed and shimmied down the dark slope. He followed her down and then onto the rocks, almost sprinting across them until they reached the tip of the pier. Water boiling over its edge. Vertigoed, he looked back—saw, across the long darkness, the foreshore thinly threaded with lights. Then, breathing hard, he turned around again and looked out into the deeper black, toward the heads where the water came in strong and deep and broke on the raised table of the reef.

"I haven't been here for ages," he said.

Alison found a curved rock on the lee side, long and canoe-narrow. The pier a heap of shadows in the night. "Lester's just a dickhead," she said. She drew her legs beneath her.

"Yeah."

"You should have seen him when he first met Dory. Talk about arse-licking."

He sat down opposite, shivering. It was like the wind was greased, he thought, it slid right against you, leaving your skin slippery where it touched. The mention of Dory triggered something inside him and he reached for her.

"Come here."

He heard himself say it. He saw his arm stippled by cold. The smell of kelp and metal dissolving on his tongue. She fended the hair from her face as he hauled her in, his hands up and down her body, claiming as much of her as he could. She responded at once, then drew herself upright.

"I just don't get why he hangs out with him," she commented.

"What?"

He rocked back, hugged his shins tight. Looked at her. Her hair silver in the pale spill of moonlight. Her makeup worn down and somehow, in this light, accidental—as though she'd been rehearsing on a friend's face. She looked like a complete stranger.

"I mean. He doesn't even like him."

"Will you shut up?" He realized, suddenly, that it pissed him off: that strange, settled face of hers. "Please? Fucking Dory this and Dory that." Words gushing up in him, frothy and cold, but he couldn't give body to them, not fast enough. "Why were you even with him? Don't you know what everyone says? What everyone thinks?"

Her expression was level. "Go on."

It occurred to him instantaneously that this was her real face, and that it was the same as Dory's—the same blankness of expression—and that that was what had been drawing him in. *That* was what he wanted to break himself against. As quickly as it came, the heady anger began to seep out of him.

She said, "So what does everyone think?"

He didn't answer.

"C'arn," she said. She leaned into him again, almost aggressively, urging his hand with her own, up over her shoulder blade. Her lips muzzling his neck.

"C'arn."

"Just that you could do better than him." His voice came out as if by rote. "Like . . . he's slow or something."

She pulled back, teeth flashing, and then she was laughing, liquidly, into the night. He waited, watching her. Sensing, deeper and deeper, how profoundly her laughter excluded him. In the distance he heard metal rings clinking against masts. The creaking of stretched wood. He would stay quiet. He'd say nothing and maybe she'd say something—one thing—that would release him for good.

Alison's face remembered itself. "Sorry," she whispered. She crawled forward on all fours and put her hands on his knees.

"Hey." He was holding her shoulders. Vance Wilhelm had been hospitalized with internal injuries—whatever that meant. Had she crawled on her hands and knees for him? Had he afterward regretted letting her? The pier, buffeted by rising waves, felt as though it was beginning to list from side to side. She looked up.

"I'll go if you want." How she said it—the words running one way and the meaning another. After a while, her mouth opened disbelievingly. "You gotta be joking." She threw his hands off her. "But okay. If that's how it is. You're up for it and Lester Long shit-talks you and then you're going every which way."

The wind grieved louder. Cutting off his every tack of thought.

"All year you're up for it—"

"It's not fucking Lester," he spat, "and it's not fucking shit-talk."

She exhaled, her eyes shining.

"Anyway," he said, fetching in his voice with effort, "you're moving."

"What?"

"Next year. To the city."

Alison ignored him. "Stuff it," she said. "They were right about you."

"We're moving too—but just to Maroomba." He was flustered by her comment. *Who?* he wanted to ask. *Right about what?* He said, "It's my mum." Then he stopped himself. Just saying it felt like some sort of betrayal.

"Look," Alison said. Now he breathed in, primed himself for the inevitable questions. But once again she acted as though she hadn't heard him. She said, "You're scared of Dory—fair enough." Her brow knitted together. "I just thought . . ." She paused. "It's different with you."

He didn't say anything.

"I just thought it'd be different with you." She crouched up, onto her feet. He turned toward her and she was smiling, lips pressed tightly together. Something about that smile. "But I'll talk to him," she said. "He'll leave you alone. Promise." She made a half-choked sound like a chuckle. "Don't worry—Dory listens to me." She held still for a moment, then started across the rocks.

Jamie turned around to face the water. Years ago he'd swum out there heaps—out where the coral was. It was easy to forget, past the reef, that you were on the edge of the great continental shelf until a rip drifted you out and one of those cold currents snaked up from the depths and brushed its slightest fringe against your body. Then you remembered. She was almost out of sight when the recognition arrived. That smile—her smile—it wasn't one-way. There was a question in it.

"Alison!" he called out.

The cry passed his mouth and coursed back into his body. Tons and tons of water moving under you. She stopped. Her body was slim and pale, a trick of light, against the black rocks.

"How's it different?" he said.

"What?"

"How's it different with me?" he shouted.

She stood in the half dark, then shrugged. When her shoulders didn't stop shrugging he realized she was crying. Jesus. He got up and scrambled toward her.

"All that time—you don't know what it's like for me all that time," she said. Her voice sounded older. She lifted her head and searched toward him with her open face. "He likes to hold my hand when he's drunk," she said. Even over the wind he could hear the bitterness. "The rest of the time—you look and you look and there's nothing there. Fucking zilch. With you, it's different."

"Okay."

"It just is."

"Okay."

"I'm sorry."

He watched as she stood there, hugging her ribs. You couldn't turn back from something like this. You saw it through and it ruined you.

"Don't go," he said.

WHEN HE WAS LITTLE he used to follow his dad down to the wharf. Watched him cast off the hawser, chug out ahead a rimy trail of grease bubbles, the chorus of curses from the wharfies. In time Jamie was allowed, on school holidays, to come along. But usually his dad would be gone by breakfast and it never felt like a missing—more like he brought the sea into their house and it braced the rest of them to know where he was, what it looked like where he was, the sea around him. Before Michael was born, before his mum's sickness. Best was when they went out in the little runabout with the two-stroke, him and his dad, and sometimes his mum as well—she'd be cradling a basket of barbecued chicken and some beetroots, sitting on rolls of butcher's paper as long as her legs—and he'd dip his fingers behind the stern and draw a white gully into the darker water.

Then Michael. When he was old enough they took him along and together they explored the whole bight of the bay. They fished for King George whiting off the southern promontory and snapper and trevally in the deeper waters. His great-grandfather had skippered one of the first trawlers in Halflead Bay: back then he could go out for six weeks over Christmas, dip in, and make enough money to fish for sport the rest of the year. Jamie loved it—the idea of his family having worked that body of water for generations. He caught his first fish when he was six—a mako—he'd never forget its spearlike snout, the long cobalt gleam of its back. His dad's hands cupping his on the reel. They gaffed it twice, behind the gills, and even when its tail flayed his arm he could barely hold in the rapture. Gulping down his dad's praise—*Not a bad effort,* he kept saying. *Not a bad effort, a shark your very first time.*

His last time, though. Over five years ago. Early evening: no luck—nothing—they'd only stayed to make it worth the long hike. The rock pier was a tricky spot: you couldn't moor a boat and it was on the undeveloped side of the dunes. No tourists out there. The nearest road was an hour off—you had to cart all your gear along the headland. They'd been about to leave when Jamie's rod bowed forward.

He grabbed it, hauled back until the rod made a tight arc.

"What is it?" asked his dad.

The resistance was strong but even. "Snagged, I think."

Michael looked back down, continued packing the tackle away. Jamie reeled in his line. It was getting dark, the sea glass-colored. The tide was coming in fast, too, washing higher against the rocks and leaving a frothy train. His mum, foraging through the lower rock pools, planted her feet—freezing her posture—every time the water surged in, and it seemed to Jamie like a private game.

"Okay," said his dad. "Pull her in and let's go."

Jamie continued reeling in. Then his line jerked hard. He leaned the rod back again—probably the reef, or a bed of sea grass—but then he felt it, there, and there—the unmistakable give and drag of a fish.

"Got one," he cried out.

"You sure?" His dad observed the weight on the line and climbed to his feet.

"Got one," Jamie repeated.

It was fighting now, weaving and twisting. The line went slack. When the charge came he was pulled forward and almost lost his footing. He looked down: browny yellow lichen. Spume churning over his ankles.

His dad grinned. "Set the drag," he said. Jamie set the drag.

They watched over the gray water together. Too dark to see anything. He fought the fish, tracking its every tension, tugging and reeling, imagining its flight through spindling reefs and sand and meadows of sea grass. This was it—this was why you waited. His dad next to him, fired up, talking him through it.

The line went spastic. It convulsed in short bursts. Jamie gripped the rod with excitement—he'd never felt a fish do this before. He glanced at his dad, who was squinting out to sea. Michael and his mum too. The sea was like this. You could wait all day and then, just when you were leaving, it might offer something up—the rubbery back of a whale, the glass-sharp glint of jumping mackerel—something. You wouldn't even know you were waiting till it came and you missed it. In the distance, something disrupted the surface of the glazed water—it was beautiful—beautiful to think it connected to him.

He tugged, reeled, tugged. His mum said, "Oh my God." He couldn't make anything out in the grayness. When she said it the second time he saw it. Wings beating furiously. A seagull. Then he heard the high-pitched screeching. It sounded human, the intonations of a baby girl throwing a tantrum. He continued reeling, the rod stooping lower and lower as he dragged the bird across the water, through the chop and, at last, to the rocks. Now it was quiet.

"Oh my God."

His dad said, "Where's it hooked?"

It had stopped moving. Jamie tried to lift the line but its body was wedged somehow, stuck in the rock scum.

"It's dead," he said.

It was enormous. Blood dyed the top of its plump breast, banded its neck—impossibly red against its white neck. Its webbed feet, limp in the wash, floated like old orange peel. He stepped toward it. The water shook its body. Then he saw, behind it, the sinuous, steely torso of a fish.

"There's a snapper too," he said, twisting around. His mum was staring at him, her face peaked but utterly focused.

"Bob," she said.

"It's on the fixed hook," said Jamie.

"Let him do it," said his dad.

He took another step. Bent down, saw the second hook, the long shanked keeper sunk in above the wing. Barbed into its shoulder and still letting blood. He reached out and suddenly the gull lurched up, screaming, flailing its big wings. Its beak gaped open: he could see right down into its pink, tattered innards. The bird was terrified—leaking something that smelled like dog piss gone off, its shrill squawks corrugating in its throat. He looked into that violent white rush and knew he couldn't touch it. No way. He jerked back and pointed the rod, trying to poke it onto the rocks, but the pliant fiberglass tip spooked the creature even more.

"Stop that," said his dad.

"I'll unhook it," he said, but he didn't move.

Michael stared at the bird, whose cries were tapering now to a dry rattle.

His mum repeated, "Bob."

His dad took the fishing rod from him. He squeezed Jamie's shoulder. "It's suffering, son. You understand?"

He nodded, but he didn't know what he meant by doing that—nodding. The bird's wings were half splayed. He watched it for a long time, churning in the water's guts. He didn't move.

A minute passed. Then he heard Michael digging around in the tackle box, mumbling to himself. He picked things up and threw them back in, metal-sounding. "Nope," he whispered under his breath. "Too blunt." A little later he handed something up to Jamie: a pair of scissors.

His dad watched silently.

So he'd have to hold it. With one hand. Should he hold its head or body? Those huge wings. The fish-flesh writhing behind it. He opened the scissors—so flimsy, with his fingers inside them. He crouched down and then it saw him—the yellow eye with its black heart—and let out a coarse shriek. That smell, that secretion of terror.

"Come on," said his dad.

"I could just cut the line," he said, not looking up.

"You will not just cut the line," said his mum. She said it so scathingly he immediately pictured the bird flying with the nylon leader hanging from one wing, the ball sinker running up and down between the swivel and hook, weighting its body into a sinking spiral.

"For Chrissake, Bob."

"He's gotta do it himself."

"Look at it."

"It's his catch." His voice firmed. "He has to do it."

Jamie bent down again. Then he stood up and backed off.

"Jesus," said his dad. There was a weariness in his tone Jamie had never heard before.

"He's crying," Michael pointed out to their parents. His voice was matter-of-fact but his face seemed itself close to tears.

His mum didn't say anything to Jamie. She didn't look at him at all as she climbed down to the water's edge. She bent over and picked up the gull with both hands and laid it on a flat rock. Then she sucked her lips into her mouth, lifted one of her Blundstones, and stomped down on the gull's head, once, hard.

The morning was blue when he awoke. Alison gone. Had she even been there? Somewhere on the water a radio dispersed its sound. Translucent sand crabs, the size of his fingernails, scurried over his shins. It was a dream. Last night had been a dream—her skin moving against her ribs, so thin over her body he could see the laddering of it. She rocked above him, coaxing her face out of the shadows. The star-drenched sky reeling. I got you, he said, when she slipped.

Now, in the shock of early morning, he was wrenched back into his body. The rocks slimy with moss. The water ice-cold and molecular. Late in the night there'd been thunder, and heat lightning—all night it had felt like it was minutes away from raining—but it hadn't rained. Already you could feel the day hotting up again. From some dark crevice the smell of a dead animal, rank and oversweet. That evening they'd laid the gull on the water and it was borne out, mutilate, into the gray drift. For hours—every time he'd looked back—he'd seen other gulls, dozens of them, circling in a silent gyre. Making black shapes out of themselves in the dusk sky. Then the light had failed. Here, he thought. He stood up, the soreness returning to him all at once. Here is the saddest place I know.

IT WAS AFTERNOON by the time he got home. All morning he'd wandered the dunes and tidal flats—too spent to think—then, strange to his own intentions, he'd set eyes on the courthouse before him. Gone in, sat down in a cool, dim corner.

At home there was a strange car in the driveway, a new-looking four-wheel drive. Out-of-towners. He watched from his bungalow as his dad came around the side of the house with two men. One wore mountain boots and a red polar fleece around his waist and walked quickly, keys in his fist. The other was a suit. His Brylcreemed hair cracking in the thirty-plus heat as he kept pace. They got into their car and did a three-point reverse and dusted down the driveway. His dad still standing by the front veranda. Two beer bottles sweating on the railing. He wore a short-brimmed hat and Jamie couldn't see his face.

Tea was a quiet affair. Every now and then Michael looked at him furtively but otherwise they kept to themselves. Afterward, Jamie plastic-wrapped the leftovers and washed the dishes. Michael dried and stacked. They worked silently, waiting to see if their parents' voices would start up. Michael's studied silence beginning to get on Jamie's nerves. Their dad came out of the living room, grabbed two bottles of wine, and went back in.

"They turned down the offer on the house," whispered Michael.

"Who, Mum?"

"Nah, the buyers."

"Why?"

But he wouldn't say any more. Jamie didn't push. Once, he'd caught Michael at the caravan park, wagging school, and hadn't said anything—he never knew whether it was out of loyalty or laziness. Once, he'd hit Michael in the mouth harder than he'd meant to and broken a tooth. *I hate you,* Michael had said, blood darkening the arches of his gum. It had only struck Jamie later that his brother might actually have meant it. That he might actually hate him. That he'd have reason. But Michael had calmed down, his face settling into an expression as smooth, cloudy as sea glass. He hadn't dobbed him in. They didn't talk to each other much, maybe, but they kept each other's secrets.

The dishes were done and then there was nothing to do.

At eleven that night his dad knocked on his door. He was holding an open wine bottle. His teeth shone chalky in the dark.

"Your light's on," he said.

"Sorry."

He stood on the concrete steps of Jamie's bungalow, swaying a little. His shadow stretched out long behind him and hung over the acacia shrubs. "Looks like no one's sleeping tonight," he said. "Not your mum either." He looked up the drive at the dark house and smiled broadly. He only smiled like that when he was drunk. "She can probably hear us."

"Dad."

"I thought I might just . . ." he patted the air above the steps, "Do you mind . . ." now hoisting his bottle—the staggering of statements confusing Jamie.

They both sat down on the steps. His dad didn't seem to know what to do with the bottle: he clamped it between his two straightened palms, rolling it forward and back, then set it down with a loud chink.

"Big game next week," he said at last.

Jamie nodded. Unbidden, his mind cast back to the school assembly—he'd been onstage—could that really have been him onstage four days ago? That person seemed unrecognizable.

His dad said, "Well, at least you won't have to move."

"Those the buyers today?"

His dad laughed. "We're all set, right? Then she tells them to bugger off. Calls the guy a tight-arse, says they can't even wait another couple of months."

"A couple of months?"

Jamie regretted it as soon as he said it. You couldn't talk about that. Not without talking about after. There was no after.

"Sorry," he said.

But this time something came into his dad's eyes. "No . . ." he said, "No, you should know." He glanced at the house again, then stared out into the garden. "A matter of months. That's what they told us in Maroomba." He spat on the ground away from Jamie. "It's her kidney. They can map it out like that. They're useless to fix anything but they can give you pinpoint bloody timelines."

Jamie froze—it was as though he'd stalled. He heard his dad's words. He'd expected them—he'd hoarded himself, day after day, against them—but now, when they came, all he could think about, obscenely, was Dory. The black tablet of his face. He hated it. He hated himself for it.

"I thought you should know," said his dad.

He could tell him: Dad, I'm in trouble—it'd be that easy—Dad, it's Dory Townsend. He wanted to, but there was no way. He knew what his dad thought of him.

"Does Michael know?"

His dad shook his head. Finally he said, "It's tough enough for him already."

The smell of wine was strong on his breath. They each waited for the other to speak. How did people speak about these things?

His dad said, "You know you can't work these holidays."

"Yeah, I know."

"I need you around the house." He fell silent. "Good boy." After a time he said it again. "Good boy."

"Dad?"

"Yeah, son."

But the distance was unthinkable. His dad took a swig from the bottle and patted Jamie's knee. He stood up, teetering with undelivered advice.

"You been fishing."

"Yeah. With Cale."

His dad's face momentarily betrayed his distaste. Then he frowned. "I been thinking. We should do that again. Michael too. Would you boys like that?"

Jamie nodded. He saw, now, how the conversation would spin itself out.

"We could take the two-stroke."

When he was little, he used to run down ahead and start the outboard motor. Turn the water over, pump out the bilge. Good boy. Now, his dad looked dead ahead whenever they drove past the wharf, its silent throng of boats.

"And your mum, she'd probably like us out of her hair."

"Yeah."

"We'll have someone come over."

You couldn't think of after, you only thought of now, and come to think of it, you didn't do that either—you were left with pools of memory, each stranded from the next by time pulling forward like a tide. *The two of you,* his mum had told him once, *you thought you were so smart—sneaking out on your secret fishing trips. You'd both come home reeking of diesel.* Her first relapse had come a matter of weeks after that trip to the rock pier. The seagull. No more time for fishing. After that, Jamie sensed a difference—a dilution—in how his dad treated them; though with Jamie, and to a lesser extent Michael, his attention turned offhand, buffered by wary disappointment. With their mum his behavior took the form of an impeccable courtesy. He moved her studio into the house. He quit his boat, started full-time woodworking. He laundered her sheets. Now, when you looked at him, five years on, and tried to see him without her, there was almost nothing left. What he'd given her, Jamie understood—what he was giving her still—he knew he'd never get back.

CALE CAME OVER THE NEXT DAY.

"Tammie told me to tell you," he said. He closed the bungalow door behind him.

"What?"

"Lester said Dory'll meet you after training on Monday."

"*Meet* me?"

Cale shrugged. "She told me to tell you."

Jamie stood up. It was Saturday: he had two days left. He guided himself, as though measuring distances, all around the small room. He made himself breathe. "I'm fucked," he said.

Cale didn't meet his gaze. "The final's next weekend," he said.

"So?"

"You know," he groped for the right words. "He might. . ." He trailed off.

"What about Wilhelm?"

Cale looked at a complete loss.

"And that Chinese chick," Jamie said. "What about her?"

No charges had ever been laid. No evidence, or the evidence was inconclusive. Some Maroomba authority came down and said so. What no one said was that Dory and his uncle—a notorious flag-waver—had taken recently to assaulting Asians in that part of the bay. The town turning a blind eye. This body, belonging, as it did, to a faceless, nameless poacher, was just another case of no one's business. More than anything, what Jamie remembered was Lester's reenactment: the sheer joy of his punches—their appalling regularity.

The conversation faltered. Cale grim-faced. Jamie felt a sudden longing to talk to him, tell him everything—he was three years older, after all, had seen that much more of the world— then all at once he wanted Cale to leave him alone. They stayed quiet for a while.

"She said they weren't even together."

"Yeah," Cale replied instantly. "Tammie said that too."

Jamie hesitated, then said, "What should I do?"

"You're fast. Use your speed."

"What?"

"Throw sand in his eyes. Then get him in the balls when his hands are up."

Jamie stopped, shook his head. The conversation was unreal. "Fuck off. I'm serious."

Cale considered him, his face rough with the effort of understanding.

"I'll do a runner," said Jamie. "Like you. Travel around."

Cale put his hands in his pockets glumly. "Nah," he said. "I don't farkin know." He sat down on Jamie's bed. "You want some mull?"

"Jesus."

Cale puffed out his cheeks, sucked them back in, then said, in a low, hurried breath, "That's why I ran away. My old man used to beat up on me." He brought out his hands, rubbing his knuckles. "And I kept telling myself. That every time he hit me, he was telling me he loved me that much—that much."

Jamie tensed. It clouded him, hearing this.

"Shit, man."

Cale closed his hands into fists. Then, doubtfully, he banged them together. The mattress bounced up and down. "Fark. That's bullshit. He never did. I don't even know why I said that."

Jamie watched on, confounded, as Cale fingered the beads on his necklace. He lumbered over to the window. "Look," Cale said, facing away from him, "I've never been any of those places either."

"What?"

"But my ex did give me this." He added quickly, "She's alive. In Cairns. Shithole of a place. She's a horoscopist or horticulturist or something."

"You're fucking hilarious."

"Easy, big man."

He straightened up and came over to Jamie and nudged his shoulder, the gesture itself ambiguous—neither playful nor solemn. "It'll be over soon, man."

Jamie pushed past, suddenly flooded with an intense rage toward his friend.

"You fucking stink of fish," he said.

Cale chuckled mournfully. "You kidding? This whole town stinks of fish."

SUNDAY AFTERNOON. All day he'd kept to himself—morning he'd spent behind the bungalow, in a lean-to built against the back wall. Hidden from the house's view. He'd sat there holed up and boxed in by his mum's old painting supplies—oil bottles, brushes, wood panels crammed into milk crates—listening to traffic along the coastal road, chatter lifting from the beaches: the stirrings of tourist summer. He'd stewed under the aluminium sheeting. The fight was tomorrow. The thought almost too much to contain, his mind recoiling between that and the thought of Alison, each contorting—neither providing respite from—the other. When the midday humidity got too much he went back inside and lay down.

Someone knocked.

"Storm's coming," said Michael through the door.

"Where's it coming from?"

"Umm, from the west. I mean, the east."

Jamie opened the door and Michael slouched in.

"Does Mum know?"

He shrugged.

"Let's go get her."

The house was empty. The reclining couch in front of the window unoccupied. "Probably at the bluff," Michael said.

"Is her wheelchair here?"

His brother checked the closet.

"Nope." A stirring on his features: "I'm gonna go look for them."

Alone, Jamie lowered himself onto the couch. The striped blanket crumpled at his feet. He nestled into the indentation of her body—so shallow—and imagined he could feel her residual warmth.

He looked out of the open window. So this was what it was like. He looked through the green foliage, over the ocean, and felt around him the heat massing in the air, the current of coolness running through it, taking form in the thunderheads. He saw the black energy becoming creatured from a hundred kays away, roaring toward shore, feeding on itself. On the headland, trees bending to absorb the weight of the forward wind.

"It's coming in," a loud voice said.

Startled, he turned to take in the room. No one. Then he sat up, craned his head out of the window. A raindrop as large as a marble plopped on his bare neck.

"Yes." That was his mum's voice. "Thank you, Bob," she said. "It's lovely."

Silence, then his dad's voice: "It's a good chair."

They sounded scrappy, as though coming through radio static. Jamie realized they hadn't made it to the bluff; they were nearer to the house—probably on the shaded veranda below— and the wind was reconstituting the sound of their voices, carrying it to him.

Now their conversation was unintelligible. Then his mum said, "Darling," just as half the sky darkened. "It's coming in," she said again.

And she was right, the storm was coming in—it was streaking in like a gray mouth snarled with wind, like a shredded howl, rendering the land into a dark, unchartered coast. The bay turning black. For centuries, fleets had broken themselves against the teeth of that coast.

"I can almost feel it on my face," his mum said.

Her voice was strangely amplified, then voided by a detonation of thunder—it shook the house; the remaining daylight dipped and then, with a rogue gust of wind that rocked the couch backward, it was raining—heavy and straight and stories high.

Jamie sat by the window. The sky dark yellow through the rain. The baked smells of the earth steamed open, soil and garden and sewage and salt and the skin of beasts. Potted music of water running through pipes, slapping against the earth; puddles strafed by heavy raindrops until in his mind they became battlefields, trenched and muddy. The wind swung westward and whipped the hanging plants' tendrils into the room. Wetting his face. He could hear them again.

"Ask me now," she said.

Sheets of water sluicing the other windows. The wind rattling them.

His dad's voice, so low as to be almost inaudible: "Are you happy, Maggie?"

A breaking of thunder ran through the sky and into the ground. Her answer blown away. Jamie sat in the shape of her body and closed his eyes and imagined the feel of the weather against her numbed face. He felt the sky's cracking as though deep along fault lines in his chest. He tested the word in his mouth: "Yes."

"I'm sorry," someone said. "Forgive me." Whose voice was that?

"Yes," said Jamie, "I'm happy now."

"Oh, you know there's nothing to forgive."

He got up from the chair. This wasn't right, listening in like this—he'd go downstairs.

Michael burst into the room, hair pasted on his forehead and streaming with rain.

"Where are they?" he wheezed. "I can't find them."

"They're downstairs," said Jamie.

"But I checked downstairs."

Michael moved closer to the window. Water dripped from his chin, his sleeves, logging at the bottom of his shorts.

"Listen," said Jamie.

Soft, shapeless, their mum's voice wafted up. Michael turned and smiled tentatively at Jamie. "Bet Mum's getting a kick out of this," he said. The storm crashed around them. Michael seemed, in that moment, caught up simply in the anxiety of having Jamie agree with him. Jamie smiled and nodded. He was always forgetting how it had once been between them.

"Come on," he said.

At the door, there came a louder voice—their dad's—broken up by the unruly wind. He was talking about finding something, saying they found something—

Their mum's voice: "That Townsend kid."

Michael glanced at Jamie.

Their dad's voice went on, scratchy and sub-audible. Then the wind lifted the words up clearly. Findings. Findings at the coroner's inquest.

"What's a coroner?" asked Michael.

"Shut up."

"Something wrong with that kid," his mum's voice said.

"I'm worried." His dad's voice. "Know why they call him Loose Ball Jamie?"

The sky raining through the rising wind. Clay pots swaying, tapping against the window frames.

"It means he doesn't go in hard. For the fifty-fifties." A fresh agitation in his dad's voice, laying open the folds of his feeling. "I'm not saying he's gutless—but he freezes."

Jamie turned toward Michael, who shrank back, face already crimped in fear.

"Let's go," he said.

"Don't," said Michael. "Please don't."

Before they left, his dad's voice floated into the room, loud and raw and plain: "You should remember."

In the kitchen he got Michael in a headlock. "How'd they find out? You little shit."

"I can't breathe!"

"You told them, didn't you?"

"Everyone knows."

"What? What'd you say?" He shoved Michael's head against the sink washboard, forced it along the metal ribbing, then dropped him to the floor. Michael's body shivering. The storm muted in here. Slowly, he felt the remorse bleeding into him. Always it came, immediately afterward. He said, "Everyone knows what?"

Michael curled into a cupboard corner. He lifted his hand to feel the side of his head. He was breathing hard when he looked up, and he didn't look at Jamie's face but at some indistinct point beneath it.

"That you're gonna fight Dory," he said in his deep voice. "And that he's gonna slaughter you."

ALL NIGHT HE COULDN'T SLEEP.

He threw on some clothes and wandered outside. The rain had stopped. Branches shuddered the water off themselves. The moon was still bright, caught in their wet leaves.

His mother had fallen asleep on the reclining couch. She was snoring softly. The moonlight poured in from the window and buoyed around her as though to bear her up. It seemed unreal. He pulled the blanket snug beneath her chin. Her mouth dropped open as though its hinges had snapped, and she snorted.

"Darling?"

"Sorry, Mum," he said. "I didn't mean to wake you."

It was as though she were swimming up from some distant pit of herself. The drugs awash in her—he saw it now. With sudden clarity he understood how lost she must feel in her body.

"God, I'm sorry," she said. Her voice was drawn thin. "I was wrong. Who gets to choose where they die?" Her eyes were barely open, one of them darting about quick as silverfish.

"Mum, wake up."

"But the boys love it here. You too." Her face loosened. She said, "You wouldn't believe."

"Mum." He shook her shoulder.

"The things I see now. But my hands."

"Mum." A pulse in her eyes and then her mouth moved. It jerked, then spread slowly into a smile of recognition.

"Sweetie." She fell quiet. They listened together to her breathing. All through her the odor of bleach, bleach sopped and smeared with a used rag.

"What is it?" she said.

A nauseous rush of answers rose up in him but he said nothing.

"The girl?" She didn't wait for his response. "And that horrible boy. Are you scared?"

He nodded.

"You're my son," she whispered. A strange shifting in her eyes, as though grass moved behind them. For a moment she looked lost. Then she said, "My son does anything he wants."

Gradually her head drooped forward. The muscles around her mouth went slack and he realized she was lapsing back into sleep. This was where she lived most of the time. He felt toward her an immense quantity of love but it was contaminated by his own venom, made sour. He wanted it to stop. When? Monday, after training? What would be enough—what commensurate with his lack? And what if he couldn't? She had come back from the hospital and the first thing she said to him and Michael was, *This won't happen to you. I promise.* He was rubbish. Whatever he did or didn't do now, he'd hate himself later—he knew that.

A truck raced by on the coastal road, ripping skins of water off the bitumen.

Her head still bowed, she said in a slurred voice, "James?" He slid his fingers into the pouch of her right hand. He'd never before noticed how loose the skin around her knuckles was.

She said, "My wine." After a long silence she said, "Will you pass it to me, please?"

"Mum."

"Your father and I love you very much. No matter what."

"Okay."

"Okay?"

It wasn't until a minute later he realized she might be squeezing his hand. "Okay."

He dreamed he was alone. The glass was cold against his fingers and forehead. He shrank away, went to the next black, steamed window, and the next, calling out as he searched. His voice sounded as though trapped inside some metal bladder. What if the paddocks were empty? And the long white corridors, too, with their waxy floors, and the dark slopes of the dunes he clambered up and down as though drunk? What if he couldn't find him?

The ocean seethed and sighed in the dark. So this was where you ended up, sick in sleep. Your night a beach and all sorts of junk washing up on shore.

AT SCHOOL NEWS OF THE FIGHT HAD SPREAD. Monday at last. Everyone watched him and no one looked him in the eye. Even the teachers seemed to leave him to himself, steering their voices around. The semis, the assembly—all of it seemed long gone, preserved elsewhere. He was being quarantined. He'd seen it before. You were dead space, you were off-limits—until afterward. Nothing malicious in it. What made it strange for him was the incongruous buzz around school—everyone getting fired up for the holidays and, in particular, the grand final that weekend. First time in five years, and against archrivals Maroomba too. The tension brinking on hysteria.

Recess he spent in the C-block toilets. What was the grand final to him? He tried to throw up but couldn't.

Lunchtime he saw her. Her friends clustered in the concrete corner of the downball court where, as one, they turned to look at him, opening apart, unfurling like some tartan-patterned flower, and there she was, leaning against the wall with large concentric targets painted in white behind her. She held his eye for a second and then the circle sealed shut. He realized he was holding his breath.

Vague impressions of classes rolled on. Each period ending with teachers saluting the team, rallying everyone for the big game. Jamie felt exhausted. Time pushed him forward. His mind wound out, one point to the next.

"C'arn, Halfies!"

He spotted Dory just before final period. Taller than everyone else. Like a dockworker in his school uniform—shirtsleeves high on his biceps, shorts tight across his quads. His eyes too close together, his hair flaxen, floppy. Like some sick cartoon of a dockworker. The corridor packed and noisy. A few people saw them, made space, straggled, but Dory disappeared into a classroom. Lester was behind him, of course, and from a distance Jamie could see his face, pinched up in anger, yelling something out.

"Fucking retard!" he seemed to be yelling.

Jamie opened his mouth.

"Fucking retard mum!" he was yelling.

Of course he couldn't be saying that. Jamie shook it off—the bog-like feeling that accompanied the thought of his mum. There was his mind again, groping at anything but what was right in front of him. In front of him—wherever he went—Dory. Huge and hard, a thing of horror. He'd been dumped on the beach by his folks. He'd bashed up this guy, hospitalized that guy. He'd killed a Chink with his uncle.

The teacher talked on as Jamie watched the clock.

You had to shut it out. You could see it on players' faces, how they approached him, ready to take damage. You could hear it in your parents' voices. You had to shut it all out, otherwise it would sprout in you like weeds.

The bell rang.

He was headed for the lockers when his geography teacher

flanked him, escorted him wordlessly to the principal's office and dropped him off there.

"Go on," said the secretary. She looked up. "Go *on*. Mr. Leyland's waiting."

Jamie knocked, cracked open the door.

"There he is," a voice boomed. Coach Rutherford. He was wearing trackies and a Halflead T-shirt, a whistle around his neck. He stood behind the principal's desk. Where was Leyland?

"I was just coming to training," Jamie said.

"Good," said Coach. He waved him inside. Then Jamie saw Leyland—on the couch obscured by the door. With him was Jamie's dad. His mum in her wheelchair. His mum—what was she doing here? Jamie stood in the doorway and didn't move. All these people. All day he'd been waiting—all those days since Thursday night's party—and now it felt as though time had pushed him forward too far, too hard. Everything collapsing into one place.

Coach said, "But today, you get a rest." He smiled curtly and closed his fist around the whistle, shaking it like dice. Jamie's dad stood up and thanked him. He was wearing work clothes, his jeans smeared with oil and sawdust. Then he turned and thanked Leyland.

"Well," said Leyland, rising to his feet, "our students, our business."

Coach left the room. Jamie didn't say anything. He was thinking of Dory, the rest of them, waiting for him on the oval. What they must be thinking. He felt airy in his own body. What they must be saying. He remembered Lester's words in the corridor.

"It's not your business," his mum said quietly, but Leyland didn't hear.

His dad moved to stand behind her chair. "Come on, Jamie."

"It's between the boys. It's not their business."

"Maggie," his dad said under his breath, "we talked about this already."

Jamie couldn't bring himself to look at them. He sensed that to witness a drama between his parents here, now, might wreck him completely.

"Jamie," said Leyland. His voice took on added weight: "I've talked to Dory. He understands—there's to be no trouble whatsoever."

His dad pushed the wheelchair out of the room.

"Alright?" Leyland asked. "It's over."

Even from the car he could see Dory. Even at that distance. Tallest in a line of green guernseys, the one moving slower, as though to a separate beat, while the others jogged in place, ran between the orange witches' hats between whistle bursts. Sprint exercises. All the way home Jamie said nothing.

When they pulled up, he got out and unfolded the wheelchair.

His dad said, "Help your mother into the house."

"Bob, I'm okay."

His dad looked at Jamie and then at the house. "I said help your mother."

The front door opened and Michael came out. He stopped—transfixed and tense—as soon as he saw Jamie, staring at him without any of his usual bashfulness. Something like concern, deeper than concern, all through his expression. Then he went over to their mum and took hold of the wheelchair handles.

"I'm going down the jetty," Jamie told his dad.

His mum turned to him with a strange, clear-eyed face. "You're allowed. You're allowed to go. You can go."

HE WALKED, ALONE, down to the jetty. It was clogged with tourist families who'd arrived over the weekend. All along the walkway were canvas chairs, Eskies, straight-backed rods thick as spear grass. A mob of fluoro jigs hopping on the water. He found a spot and sat. Someone had a portable radio and music streamed into the air in clean, bright colors. The bay a basin of light.

Could that really be the end of it? Leyland talking to Dory? What would he have said to him? That the school needed Jamie fit for the final? That Jamie's dad had begged Dory to spare his gutless son? That his mum, in that wheelchair, was dying? He sat in the midst of the jetty's hurly-burly, watching and listening. He felt the need of explanation. Here's what he could say to Dory—no, he could say anything, all the right things, and it still wouldn't be enough. Maybe things could be normal again. He'd finish school, run onto the field on Saturday and run off two hours later. He'd take up the job at the fish plant, or, better yet, he'd talk to John Thompson. His dad would take the sheets in. *Stop.* They'd pot the ashes under the waratahs; leave a handful for the bluff, throw it up and the wind would probably shift and putter it into their faces. She'd like that. No—you didn't think of that.

He got up and started walking. He'd sat there long enough— training would be done by now. He walked down the main street and past the wharf. At the tidal flats he took off his shoes and kept going. He had an idea where he was going but nothing beyond that. Sand spits sank into ankle-deep shoals. The night had been cold and the water chilled his feet. The sky flat and blue with mineral streaks. He passed the rock pier and started picking his way through the sedgeland— sharp, rushlike plants grazing his legs. At every step he dared himself to turn around, but he didn't. He followed a rough trail marked with half-submerged beer bottles, clearings where blackened tins from bonfire rockets were set into the dirt like sentinels.

And Alison. How would he have any chance with her other-wise? He stepped on solid-looking ground and sank to his knees.

The bile rose up in him. Roundabout here was where they'd found the poacher's body. Half stuck, half floating in the marshy suck. No—nothing was worth that. And in that moment he realized, deep as any realization went, that that wasn't what he was afraid of at all. He had to see it through.

He came to the shack in the middle of a muddy clearing. A man sat out front on a steel trap doing ropework. He was surrounded by other traps and old nets, dried and sun-stiffened in the shapes of their failure. It must have been Dory's uncle. He didn't look up.

"Dory," he called out. "One of your little friends is here to see you."

Jamie moved closer. The sides of slatted wooden crates were laid end to end over the mud—a makeshift path—and he stepped onto them. He saw the man's hands, shot with swollen veins and spidery capillaries. The waistband of his shorts cutting deep under his beer gut.

"Dory!"

"I'll come back," said Jamie.

The screen door opened and there was Dory, his body blocking almost the whole space, eyes narrowed in the sun. Hair over his eyes. He was wearing trackies and a stained singlet. He rubbed the bristles on his chin and cheek. Then he came partway down the crate-board path.

"You're here," he said. He sounded surprised.

"Offer him a drink," said his uncle. "And get me one while you're at it."

"We're out," said Dory.

His uncle looked up and chortled, his face orange and unevenly tanned like an old copper coin. Then Jamie heard a whoop from inside the hut. He saw movement behind the boarded-up windows where the wood had rotted off.

"The fuck you doing here?" said Dory in a low voice.

Jamie stared dumbly at him. "The fight," he managed to say.

Dory surveyed the entire clearing behind Jamie. "It's off."

"Why?"

A disgusted look came over Dory's adult face. "Why?" He glanced, almost involuntarily, over his shoulder, then came a step closer to Jamie and said, "You dunno what the fuck you're doing, do you?"

Lester appeared at the door. "This fucker," he shouted, his face splitting into a grin.

"Jamie?"

Alison—that was Alison's voice. She emerged from the hut in her school uniform like some sort of proof. Even here—deep down in this plot of filth—her dress was clean. The mud didn't touch her. She looked at Jamie with an expression of dark intensity.

"I thought . . ." He tried to make his voice firm. "There's squid now, down the jetty," he said.

She hesitated, then walked toward him, then stopped beside Dory. Her face still amok. Then she put her mouth to Dory's ear and after a moment he laughed, a deep, throttled hack of a laugh.

"See," said Dory's uncle. He lowered the greased rope onto his lap. "Here's what I don't get."

"Alison," Jamie went on. He spoke only to her. But his voice faltered, undercutting what he wanted—what he was trying to say.

"Don't you boys go to school together? Why come all the way out here?"

"Can't hide behind his retard mum here, that's why," said Lester.

Dory gave out another guttural laugh. Then, turning his back, he said, "Just fuck off, Jamie. Okay?"

It wasn't as though he'd planned anything. He hadn't known

exactly what to expect. But this—Alison, her shoulders neatly narrowed as though pinned back, spinning Dory around and hissing into his ear, the old man leering on a crab trap in a crater of mud—this wasn't part of it. He stepped up to Dory.

"Okay then," Dory said.

Jamie held up his arms but the first pain came in his stomach— he could feel the air being forced up, spraying out of his mouth. He cradled his stomach and then there was a heavy knock to the side of his head. He sat down. The ground tramped with mud like a goal square.

"Fuck you up!" Lester hooted.

"Right," said Dory's uncle. "Now I get it."

Alison stared at Jamie with a stunned expression. Then slowly, stutteringly, she started laughing too, a thin, uncertain trickle into the air.

Was that enough? The air felt hot in his lungs. He waited for his breath to come back. He stood up. He looked at Dory and realized he'd never looked at another body—not even Alison's— so closely: the hard-knotted chest, the scabbed shoulders. The face a hide stretched over a seat of stone. When it came, he swung at it but his own head whiplashed back.

Seated again. His throat burning. His vision broken into scales. Stay down. Someone's voice—a whisper—he looked over to where Alison had been standing but she was no longer there. On the rock pier that night, under the hot stars—she'd said it into his mouth. She'd been there with him, watching the water wink, moonlight on the surface and then underneath, too, the glow of shucked abalone shells . . . *It's different with you.* He could still hear her laughing, and Lester yelling—he sounded angry, too angry—as though by proxy for Dory. When his sight returned he saw Michael drop his bike and wipe the sand from his eyes.

"That's enough!" His dad—breaking through the sedge into

the clearing. Of course, thought Jamie, slogging through the mire of his mind—Michael. Michael had followed him.

"Stay down."

But who was speaking? The voice was too soft.

"You alright, son?"

"Just stay down." Jamie twisted around and realized, with mild surprise, it was Dory muttering to him.

His dad arrived at his side.

The only sound left was Alison's laugh, which, somewhere along the line, had turned inside out, into a sequence of hollow sobs.

"Let's go, son."

He searched his dad's face—he was ready, now, to accept all its familiar reproaches. But the face he saw was different: shaken loose from its usual certainty. Frowning, though without heat, Jamie's dad bent down, picked Jamie up. At his dad's touch a tremor ran all through him.

"Boys, ey?" offered Dory's uncle with a smile.

Jamie's dad looked at him flatly, then turned away. "Come on, Jamie."

Alison was still standing halfway down the crate-board path, next to Lester. Her arms were crossed low over the front of her school dress, over her stomach, as though it were she who'd just been gut-punched. Her sobbing had subsided. Jamie half made to approach her when his dad squeezed his shoulder.

"Son," he said in a low voice. He shook his head.

Alison's mouth, her eyes—now turned toward them—seemed slowly to shape themselves into a leery cast. She rushed up to Dory. "Wait!"

Dory said something back to her.

"What I wanted?" she cried.

Dory turned toward Jamie and his dad. The expression on his face—a mask concealing another mask, and behind that—

what? Minutes ago, Jamie would have said there was nothing: a dark gale thrown into a room and trapped. Now, he didn't know.

Dory gripped Alison's forearm but she flung his hand off.

"Rubbish is rubbish," muttered his dad. "Wherever it comes from."

"You're letting him off!" She was tiny next to Dory, furious. "You know. You *know* what he said! What he did!"

Everything became quiet. An ocean wind swept over the swale, heavy with salt, carrying the faint shriek of seagulls.

"I told you," Dory replied. His tone was impersonal. It occurred to Jamie unexpectedly that Dory might be talking to him. He looked and looked at Dory but could no longer induce himself to feel anything.

"Come on," said Jamie.

He reached up to touch his face and the touch came earlier than he'd expected. His face was numb. This was how it felt. His mouth tasted of mud, and blood, and it was smiling.

"Jamie?" murmured his dad.

He felt them all watching him, felt the sun warm on his face. A gold-tinged rope of spit dangled from his lips. Dory squared his body around. His demeanor was slack, drained of intention, like a sprinter's after crossing the finish line.

"I'm still here," said Jamie. "Come on."

It hurt to speak: his jaw felt locked and he was pushing, pushing down on it.

"That's enough, son."

He stepped clear of his dad. "I said I'm still here!"

Dory was stumped, you could tell. It didn't make sense. He took a deep breath and then came at Jamie, his arm outstretched. Something grainy about his face, unfocused. Something sounded like balsa wood breaking and suddenly Jamie's dad was on the ground, lying on his elbow, his face flecked with dirt. Everything froze. Then Dory hit Jamie as well: it felt like pity, and Jamie was down, too, in the midst of the mud and the shattered light. Bursts of color so bright they must speak, surely, for something.

No one talked. Then Dory's blunt, blurred voice: "It was an accident."

Alison's voice started up: "Stupid . . . stupid . . ."

Lester: "Shut up, cunt."

"I didn't mean to hit his dad—he jumped in. He just jumped in."

"Jesus," said Dory's uncle.

But what if this was all of it? What if, when you saw things through, this was all that waited for you at the end? He lay on the ground and saw the black line of mud and the yellow lines of sand and sedge and then the bottle-green ocean. How wonderful it would be to be out there on the water. The wind scoured in and stung his eyes until they were wet. He'd watched her paint, once, at the courthouse. It was before dawn and he was half-asleep. Blue and blue-green and then dark blue. A hasty white swath. He watched as she turned the bay into a field of color. Then he looked out and, in his grogginess, saw it all through her eyes—the town, the dunes and flats, the foreshore with its man-made outcrops, the bay, sandbars, reef and deep sea. All of it motionless—slabs of paint, smeared on and scraped off, just so, fixed at a time of day that could never touch down. And here was his father, picking himself up from the black sludge, his face in its old grief. Here was Dory, who, despite everything—his emptiness—seemed uninterested, or incapable, of holding Jamie's hate. Michael, who still could. Alison. Watching from within her immaculate uniform. Only Lester's face brimmed with epiphany—a line had been crossed—and nothing had changed.

His dad got to his feet. He was shorter than Dory but spoke straight up into his face.

"That's enough."

They looked at each other and then Dory looked away. A second later, Alison coughed into her hands and ran inside the shack. Michael waded into the mud and helped pull Jamie up. His face, Jamie realized, bore the same clear, graceful expression Jamie had last seen on their mum's face—his hands on Jamie's wrists surprisingly strong. Again—despite everything—he'd chosen to come. Jamie felt himself falling apart. Now, as Michael hauled him up from the ground, he braced his pain against his brother's strength. His dad held him under the armpits. Now, for the first time, Jamie gave over his weight to them entirely.

His dad tightened his embrace. He said, "You okay?"

Michael, face tracked with mud, went to pick up his bike, steered it around. He wheeled it close by them. Jamie held fast to his dad's shoulder. At the edge of the clearing his dad stopped, turned, as though to kiss him on the head, then said, "You're okay, son." They started the long walk home.

Hiroshima

KEEP A STRAIGHT BACK, Mrs. Sasaki says. Wipe the floor with your spirit. The floor is still cold from night and stings my knees. On my left, Tomiko makes her back straight and stretches out her legs behind her, left, right, like the morning exercises. She holds each leg for two breaths, in, out, in, out. I look away from her. I look down and see my face in the shiny wood. It looks half-asleep. The rag hides and then reveals my face, left, right, like a spirit peering through the wood. Father knows many stories about tree spirits. The biggest tree at his Shrine in the city is older than Grandfather—than Grandfather's grandfather, he says. The shadows are large and cool even in summer. But Father says its spirit is young in appearance, maybe as young as me. Camphor, he says, teaching me the name. Father's garden is full of spirits. I like it there. Maybe I am a spirit of the pine boards in the hallway between the entrance and the main room. In this Temple up in the hills. I am safe here. Spirit? So foolish, little turnip. This is what Big Sister calls me. Her face is white and filled with the Yamato spirit and I think of it every night before going to sleep. I want to look like her. You don't become a spirit until you die, little turnip. Honorable death before surrender. She says this a lot. The radio says this a lot. Mother says nothing when Big Sister says this, wearing her designated nametag and armband and headband. She looks like a warrior when she comes home from mobilization. Covered in gray dust like she is made from stone. Left, right, on the floor—my knees don't hurt like they did at the beginning but being in this position makes the emptiness of my belly feel even bigger. Do without until victory! After we recite the Imperial Rescript on Education at assembly each morning, Mrs. Sasaki reminds us we are all small citizens. Sometimes, after I dip the rag in the bucket, the wooden floorboards squeak like small dogs. *Hungry!* they yelp. *Hungry hungry!* My spirit smiles back at me, more open-eyed now. Some of the younger children like making this noise; when three or four of them do it at the same time they giggle. Children, says Mrs. Sasaki. Citizens.

Last night there were no warnings and it was hard to sleep. Behind the paper door where the teachers sleep, the radio did not speak but made the sounds of a sick person breathing. My mat is four mats away from the radio. I sleep in the front corner of the room with all the other girls, next to one of the stone Buddha statues. The boys sleep at the back of the room by the Temple doors. If I lie down and look at the ceiling, on my left is Tomiko and on my right is Yukiyo. Tomiko is my friend and Yukiyo is one year older than me but she is nice. She is in the fourth grade. Two days ago, Yukiyo told me her father is a science teacher at the Prefectural Technical School and chief of the air-raid evacuation team in Yokogawa-cho. She said he was studying in Tokyo to be a doctor but went to China to fight our reviled enemy after the Manchurian Incident in the sixth year of Showa, period of enlightened peace. Father went to China too, I told her. He hurt his legs serving the Emperor with unquestioning loyalty. She nodded in approval. I did not tell her he came back to become a Shinto priest in Zaimoku-cho. Mother says we are at war and that some people do not wish to be reminded of the gods. She tells me to press my hands together for those people.

After cleaning we eat soybean rice. We have eaten soybean rice every day since the last Visiting Day. Tomoe says out loud that she hates soybean rice as much as she hates the American beasts. She is a sixth grader and everyone laughs. But I see Mr. Sasaki, who is married to Mrs. Sasaki, give her a look like the one Father gave Big Sister on the ferry. Then, like Father, he looks away. Father's face is wet from the rain and he turns to look at me instead of her. Mr. Sasaki is a teacher from my old elementary school in the city. Now he lives in the hills with us. Waste is the enemy! I say in my head. My sister's face is shiny with spirit. Do without until victory! I remember the story of the little boy-prince of Sendai. He says to his servant: See those baby sparrows in the nest, how their yellow beaks are opened wide, and now see! there comes the mother with worms to feed them; how happily the babies eat! But for a samurai when his belly is empty it is a disgrace to feel hungry. I do not like soybean rice either but I like it better than pounded rice balls with bran. Or parched soybeans. We third graders are allowed to choose the bowls with parched soybeans before everyone else. The sixth graders are allowed to choose the bowls with rice. All of us weigh the bowls with both hands. On our first day here we had luxurious food: rice with red beans, then red and white rice cakes in the nearby village. See, children, said Mrs. Sasaki to the younger ones still crying for their mothers, is it not better here? But the night before that, at home, I had had sweet rice cake dumpling with bean paste, with extra sugar Father brought home from the Shrine. It was my favorite meal in months. We set an extra bowl at the table for Big Brother, who is with the Emperor's West Eighty-seventh Division in the confidential place. He has been confidential since the Chinese Incident in the twelfth year of Showa, period of enlightened peace. Everything is given to the holy war but everything about the holy war is confidential. We must press our hands together for Tojo-san and the leaders of

His Imperial Majesty's government. No, we do not say Tojo-san anymore, little turnip. Koiso-san, says Mother. Suzuki-san, says Father. No, says Big Sister. Just press your hands together for the Fatherland. Mother has a photograph of Big Brother wearing a khaki uniform with a rifle in his hands and a dagger on the right side of his belt. It was taken at Ujina Port. We made a photograph to send to Big Brother too. Look here. Don't blink now. The man's rabbit teeth above the box, the sky behind him dark and green-looking. Your brother Matsuo held you when you were a baby, Mother tells me, and said you were as strong as a carp. At night, sometimes she unfolds a letter from him. I was promoted to First Class Private, she reads. I am grateful that I have skill with the anti-aircraft guns. If you can spare it, please send some ink and a safety razor. And some cigarettes, if you can spare it. *Banzai* to the Emperor. Well, good-bye, and good-bye to Sumi and little Mayako. Mayako—he is talking about me, but I do not remember him.

At exercise time I run with some of the others to the top of the hill. Running is good to stop the cold but bad for the hunger that comes after. The day is white and clear and cloudless. From the top of the hill we can see another hill, and behind that, the ocean. The ocean is a darker blue than the sky. Behind the hill is the city. We are safe here. Then from behind the hill the warning sounds. The sound is weak, then strong, like the wind. We look over the hill and over the ocean. I do not see anything when a boy says, There's only one. Everyone knows the cowardly Americans drop bombs only when they have hundreds of planes, grouped like geese, when the sky sounds like heavy thunder. When it is a single plane, says Big Sister, it is either taking photographs or dropping handbills. The plane passes far away to our left. Takai, a tall sixth grader, tells a group of third graders to be China, then some others to be Americans. The rest of us organize ourselves into His Imperial Majesty's forces. Like Father, I am in the Fifth Division. Evacuation! At Takai's signal, our enemies drop down to their bellies and put thumbs in their ears and fingers over their eyes, just like we have been trained in school. The rest of us pick up stones and clods of dirt and throw them at the enemy. We charge and fall on them with our knees and elbows and bamboo swords. One hundred million deaths with honor! Defend every last inch of the Fatherland! Big Sister says this, taking the words from the radio. Father looks at me instead of her. The soft rain runs down his hair and down his face. Everything is the same color in the rain. One hundred million deaths with honor! I say after her. We are fearless. Pilots of the Imperial Air Force transform themselves into human-guided missiles and crash into the enemy, sacrificing their lives for the Fatherland. I lie dead on the ground, looking into the deep blue sky, overwhelmed with a glorious feeling of happiness. *Kana kana kana.* We will defend our nation through all eternity! Some of the children are crying. I am filled with such love for my nation I forget my hunger and nearly cry too.

The radio is sick again that night. It coughs and wheezes. Behind this is the small noise of the weak ones trying to hide their weeping. Outside, the wind comes in from the black bay and over the city into the hills. When we were evacuating, the truck stopped on the top of the first hill and we looked down behind us and the city looked like an empty rice bowl with a piece broken off where the ocean was. The Temple is dark and silent except for the radio and the small sniffing. I lie on the straw mat and think of Big Sister. It is the holidays and she lets me come with her to mobilization. She has recently joined the Young Women's Volunteer Corps and the Students' Patriotic League by over-telling her age. We do not tell Mother. We catch a streetcar to Fujimi-cho where there are hundreds of students and some soldiers gathering around a large building. It is hot. Big Sister insisted that we both wear our padded air-raid hoods and now the sweat from my neck runs down my back and the backs of my knees. A man from the Volunteer Corps approaches Big Sister and gives her a basket. His shirt is open and the skin beneath it is the color of concrete where the dust sticks to his sweat. He does not check her nametag. When he smiles at her she looks away from him for too long, the way a cat does, and I realize they know each other. This is little turnip. Mayako, I correct. I prefer Mayako too, he says, bending down. It's a strong name. See over there? Watch this. He jogs back to the building and picks up one end of a long two-handed saw. Someone holds the other end. Someone cries out from the roof. Clay tiles and paper doors fall to the ground. Dust rises up and through it Big Sister's face is full of light. She is explaining it to me, the demolition, the need to create fire lanes, but I am more interested in watching her friend's arms as they work—left, right—across the beam, exactly the same speed as the man on the other side of the saw. Everywhere things are falling. More cries, and two soldiers climb to the tops of two ladders with ropes trailing behind them; then, when they climb down and walk away from the building, ten, maybe twelve, men pick up the two ropes and all of them strain toward the street until both ropes are straight. Big Sister holds my hand. The building groans like a tree, shivers, then falls into itself with an enormous noise. Isn't it glorious? she says. The air fills with dust. Cover your eyes. The Fatherland, a voice cries. If the building was a tree it would have died. All things come to *kami,* Father says. He is alone in his Shrine garden in the city. Is it one of the eight million *kami* now? I will ask Father. I will ask Mother on the next Visiting Day to ask Father. The idea excites me, and I try to keep the loudness in my head.

Mayako? It is Tomiko. Yes? Do you hear the warning? It is nothing but the wind. It is the wind, I say. We are safe here, says Yukiyo. You will be safe there, says Mother. My son is gone and my eldest daughter wants to follow—you are my heart. If I die, at least my heart will still be alive.

I am safe here, Big Sister says to Mother before the evacuation. They are in the kitchen and I can hear them from the outside yard where I am trapping cicadas. You are permitted to go, says Mother. You are of the age, Sumi. You will go with your sister. But I am safe here, says Big Sister. What do you mean, safe?— every night there are the warnings. But no bombs, says Big Sister—the planes fly over the city but do not bomb us. There are bombs, says Mother. My friends know students mobilized at the central telephone office, says Big Sister. In Kobe there are bombs. In Yokohama there are bombs. In Nagoya there are bombs. Tokyo, says Mother. Yes, in Tokyo. But not here—we are lucky here. What of the handbills the Americans drop? Mother asks. On the farm Tomoe tells everyone the American handbills look like money. But on one side only. What is on the other side? It is forbidden to read them. Her father works in the Mitsubishi shipyard in Eba and picks them up without looking at them and delivers them to the Prefectural Office. We are safe here, says Big Sister. I will stay. Her face is white, even through the dirty kitchen window. Your father will decide, says Mother. Yes, I say in the darkness to Tomiko, we are safe here. Then the wind picks up and I imagine I can hear the engines of a B-24 behind it. Father taught me the difference between the sounds. It will also depend on how high they are, he said. The *natsuzemi* cicada says *ji-i-i,* the *higurashi* sounds like a bell: *kana kana kana,* the *minminzemi* makes the sound of the lotus sutra. Do you hear that? It's a plane. The wind blows under the door and across the rows and rows of mats and I am back inside the dark Temple. It's your belly, I say to Tomiko. The radio coughs. Tomorrow I will find wild herbs to eat with my potatoes, whispers Yukiyo. And my mother said she will bring me more pickled apricots next Visiting Day. I lie back and put my hands on my belly and listen to the wind. It sounds like dry grass moving. I breathe in and out—one, two, one, two. The best and most rare cicada, Father says, is the *tsukutsukuboshi,* which sounds exactly like a bird: *chokko chokko uisu.*

Mayako. Mayako? *Chokko chokko uisu.*

White rice—bowlfuls of it. Eba dumplings with ground wheat and mugwort grass and sugar and lots of sugar. When the Fatherland wins the war we can eat anything we like. Heaped bowls of silvery white rice. Be patient, says Mother. Waste is the enemy, says Big Sister. Big Brother holds out his dagger and on the tip there is a big stewed white radish. Good-bye, little Mayako. He looks like the man in the photograph.

The soybean rice is cold. When I open my mouth the cold air of morning comes in. *Be filial to your parents,* we chant together, *affectionate to your brothers and sisters; as husbands and wives be harmonious; as friends true; bear yourselves in modesty and moderation; extend your benevolence to all.* Tomiko and I gather flax in the hills behind the Temple. The day is bright and still cold. Kites and carrion crows fly around us. The crows are evil spirits with black eyes and I am frightened. *Karasu ni hampo no ko ari,* Mother says. The young crow returns its filial duty and feeds its parents. Don't be frightened, child of my heart. When I tell Father he smiles. The proverb is from China, he says. China is our reviled enemy, I say. The Chinese are godless bandits. He looks away from me for a long time like a cat. Yes, he says. I look for the flower stalks of butterburs and field horsetails and dig up pine roots. The cicadas say *ji-i-i.* Some of the boys go to the villages three hills away for potatoes. When they come back we go to the farm in the nearby village and work. The village boys tease us about our feebleness. Be careful or you will faint, city dweller. Be careful or your hands will blister, city dweller! See, she holds the shovel like a firecracker . . . be careful or it will explode . . . *pika don!* In the line of students everyone is older than Big Sister but she has the strength of two women, passing baskets of sand and rubble from hand to hand, left to right, without stopping. It is white-hot on the street. The air is still dusty from the dead building. Her face is shiny, full of Yamato, and often she looks at the man who moved the saw, left, right. At my old elementary school in the city we farmed the playground for sweet potatoes and eggplants and squash. Turn the soil over, one time, two times, three times. One time, two times, three times. Mr. Sasaki gives the same orders here. He is nice to us. Now my mouth is hot and dry. I am no feeble city dweller. I turn the soil with my spirit. One time, two times, three times.

I am in the Fifth Division on the hill again when some boys cry out from the river. The water is cool and the leaves are green. The stones by the water are covered in moss. There are more than fifty types of moss in Father's garden. The shadows are large and cool. He is always alone there. I like the sound of water running over the stones. Father says the water is singing of impermanence. I am thinking of sweet potatoes and eggplants and squash. There is great excitement because some boys have caught a dragonfly. It is bigger than three thumbs. It is an Emperor's dragonfly, boasts Takai. Is it a female? It is a female, says Takai. He ties it with flax to a cherry branch and the dragonfly spreads its four wings and moves them so fast they look like they do not move at all, and holds them so wide they look like they hold every color—colors of pine oil and wet stone and metal. Don't blink now. We come close and hold out the captive prisoner and sing, *Konna dansho Korai o, adzunza no meto ni makete, nigeru wa haji dewa naikai* . . . O King of Korea, are you not ashamed to flee from the Queen of the East? I try hard to remember the folktale. A male dragonfly comes immediately over the water. Someone catches it and we laugh happily, passing it from hand to hand.

When I was your age, Mother says, I liked nothing more than to dive into the Kyobashigawa River from the streetcar bridge. We played there all summer, my sisters and I. Then the city installed lily-of-the-valley lanterns in the Hondori shopping district. We would walk back and forth for hours, never looking down, and when it turned to night it was like walking under a curved ceiling of moons. Smoke from the chestnut grills rising like clouds. There were lights on at night? Yes, child of my heart. They are gone now, of course, they were metal. But then, you could walk under the moons all through the night, all the way from Nakajima to Shintenchi, where there were shops and movie theaters and music halls and cafés and restaurants.

Tell me of when you met Father. When I met Father, we went to the Prefectural Industrial Promotion Hall to watch a tap-dancing concert. Afterward we went to a restaurant where they played jazz on a gramophone. It was music straight from heaven. Happy and sad at the same time and no one knew how to dance to it. The water is cold. Hiroshima is the city of rivers, Father says. Seven rivers run through it, each with a *kami*. You don't become a *kami* until you die, little turnip. Let's go, Mayako. She is wet, says Tomoe. The wind makes the water cold. Now the sky has changed color. Mrs. Sasaki will punish her, says Tomoe. No swimming in your clothes, says Mrs. Sasaki. Masachan got the pneumonia and went to the clinic in the city and did not return. Tochiki and Akira and his friend with the small ears were taken by Mr. Sasaki back to the city. Maybe they were naughty too. I will come later, I say. I think: When my clothes are dry. When I was your age, Mother says. It feels like a long time since the last Visiting Day. Do without until victory! Then you become one of the eight million *kami*. I will tell Mrs. Sasaki you are digging pine roots for dinner, says Tomiko. The light is changing into the color of our watercolors and on the blue hills a bird cries *hoo hoo*. Farmers hear that, says Father, and they know it is time to plant the millet. He teaches me the name: *awamakidori*. The wind is loud now. There are kites above me in the watercolor sky and everywhere the sound of cicadas. Father teaches me the difference between the sounds. That is a B-24. That is a B-27. And that is a B-29. Father went to China and

served the Emperor with unquestioning loyalty and hurt his legs
and now he serves the Emperor as a priest in his Shinto Shrine in
the city. The shadows are large and cool in the garden. You are
like Matsuo, your brother, he says. Big Brother is wearing a
khaki uniform with a rifle in his hands and a dagger on the right
side of his belt. Father sighs as if I have been naughty. And you
are like your sister too. *Kanai anzen:* may our family be preserved. You do not have to stay here, Mayako. I look around.
There are maples and pines and cherry trees and small green
hills and stone basins with running water and *nanten* shrubs
with red berries. If you have an evil dream, you can whisper it to
the *nanten* first thing in the morning and it will never come true.
There are yellow peonies and irises with flowers like purple tissue paper and lotuses with leaves like cups. There are rocks with
more than fifty types of moss. I like it here, I say. Yes, I know you
do, says Father.

Do without until victory! I am under a gingko tree and behind
it the sky is darker, the color of dry dirt. I will walk and dry in
the wind. The watercolors are gone. Takai's friend tried to eat
the watercolors and was punished by Mrs. Sasaki. I imagine the
smell of potatoes, with spices. Butterburs and horsetails. It has
been so long since the last Visiting Day. Yukiyo and Tomiko were
angry because Mother did not follow the rules and brought me
luxurious food: two pears, and rice with red beans, and sesame
seeds mixed with salt. Their mothers did not bring so much.
I give them sesame seeds to chew. Where is Big Sister? I ask.
Sumi could not get a travel certificate, says Mother, even though
she is eligible for evacuation. She tells you to work hard on the
farms to help with the food shortage. Yes, I will. Sumi is a loyal
subject, says Mother. In the day she is mobilized and at night she
works at the munitions factory. I see her in the rain with her face
shining. Father does not look at her. She tells you to remember
the way of Bushido. Mother sleeps with her head on the summer

clothes she brought for me. Now they are wet, and cold against my skin. The wind is loud. That night the room is full of darkness and whispering. Her hair smells of chrysanthemum and pine oil and as I sleep I try to keep the smell in my nose. The Emperor sits on the Chrysanthemum Throne and is our Father. Flowers fall from the sky. My eyes are heavy and Mother stands next to the truck. The other mothers are already inside the truck, crying. I want you to have this. Look here, says the man with the rabbit teeth. The sky is green like the leaves of the plum tree before night. I stand in the middle and sitting on my left is Mother in her best kimono and sitting on my right is Father in his white *joe* with his headgear and standing behind me is Big Sister in her designated nametag and armband and headband from the Volunteer Corps. We look into the box. Mother is holding the photograph of Big Brother in front of her stomach. Father has one hand on the bronze statue of Kannon, Goddess of Mercy. Don't blink now. But everything turns white—the box disappears—and I blink. I have been naughty. It's only the magnesium flash, says Father. He laughs at me and says, Don't worry. The air feels like it wants to rain. The clouds are green. The military mail service sent this back with the last letter, says Mother. I want you to have it. I look down at the photograph. Big Brother is not at the confidential place? I ask. When I look up Mother smiles strangely at me and I see she is crying. Your brother is safe now, she says. She steps onto the truck. Many of the children are crying. I do not cry. Now, by myself on this cold hill, in the night wind, I cry. Mother.

Mayako? I think Mrs. Sasaki will punish me but it is not her. It is Mrs. Tamura, another teacher from my old elementary school in the city. She comes sometimes and sings and tells folktales. She was strict at the school but she is nice here at the Temple. Mrs. Tamura comes out to the front of the Temple and says, What's wrong? Someone else brings me a bowl. It is Mr. Sasaki.

I am late and cannot weigh the bowls to choose the heavier one. Forgive me, I say, I want to go home. But you are safe here. Forgive me, my sister says it is safe in the city. Your mother and father want you to be here. It is the order of the prefecture and the government. Forgive me, I want to serve the Emperor and be a shattered jewel. The two faces, in the shadow, could belong to anyone. Mayako, says the woman, there will be another Visiting Day soon. Eat, says the man. I press my hands together. *Kanai anzen:* may our family be preserved.

Mrs. Tamura does not sing that night. I lie on my back. Tomiko is on my left and Yukiyo is on my right. Everywhere there is the sound of sniffing. Mother is on my left and she smells of pine oil and chrysanthemum and close to her body she smells like dust and sweat. I am on her right. Mrs. Tamura says softly to me in the dark, You cannot go home now, Mayako. The truck can come only once every few weeks and it just left today. I feel her lips against my ear. They are just over that hill, she says. Think of that. Just wait for Visiting Day. She smells like spiced potatoes. Do without until victory! There is a warning. The radio speaks. The wind is loud under the Temple doors. Is that the sound of a B-29? It is only a single plane. It is honorable to follow the jeweled path for the Emperor. The radio is sick again. Takai says the American beasts sometimes drop leaves of tin from the sky to make the radio sick. All around us is soft rain. Big Sister and I wear our air-raid hoods, Father wears his white *joe*. The ferry makes a deep sound like a plane far beneath us. Everything around us is washed until the water is the same color as the sky. We are visiting the Shrine on Miyajima Island to press our hands together for good luck with the evacuation. Sumi, says Father. You must go with Mayako. I will stay, says Big Sister. You are in the sixth grade, he says. You are eligible to go. Forgive me, I will not evacuate. It is the order of the prefecture, says Father, and there is not enough food in the city. To bear what you think you cannot bear is really to bear, says Big Sister. Father bends down to speak closer to her. His face is all wet. Sumi, you will be safe there. Through the rain I see the big *torii* archway to the Shrine on Miyajima Island. It floats like a red spirit above the water. Forgive me, I will not run from danger, says Big Sister. Water drips down from the rim of her air-raid hood. You taught me the story of the son of Ieyasu—honor won in youth grows with age. You fought the enemy in Manchuria. I am not a child. I know the way of Bushido and I will fight like you. Who will look after your sister? Mayako goes with the school, says Big Sister. She will be safe. I do not want to go, I say. If the bombs come, says Big Sister, I will stay and die like a shattered jewel. Her face is bright. How is it so bright when it is raining? The air smells like Ujina Port. Sumi, listen to me. Go with Mayako. You will both be safe in the hills. Big Sister says, Anyone who thinks the Fatherland will lose is *hikokumin*. Traitor. Father is silent for a long time. Then he looks at me instead of her. I will be a hero-spirit like you, says Big Sister. One hundred million deaths with honor! Honorable death before surrender! Defend every last inch of the Fatherland! There is no dust on her face but it looks like stone. Father does not look at her. He looks at me. One hundred million deaths with honor! I repeat after her. Then I say again, I do not want to go. You will go, says Father. You will go, says Big Sister. She looks like a warrior. It is only for a little while until we win the war, little turnip. And I will come to visit you. Promise? I promise, little turnip. The rain comes down without noise. Over the wind the all-clear sounds. Someone in the Temple is softly crying. Then far away another B-29. I see leaves of tin falling like cherry blossoms. I smell pine oil and chrysanthemum. Child of my heart.

If I cannot go home, I will write a letter. I tell Mr. Sasaki before our morning stretches. *Should emergency arise,* we chant together, *offer yourselves courageously to the State.* There is lice inspection instead of cleaning. A letter, that is a good idea, says Mr. Sasaki. He nods. *So shall you not only be our good and faithful subjects, but render illustrious the best traditions of your forefathers.* The morning is hot and clear. There is a warning and the roar of a single B-29. The noise drags across the blue sky. The boys go to train in Morse code and the girls make straw sandals with Mrs. Sasaki. The all-clear sounds. I will do without until victory, but with my family. I go outside to write the letter in my head. Dear Father and Mother. Thank you for the pears and the rice with red beans and the sesame seeds mixed with salt. Thank you for my *yukata* and wooden sandals. It is hot here. We are taught to make straw sandals here. Yesterday we ate potatoes. *Banzai* to the Emperor! The Imperial Rescript on Education says, *Should emergency arise, offer yourselves courageously to the State.* Please let me come home and work on mobilization. I will be safe there. I take out the photograph. And thank you for the photograph. Over the light wind there is the roar of another B-29. Just a single plane. The Americans use their planes to take photographs, says Big Sister. It is hot outside. I hear the sound of the *higurashi* cicada—*kana kana kana.* There are kites and crows in the blue sky. I imagine I hear the song of the *tsukutsukuboshi,* which says: *chokko chokko uisu. Chokko chokko uisu.* All around me are the eight million *kami.* I look in my hand. On my left is Mother and on my right is Father. Behind me is Big Sister. The paper is mostly gray. Then everything turns white and the left side of my face is warm. Don't blink, says the man with the rabbit teeth. Don't worry, says Father. He laughs at me. Don't blink. Look here.

Tehran Calling

THE SECOND ANNOUNCEMENT WOKE HER. Sarah turned to the window: nothing—night—then, swimming up through the blackness, an image of her face. The cabin lights coming on. She couldn't remember falling asleep. All around her were dark-eyed women dabbing off their makeup, donning head scarves and manteaus in silence, as though beguiled by some lingering residue of Sarah's sleep. Sarah put on her own scarf, felt the knot of cloth against her throat.

The city came up at them like a dream of light. White streams and red, neon lava, flowing side by side along arterial roads; electric dots and clusters of yellow, pink, and orange. She thought of Parvin down there, working her way between those points. With a mechanical groan from the undercarriage the wheels opened out. The plane banked, decelerated, then seconds later they were touching down, roaring to a stop in the middle of a vast, enchanted field. Runways glowed blue in the ground mist. Taxiways green. Lights around them blinking and blearing in the jet fuel haze. Sarah checked her watch: 4 a.m. local time.

Inside the airport, Parvin was nowhere to be seen. Sarah hurried through the terminal, pursued, it felt, by photographs lining the walls: faces of men in gray beards, black turbans, their expressions strained between benevolence and censure. Despite the hour, the airport was implausibly, surreally busy.

Low-wattage light pressed on her nerves as she walked, coercing her body into its familiar anxiety: rushing to work through underground tunnels, the digital alarm still ringing in her ears, toothpaste still bitter on her tongue—suspending herself in the slipstream of other bodies. Staving off sleep. She wore a long black overgarment and black cotton scarf. All the women wore long overgarments and head scarves. This shook her a little—she'd expected more visual disparity. She'd expected to be surprised by it. Around a corner an electronic sign pulsed: IN FUTURE ISLAM WILL DESTROY SATANIC SOVEREIGNTY OF THE WEST. It was too early, and she too tired, to burrow beneath the threat. Keep moving, she told herself.

Large glass windows separated customs from the arrival bay. Retrieving her bags, Sarah noticed a young man watching her through the glass. She stopped, waited for some bodies to interpose, then shuffled out behind them. He was still there. Slight figured and clean-shaven, nondescriptly dressed. He hadn't taken his eyes off her. A slow warmth rose up from her abdomen. She'd read too many accounts, before coming, about the plainclothes police in this country. She lowered her eyes, withdrawing into her scarf, and then, without warning, he was beside her.

"Sarah," he said.

She froze.

He said, "I am Parvin's friend."

Her posture, she was aware, was one of almost parodic decorum—a sister of the faith, scrupulously observing the veil—but there was no part of her spared to find it funny. She'd barely landed. Now she was shocked awake, her mind instantaneously compacted in fear, fixed on the image of a small dark room . . . a metal chair in the middle of it.

"Parvin. You know?"

She didn't speak. What if it were a trick?—to elicit information? An admission of association?

"Come with me," he said. For the first time his English seemed weighted by a heavier accent.

She looked up but he hadn't moved. He reached into his shirt pocket. "Here," he said, and took a step back.

It was a Polaroid. Parvin, her jaw dangling open in the middle of some mischief, one hand brushing back her purple-streaked hair, the other squeezing Sarah's shoulder. Both their faces upwardly flushed by the candlelit cake before them. Sarah recognized it from her thirtieth birthday. Five years ago. Parvin had taken her to a sushi restaurant near the Chinatown lions and, after the complimentary snapshot, had persuaded the waitstaff to sing "Happy Birthday" in Japanese. They'd filed away, smiling tightly, harassedly. How hopeless that whole occasion had made her feel, Sarah remembered—turning thirty—yet even so, looking back now, she was stifled with nostalgia.

"Good," said the young man. He leaned in closer. "Now. Please. Come with me."

HIS NAME WAS MAHMOUD and he was a family friend of Parvin's. She shouldn't be afraid. Also, he was the leader of the Party. Parvin worked with him now. Why hadn't she picked Sarah up? She had been busy with last-minute responsibilities. He spoke rapidly, in a tone suggesting he didn't want to explain any more than he already had. He assumed Parvin had told her about the rally in two days' time.

Sarah sat with him in the backseat, wondering what responsibilities could possibly have kept her friend at this hour. It was hard to tell whether dawn had broken. A faint glow massed behind the smog but it could have been the electric ambience of night—caught and refracted in low-lying haze. In the driver's seat a heavily stubbled youth named Reza steered their car, an ancient Ford, like a bullet into the city.

"You have come at a busy time," said Mahmoud.

"Where are we going?" She wound down her window. A warp of gasoline and exhaust filled the car and she quickly closed it again. Behind the brief scream of wind she thought she'd heard the sound of drums. "Where are we meeting Parvin?"

The two men conferred in Farsi.

"You have come during Ashura," said Mahmoud. "Our holiest week."

She nodded impatiently. Reza glanced up into the rearview mirror.

"Your hotel is near one of the largest processions," Mahmoud went on. "If you would like to see—if you are not too tired—"

"Hotel? I thought that was just for the visa." Parvin had arranged the letter of invitation from the hotel, had assured her it was just a formality. "I'm staying with Parvin," she said.

The car swerved left. Sarah slid over and smacked into Mahmoud, who flinched, then, as she disengaged herself, smiled stiffly down at his knees. Inexplicably, his reaction riled her. Reza twisted half around from the front seat, made a comment in his skipping Farsi. A short silence ensued, then Mahmoud translated, "He says there are one thousand accidents a day in this city." Reza caught her eye in the rearview mirror and gave her a civic nod. After another silence, Mahmoud said, "We thought it would be better. At the hotel."

"Why?" She frowned, shook her head. "I don't understand."

The lines on his face were so shallow, like lines on tracing paper, and this, with the way his lower lip turned outward, gave him the slightly churlish air of a child. He said, "At least until the rally is over." There was irritation in his voice. "Parvin will explain—she comes to meet us in the afternoon." Then his face closed off completely to her.

Sarah slumped back in the deep seat. As they drove, the sky around them lightened, lifting the concrete landscape—block after block of squat, square buildings—into blue relief. Sarah swallowed repeatedly, trying to clear her throat of its sooty taste. She had no choice—she'd wait for Parvin. Her body felt suddenly spent beneath her clothes. Her head still fumy from the flight, the sleeping pills she'd taken. And now she'd offended this smooth-cheeked boy—this reluctant guide of hers—Mahmoud. She pressed her face against the glass. The city was stilled, caught in the subdued minutes before sunrise. A woman tripped out of a cinder-block doorway, holding her scarf down against the wind. In the distance, the constant shudder of drums. All at once Sarah was overpowered by the strangeness of where she was. Loneliness dropped on her with the speed of a black column.

THREE MONTHS AGO, she'd been a senior associate at Pearson, Peelle and Sloss—one of the top-tier law firms in Portland. She'd had a private office with a river view, a private understanding with management with regard to her next promotion, a reservoir of professional goodwill accrued, it sometimes seemed, by virtue of having not yet majorly screwed up. She'd paid off half of a two-bedroom apartment in the Pearl District, exercised almost daily to keep her body in good shape. And—back then—pathetically, she knew—she'd had Paul. She would return from her morning exercise to find him still ensnared in their bedsheets, or shaving behind a blade of light from the bathroom, frazzle-haired and stumbly, seeing her and hauling her body—buzzing and taut and alive—toward his own. He was the aberration of her life: the relief from her lifelong suspicion that she was, at heart, a hollow person, who clung to hollow things.

She unknotted her head scarf. She'd pleaded jet lag as soon as they arrived at the hotel and Mahmoud, who seemed already uncomfortable accompanying her into the lobby, had quickly taken his leave. Upstairs, someone had forgotten to draw the curtains and the room was blanched with golden light. The eastern windows were level with the top of a large plane tree—so close Sarah could reach out and touch its leaves. It cast a fretwork of shadows on the floor.

She removed her long black overgarment and threw it on a chair. Her shirt underneath was drenched. She peeled it off, then her jeans, and abruptly caught a glimpse of her reflection in a bathroom mirror: slender and olive-skinned, a body in accidentally matching bra and underwear. A small wad of undeclared U.S. dollars was gauze-covered and bandaged to the back of her knee. She looked mysterious, glowing—there was a different sun here, somehow; more impersonal. Incandescent. Well, this was what she wanted, wasn't it? She was in the desert now.

They'd met at work. At first he'd been just another good-looking suit in Banking, three floors up, with good teeth, arms that filled out his sleeves when he leaned, the way men always leaned, double-elbowed, on bar counters. He had the salt-and-pepper hair that, on some men, draws more attention to their youth than their age. He was divorced—no kids. He was her professional senior. She'd dealt with him on some statutory debt recovery claims. One day, at Friday drinks, he brought up the last file they'd worked. Their client had been demanding payment from a company in Chapter 11 but had been low on the list of creditors. The firm had all but counseled forfeit when Sarah developed a submission for priority and, against all expectations, won a good settlement. It had been a tough case. Paul admired her work and said so. Despite her proficiency, work had for so long devolved into sets of empty, unaltering rituals for Sarah that she was capable of registering his comment only as some kind of code. Already, she found herself deferring to him for meaning.

He took her to a seafood bistro near Seven Corners where even the water smelled like mussels. They ordered crabs. Paul rolled up his sleeves and broke open a pincer, his fingers with their perfect square nails glistening in the meat's steam. She found herself transfixed as he slurped the wet flesh. As though to hold up her end of the deal, she tried to eat sexily—imitating the way women on TV pursed their lips, leaving the tip of each morsel visible—but ended up dripping grease down her chin and forearms and onto her blouse. He didn't notice, or seem to. They went on to a small jazz club in an Irvington brownstone that looked, from the outside, like a B&B. The music, breathless and wheezy, mixed with the alcohol, and, when he righted his chair away from her and leaned toward the band, wrists on his knees, his expression almost narcotic in its concentration, she shocked herself by arching over and kissing him on the side of his neck. He turned to her with a look of surprise.

The door of his apartment was cold and hard against her back. She popped up on her toes. His hands were all over her body now. It was dark. He reached under her shirt and pulled it up, over her face. She tilted her head back. The collar caught under her chin. He kissed her through the fabric, roughly, the taste of his mouth salty with the taste of her body. She felt heavy in her legs. The metal of his belt buckle shocking her skin.

"I can't stay," she said.

"I'll stop," he murmured, somewhere around her navel. His fists were tight on her waistband, tugging.

"No." She reached down and outlined his shoulders, tense with exertion. His tendoned neck. "I mean, I've got a brief due tomorrow." For a moment everything was suspended but the words, the image of her keyboard blue-lit by her screensaver. Why had she said that? He continued below in the darkness. Maybe she hadn't said it aloud. She lifted her legs one by one. "Turn around," he ordered.

She turned around. The air was cold against her bare skin but still she felt woozy with warmth. The music from the jazz club

banged around in her head. She had never done this. She had
never turned around like that. She was a girl who'd always
undressed under the covers and now she was naked in the hallway of an unknown apartment with a man she barely knew
behind her.

"Wider."

From an adjoining apartment a telephone started ringing. She
heard him undo his buckle, unzip. She could feel the heat of him,
her body nervous with want. He spat into his hands and slick-
ened her. A shudder ran through her, was forced from her mouth
as noise.

"Wider."

Someone answered the phone, a muffled, stale inflection in
counterpoint to his spongy breathing. His wet hands gripping
her hip bones. His fingernails. All of a sudden she needed to see
him. She needed to see his face. She twisted around and looked
at his face. It was creased in anger—his eyes closed—a snarl on
his lips. She bit back a cry. She didn't know him. This man who
was fucking her. Then she looked again, closely, and realized the
look on his face wasn't anger at all.

He was gone when she awoke. The room grown strange in its
size, the white glow through the shutters. Except where her body
had lain the bed was cold. *Stupid,* she thought, *Stupid, stupid,
stupid.* The secretaries would have a field day. Why was she
thinking about the secretaries? *Stupid!* She got up, squinting
in the dim burn from the windows. Then she saw them—her
clothes—neatly folded in a chair. The bastard. Later, she would
tell him it was preposterous to think a woman wouldn't interpret
the scene as she had. She dressed quickly, quietly, as though
under orders. By the time she'd finished she was so shaken that
when, on her way out, she saw him at the kitchen counter, still in
his boxers, pen in hand, correcting her brief in the light from an
open fridge; when he called her name and she heard how it

sounded on his lips, it was unfair—an unconscionable situation—because she'd been rendered wholly susceptible and was no longer in any state to resist.

The air-conditioning unit clicked twice, made a rattling sound, whined off. Sarah tried it again, then gave up. She lay down on the bed. The sheets were cool, the pillowcases so starched they creased like cardboard. The shadows thrown by the tree boughs against her skin looked like the written language here: half-open mouths, fishhooks, sickle blades, pregnant letters with dots in their bellies. An alphabet refracted in water. She closed her eyes. Again, the faint thud of drums. After a while—unable to sleep—she got up and turned the bath spigot, conscious of the waste but past caring, letting the water run as white noise.

THE PHONE RANG. Sarah woke up—how long had she been asleep?—into an awful smell: like fruit gone bad, sink water left too long. She struggled to place herself inside it. No one answered when she picked up the receiver, the only sound a faint hum of song. The sun was high outside. She realized now: the smell had worried her since she'd first arrived in Tehran—suppurating as though from some open wound beneath the city.

Three short knocks at the door. She floundered up.

"It's you!" exclaimed Parvin in a hoarse voice, lunging her arms around Sarah's neck. "You made it!" Sarah held on to her, startled by the force of her own relief. They both pulled back. It was disconcerting to see Parvin's face cropped by the black scarf.

"Oh, Sarah." Parvin, smiling steadfastly, seemed on the verge of saying any number of things, but said nothing.

"What's going on?" asked Sarah. "Why can't I stay with you?"

Parvin glanced behind her. In the hallway was Mahmoud, wearing dark slacks with a white shirt buttoned up to his Adam's apple. He looked fleetingly at Sarah, then shuffled his body completely around.

"He told you that?" Parvin lowered her voice: "It was just a precaution."

"A precaution against what?"

Parvin hesitated. "There have been a few arrests." She sidestepped Sarah into the room. "But they tend to crack down during religious holidays. My God, it stinks in here." She swung around. "No—I'll tell you all about it, but right now"—she waved with both hands—"go get your things. We're late."

Sarah dashed into the bathroom. She would save her questions. In the bathtub, the water was cloudy, tinged with mineral colors. She turned off the faucet and suddenly the sound of the outside world flooded in: drumbeats, unmistakable, in every distance, cymbals, the occasional flare of an amplified voice. She thought she heard children's footsteps.

"Sarah!"

The din on the street was astonishing. Noise collected and chafed, it seemed, in the folds of fabric next to her ears. The sky was white, overcast, and beneath it wind gusted, fitfully, as if trapped. They were going to her parents' house for a meeting, Parvin shouted, but first she wanted Sarah to see this. They turned into a chaotic market: shop after shop spilling wares onto the road—hats, shirts and shoes, electronic gadgets that blared a cacophony of tones and trills as they walked past. Sidewalk barrows were packed with green plums and big yellow limes and red-black mulberries, with dates, raisins, and nuts of every description. The dull sheen of the sunlight heightened and contrasted the rows of colors.

Parvin turned toward her. "I'm so glad you came," she called out.

Sarah grinned. For the first time since landing she felt completely safe. She was still taking note of the new heft of Parvin's body underneath her robe, the untidy fringe of brown hair—her natural color!—underneath the hair-clipped scarf. Even her eyes seemed more naturally brown. She looked like a rougher, truer version of herself.

"Where were you this morning?" Sarah asked.

Parvin held up her hand. They rounded another corner and abruptly the air turned thick with deep-throated cries, the crash of cymbals. A mourning procession. It looked, Sarah was stunned to see, exactly how it looked on newsreels: young men straight-backed behind enormous drums; behind them, moving in block step, men clapping their chests, throwing iron chains over their shoulders like dinner jackets. They were all bearded; all—she thought with reflexive guilt—indistinguishable from one another. Men in loose black robes and green headbands. Men with tunics open to their navels. Men naked above the waist—their backs swollen, flayed, slug-shiny in the light.

Sarah let go of her breath. This was why she'd come—to see exactly this—the city as it was—the proof of this place unthinkably outside herself.

Now an enormous square canvas floated down the street, hoisted on two poles and luffing like a sail in the wind. It depicted a black-bearded man. His eyes soulful, mascara-dark, watching everything. The street was full of these pictures.

"Imam Hussein!" shouted Parvin. The loudness of her voice almost tipped it into cheeriness.

He was shown in deep green robes and a black turban, and—with his gentle, cowlike eyes—looked bizarrely like an oriental Jesus. What had Parvin said about bin Laden? That it had to have been a mistake: that no one so soft-spoken, with such kind eyes, with that flossy beard, could have been responsible. It was difficult, sometimes, to tell when she was joking.

"Grandson of the Prophet." That was Mahmoud speaking—he'd caught up with them from behind.

But Parvin was already pushing farther into the mayhem. They came across a low gnarl of bodies: a man with white pants lay on the ground bleeding from his scalp, his hands interlocked around his head as though to improvise a basin. People converged, crouched over him, then kept onward. Sarah realized with horror that they were dipping their sleeves into his blood.

"Why are they—"

The drums drowned her out. She rooted herself within the milling mass and said it again, louder: "Why are they doing that?"

It was a street show extravaganza and she was being scripted, deeper and deeper, into panic. A test, she reminded herself. She could write her own part. Both Parvin and Mahmoud were a short distance ahead, on the opposite sidewalk—Parvin beckoning to her. Parvin, who'd assured her a few months ago it was worth coming just to see Ashura. There was a huge black cauldron behind them. A tarpaulin making the sound of surf as it flapped in the wind—something white and woolly weighing down its center. Sarah came closer, then shrank back. The carcass of a headless sheep—blood still dribbling, gel-like, from its stump, darkening its matted collar. On the sidewalk, spectators threw up their hands and wailed.

Parvin shoved a plastic cup into her hands. "Tea," she said loudly.

Sarah twisted back toward the parade.

"He is okay," said Mahmoud. He pointed at his head.

"He's not okay, he's bleeding!"

A troop of women and girls poured down the street, coalescing around the prone figure. They were dressed in full black chadors—covering everything but their shoes and faces—and their faces shone out from within their black hoods like beacons of pale grief.

"You are thinking 'What a barbarism,' " shouted Mahmoud. "You are thinking, 'There is much violence in Islam.' "

Some of the women, Sarah noticed, wore white sneakers. They were keening to music that crackled from a ghetto blaster. White and yellow tulips sprang from their hands.

Mahmoud pointed at his head again, a certain shyness in the gesture. Sarah realized her head scarf had slipped down to her neck. She quickly pulled it up over her hair, turned back to face him.

"I was thinking 'Poor sheep,' 'Poor man.' "

"The man," he replied with a small smile, "he cuts his head to remember the imam's suffering."

"And the sheep?"

From nowhere, a bearded figure in a black gown and white cap brandished a metal rod in front of her face. She cringed, closed her eyes, then felt the spray of water on her cheek.

Both men enjoyed this. "Perfume," explained Mahmoud, "for pilgrims."

Parvin cupped Sarah's elbow in her palm.

The man walked away. There was a metallic tank affixed to his back like a rocket pack. Sarah's face smelled of musk and amber. Dime store deodorant. She made a decision. She swiped the wetness of her cheek onto her fingers and made to flick it at Mahmoud's face, his smooth-skinned jaw.

"Please," he said, taking a step back.

She flushed. "We're all pilgrims," she said.

* * *

LONG BEFORE SHE'D SET FOOT on its streets, this world had already conspired to throw her off balance. When Parvin first told her she'd founded, with typical slapdash resolve, a weekly call-in radio program agitating for women's rights reform in Iran, Sarah hadn't known what to think. Back then—four years ago—no one did much thinking about Iran. At most, people in her circle were predisposed to a vague solidarity with the country—arising from the sense that any place reprehended by an administration itself so reprehensible couldn't be all that bad.

Parvin had her own ideas. She taught herself how to produce an audio program at a local college; how to stream it online to a company in Holland, which then broadcast it live, via shortwave radio, into Iran. Shortwave—what did that even mean? Her show, *Tehran Calling,* was live, direct, unrehearsed: its proclaimed mission the complete political, economic and religious liberation of the Iranian woman. Its callers broke the law— risked their lives—every time they called. Sarah indulged her friend's effusions. She'd become used to them. Ever since they'd met in college, Parvin had enthralled herself with one cause or another. What was surprising to Sarah was that Parvin had actually chosen this cause: she'd always been close-lipped—even cagey—about her past in Iran. She'd left as a teenager, Sarah knew that. Her parents had sent her to Europe. Beyond that was a studiedly offhand trail of red herrings: a Swiss boarding school, a German boyfriend, an older divorcé who'd been an offroad racer, a father who'd been a university professor. Sarah could never have predicted that the show would make Parvin a minor celebrity in the Persian reformist movement—let alone that it would pave the way, ultimately, for her re-emigration.

The truth about the show: Sarah had always had trouble taking it seriously. For one, everybody who called in spoke English. Of course it was a show in English, but how could she take seriously the oppression of this far-flung people who were not only English-speaking—but so liberally educated? Who could afford to make these regular international calls? Her misgivings were foolish—she knew that. But on the occasions when Sarah had dropped by the studio, she'd repeatedly heard words like *oppression,* lectures laced with jargon and political-science abstractions, and it didn't help that Parvin seemed to absorb, expansively, unconsciously, the heavy Persian accent of her callers. To Sarah it seemed that, as the show grew in popularity, it developed more and more a sense of staged parody.

Once, she'd stepped in near the end of a show and heard a thickly accented male voice ask: "What do you look like?"

Parvin had thrown Sarah a look—a look full of slyness, scorn, self-mockery—and instantly it had dawned on Sarah that Parvin had changed, that she'd drawn away, steadily and for some time, from that side of herself. The side that Sarah knew.

"I think you are ugly," the man said. "Your voice is ugly."

The rest of the hour slid into bewildering invective: Parvin was a monarchist, she was un-Islamic, she was funded by the CIA, she was completely ignorant. Not once did she hang up. She let her callers talk. It wasn't until much later that Sarah learned she'd stumbled on the anniversary of the 1999 student uprisings; then, in the small, too-bright studio that evening, Sarah had struggled to puzzle out her own feelings. She'd never seen her friend like that. Where was the headstrong, irreverent Parvin? the hot-tempered disputant? the career radical who nevertheless prided herself on maintaining professional irony at all times? Where was the strength and variousness on which Sarah had always drawn—and often over-relied? She should say something. What should she say? How to navigate that space between sympathy, tact, unconcern?

A sign above the mixing desk read: PLEASE LEAVE THE STUDIO IN THE SAME CONDITION.

"The thing is," Parvin anwered her later, during the drive home, "they're right." It was nighttime now; as she talked, cigarette smoke vented from her mouth and shredded out the open crack of her window. "I was born there, but still. You need to be there."

"They shouldn't talk to you like that," said Sarah. She thought of the man's voice—all those voices—faceless and hateful. Those accounts of killings, rapes, finger amputations, related in attitudes that seemed possessive, even petty. If those things were happening, she felt instinctively, they couldn't be happening to those people calling in. Mostly, she realized, what she felt was anger. What she'd meant to say to Parvin was, *You shouldn't let them talk to you like that.*

"It's their right," said Parvin.

"Doesn't it piss you off, though?"

But her friend was resilient, she was preposterous, amazing. Probably there was something wrong with her. Something missing that, in everyone else, assorted actions by the need to be liked and the anxiety that you weren't.

Set in these habits, they grew apart. By then Sarah had met Paul, and Parvin, to Sarah's mind, had reacted gracelessly. She couldn't concede how frustrating it might be for Sarah— watching Parvin sink into a world so at odds with the Iran everyone now heard about: the place populated overwhelmingly by brand-conscious, recreationally drugged youths; riddled with online networking sites and underground dance parties. If there was indeed a tyrannical regime, it seemed the citizenry had opted out of it. This version of Iran, especially being countermainstream, struck Sarah as authentic. Parvin, she felt, was being exploited by a native audience that kept insisting—for whatever reason—on its own victimhood.

For a long time Sarah deferred to Parvin's background, probing her friend only lightly about these discrepancies. Later, in efforts to prove the baselessness of Parvin's concerns—the audacious sham of the regime—Sarah began marshaling facts: that during the embassy takeover, for example, people had been bused in from the provinces and hired to burn American flags and shout anti-American slogans in exchange for free food, that they wouldn't start until the cameras were rolling and, if there weren't any video cameras—if only still photographers were present—they wouldn't even bother shouting but just punch the air in silence. It was a country busy with its own deceptions. It neither wanted nor needed Parvin's help.

But Parvin kept on. Three years in, she downgraded, then quit her job with an events coordinating company to dedicate herself to the show. She hired an assistant—with what funds, Sarah never learned. Then she asked Sarah to stop coming to the studio altogether. Sarah's presence and comments, she felt, belittled her efforts. Not long after that they stopped speaking.

"It's what she wants," Paul consoled her.

"What?"

"For us to talk about her. While she suffers, nobly."

Sarah shifted under the bedsheets and thought about her friend, bracketed by her headphones in that dark, windowless studio. It depressed her. "You don't know her at all."

"You know what your problem is?" He traced a path of intersecting loops, a figure eight, around her nipples.

"Which one?"

"You take everything so personally." His face sank into thought. "Can't you see? It's *her* who doesn't know *you* at all."

But what was it Parvin didn't know? Hadn't she seemed sure of her knowledge when she'd declared, during their last conversation, that Sarah had ransomed herself to Paul? That she'd become blind to the needs of those around her—and now lived a useless life? At the time Sarah had considered those words unforgivable. Then she wasn't sure. For as long as she could remember, she had indeed felt that she hadn't lived in the strong, full-bodied current of her own life; that at some point she'd been shunted to one side, trapped in its shallowest eddies. She was capable of velocity but not depth—there wasn't enough to her. It was Paul, when she met him—as gradually she got to know him—who seemed to suggest the possibility of a deeper, truer life. He could anchor her. That was what Parvin could never understand. That it could actually be—had actually been— Sarah's choice.

She made the decision to love him and she did. He walked into a room and stood still. His face clouded when he planted himself behind her, bobbed above paper bags as he carried them up the stairs. When he cooked for them, he rolled up his sleeves and tipped and tilted the frying pan in a half-haute style that never failed to delight her. When he made their bed, he made it a point to billow the sheet out over the mattress in a single flourish. She loved the striations of his character—how, at work, he became serious, taciturn, giving himself over to the duties of the profession in the old sense. They lived together, worked together. Once a year they visited his family home in New Hampshire. It was there, in that large house in that large clearing, that Sarah finally realized how much Paul's character had been governed by his parents' easy formality; there, watching them attend their shared days, that she'd allowed herself to extrapolate—impossible not to!—her own future with their son.

Her first visit, she'd endlessly explored the wooded backyard that gave onto a lake the locals insisted on calling a "pond." One hot afternoon she convinced Paul to swim with her to the opposite shore. The water was the one place she felt more comfortable, could lead the way. Unexpectedly—charmingly—he was a nervous swimmer, and she set a slow pace. They swam a good mile or so, then pulled themselves onto a boulder. The rock almost too warm. Once the sludge and sand had settled, the water over the edge became so clear that they could see all the way down. Gnats and dragonflies skated the liquid surface. Beneath, shapes of fish trolled the leaf-tramped bed. Sarah ducked her head underwater. When she opened her eyes she caught sight of two brown-spotted trout within arm's length; she tracked their languid movements until suddenly a sleek, almost metallic gleam of black and white crossed her vision; she turned, saw—bewitchingly—the beak, the folded, streamlined wings—it was a loon—gliding steadily into the cool depths. She spluttered to the surface, mute with excitement, and saw Paul lift his head from the rock and smile at her as if he understood completely, and right then she knew, cross her heart, in all her life, that she'd never been so happy.

Parvin left for Iran. The news, when it came a year ago, seemed abstract and out of place in her life. At last, part of Sarah admitted that she had misjudged her friend, had taken her at far less than her word. But the rest of her—the part given over to Paul—took ever more pleasure from him and, in her mind, day by day, proffered it to Parvin as rebuke.

"THIS MORNING," SAID PARVIN. They were walking to the car, back along the smoke-drab streets. Mahmoud locked in step behind them. "What can I tell you about this morning?"

On both sides of the road, multistory walls had been painted over in gaudy murals: Shi'ite saints, mope-faced martyrs in army uniforms, garlanded with flowers and butterflies and rainbows. Publicly rendered paradises. Beneath one mural a thoroughfare was strung with fairy lights, an Internet café crowded with youths. Walking past, Sarah glimpsed girls in heeled boots, girls with colorful hijabs, sunglasses perched on top of them.

Here she was, she thought—with Parvin—in the place itself.

She'd bought a ticket—that was all it took!—and stunningly, almost unimaginably, she was *here.*

That morning, Parvin explained, while Mahmoud was picking Sarah up from the airport, Parvin had met with members of a sympathetic group. A drama company from one of the city's smaller universities. It was urgent, they'd said. They needed to speak to someone high up in the Party.

Mahmoud walked behind them, leaving a buffer between his body and theirs.

"I thought the worst, of course. They'd found us out. Or they were gathering all their people to attack us on Thursday." She looked around, askance. "It's happened before."

They passed a jewelry shop glittering gold, silver, crystal. Out front, a group of men were arguing animatedly. They all had the same puffed-up hair, all wore what looked to be hand-me-down suits from the eighties. Across the street, Sarah saw the upper half of men's bodies draped over scooter handlebars, the bottom half of their faces darkened by short beards. Mahmoud caught her eye and held it coolly for a moment.

"What it was," said Parvin, "was they'd put together a play. That was the big secret."

"A play?"

"Oh, Sarah—you should have seen it." She pinched up the thigh of her robe as she stepped over a reeking culvert. Ruts ran all over the road and sidewalk, trickling waste into the gutters. "One of them had a little sister. Thirteen years old. She wanted to be an actor too." Parvin scaled her voice back. "Last month they arrested her—for 'acts incompatible with chastity.' "

"What's that mean?"

"Then they held her for two weeks of tests and interrogation." She spun around to face Sarah. "Were you searched? At the airport?"

Sarah shook her head. Parvin nodded, walked on. Unbidden, a particular case from her pre-travel research surfaced in Sarah's mind. Zahra Kazemi, Canadian journalist, detained for taking photos during a protest—then beaten, with a guard's shoe, into a coma. She remembered the picture she'd seen: a late-middle-aged woman, her baggy chocolate-colored sweater lending her a girl-like air. She remembered the camera hanging from her neck, its black lens a well beneath her own calm, deeply settling face.

"Last week," said Parvin, "she was hanged. This little girl. All this is in the play. It's sentimental, and a bit slapstick, I'll admit, for a tragedy—but they only had a week to throw it together." A steeliness Sarah had never heard before now reinforced her friend's voice. Parvin flipped her thumb—a hitchhiker's gesture—behind her, toward Mahmoud. "But he's not a fan."

"Too much!" said Mahmoud. Sarah turned. His Adam's apple jogged pronouncedly above his collar. "I said it is not a play for Ashura."

"It's the perfect play for Ashura," Parvin spat. "It's a very religious play."

They'd reached the car. Parvin stood by the passenger door and stared directly at Sarah. "Those *men*," she said, curling her mouth on the word, "those men of God, do you know how they enforce God's law?" She'd brought her voice under control, but tension clenched her shoulders and neck. "They kidnap this girl on an immorality charge. Then they test her—but find out she's still a virgin."

"Parvin," Mahmoud implored. "Please get in the car."

"So what do they do? They marry her, so they can rape her. They rape her—so they can kill her—so she won't go to heaven, where all the virgins go." Her nostrils flared in the middle of her rough, square face. "Men of God," she said.

A block away, drums were beaten as though into the ground, trembling the very concrete. Mahmoud's eyes searched the street.

To her surprise, Sarah felt a swell of sympathy for him—even as she found herself exhilarated by Parvin's rage. No one else she knew, it occurred to her, would ever dare speak so critically of Islam. Parvin got in the car. She looked down at her lap for a long time. Then, in a softer, effortfully lighthearted tone, she said, "And what about Sarah? If she has to wait till after Ashura, she'll miss the play."

"How long are you staying?" demanded Mahmoud. He pinned her with his gaze.

Sarah smiled weakly. "Six days."

The engine clattered to life and they pulled away, the parade diminishing behind them. Mahmoud drove and didn't talk. Parvin was quiet now too. They merged with traffic on a busy one-way street and seemed to drive directly into smog. Sarah looked out, her head as clouded as the air, the thoughts within it churning shallow and fast. It felt inconceivable she'd been here only a few hours. She slackened her attention and almost convinced herself she was home again: slate-gray sky, concrete-walled compounds, poured-cement yards, a roofline rife with billboards and signs. But wherever she looked, just underneath the outside of things, something was always slightly off: ordinary buildings listed toward, or away from, one another—their lines never quite plumb; straight roads turned into alleys wending into dead ends. And words—words everywhere—on trucks, street signs, T-shirts—seemed like language that had been melted, meandering up and down like quavers and clefs on invisible staves. The car climbed to higher ground. Sarah stuck her whole head out the window, letting the wind crunch her scarf against her ears. On every other corner she thought she heard an English-speaking cadence—recognized someone from home—but then the realization set in. Parvin was here. Otherwise she was alone. People looked at her and understood that. She was completely extraneous.

———

As they repaired to the quieter, more affluent boulevards of northern Tehran, it felt like they were entering a different country. At one point they crested a rise and ahead, through a green canopy, materialized the full spread of the Elburz Mountains, stately and snowcapped, slopes dappled with sun and cloud and shadow. Mahmoud turned up a narrow street. They stopped in front of an old, weatherworn villa, which, Sarah was astonished to learn, belonged to Parvin's family.

What she noticed first, entering the room, were the women seated at the long dining table. They'd shed their robes, four or five of them, and their hair was uncovered. Several men were present, too, standing across the room next to a set of ornate sofas. Mahmoud immediately joined them. Platters of bread, goat cheese, pistachios and yoghurt were laid out on tables.

Conversation paused when Sarah walked in.

"This is Sarah Middleton," announced Parvin, pushing her scarf back onto her neck like a hood. "Who I told you about. My best friend." She repeated the introduction—more emphatically, it seemed—in Farsi.

A couple of the women nodded to Sarah. "Come, sit down," said one. She sat by herself at the far end of the dining table.

"Thank you."

The woman poured tea into a glass shaped like an egg timer and handed it to Sarah. She slid a vase of pink-blue gladioli out of the way. "My name is Roya," she said. She was young but there was a subtle dourness about her face that weighed on her features. Her body was stout, small-breasted, and she wore a tight T-shirt with a Chinese character embossed on it. It seemed on her almost a parody of youthful fashion. She said, "So you are the one."

"The one?"

"The one whose heart is broken." She peered into Sarah's face. "You must forgive my English."

Sarah turned sharply to Parvin at the other end of the table. She was absorbed in conversation with the group of women. Sarah turned back. Who was this woman? What did she know? Her comment felt to Sarah almost spiteful. Now Roya leaned in closer.

"I have wine too," she said.

Sarah gave a terse shake of the head.

"It is made by my parents. I know where they keep it upstairs. And their opium, too—if you prefer."

Mahmoud said something aloud and immediately the men unbunched and came over to the dining table. He was the shortest of them all, Sarah saw, yet they all treated him with noticeable deference. Sarah stood up. She felt like being alone.

"No," Parvin called out from across the table. "Stay. You should stay."

"I will translate for her," said Roya. Parvin smiled at both of them before turning back to her discussion.

Something occurred to Sarah. "You live here?"

Roya lifted her hand to her mouth. "She did not tell you?" She rested her chin in her palms—an awkwardly coquettish effort to frame her face. "I am her sister."

Sarah sat down and sipped her tea. She felt acutely unsettled. It was in keeping with Parvin to withhold details, but all this?— this sister from an erstwhile life? This baroque villa? What else hadn't her best friend told her?

"Are your parents here?"

"They are away because of the rally." On seeing Sarah's expression, Roya amended, "I mean, they are in Turkey for vacation. They give us the house for the rally."

The meeting began. Mahmoud spoke first and others—in particular Parvin—interjected. It soon became clear, as Roya confirmed during the course of her choppy, digressive translations, that they were again arguing about the play. Parvin wanted to stage the reenactment—in the square where the rally would be held—of the young girl's torture and execution. Mahmoud said it would be too dangerous. The square would be watched by religious militia. Such a reenactment would mock the official passion plays of the Battle of Karbala. Sarah tried to concentrate but she felt, as Roya jawed in her ear, the room, the crowd of strangers, their heated back-and-forth—everything—all receding from her as though she were in her mother's house again, watching the plants in front of the living room window curl into chalky remnants of themselves. Parvin was gesticulating. Sarah, watching, now felt a delicate tenderness toward her: she had, at least, acknowledged Sarah's heartbreak—if only to her sister. She'd said to her sister that Sarah was the one. Had she also told Roya that for the last three months—since Sarah had quit her job—she'd crawled back to her mother's house? Eating, not talking, blanking out and coming to with undirected terror? Awakening constantly as if from afternoon naps into darkness? Even now, those months seemed to Sarah a dim fantasy. Those honest, initially unbearable conversations she'd had with Parvin about Paul all seemed suspensions of lived memory. They'd talked like suitors, careful with one another, and in the end, when Parvin had extended the invitation, it hadn't been assurance or exhortation that had convinced Sarah to come to Tehran but the note of vulnerability she'd detected in Parvin's voice when she'd stated, simply, *I want you to see what I've been doing.*

Someone was saying her name. She blinked, focused on Mahmoud. He said in English, "Sarah, what do you think?"

Everyone watched her silently. She hauled her mind back to its present circumstance: the rally, the play. She sensed Parvin glowering in her direction.

She said, "Well, if it's dangerous—"

Mahmoud's mouth twisted up at one corner.

Parvin broke in, "What does she know? She's only been here half a day."

"And how long have you been here?"

"Mahmoud," said one of the women.

"No," he declared, "was she here in 1999? When we went out on the streets and—and Hassan and Ramyar and Ava were taken? And she"—pointing to Parvin—"was in her radio station in America, telling us to go out on the streets?"

Parvin said, "I didn't have a show in 1999."

"Last June," muttered a young dark-haired woman.

"I'm as politically committed as anyone here."

"She was not here in 1999," said Mahmoud, "and she was not here last June."

Parvin turned directly toward him. "I'm here now," she retorted, but her voice inflected upward, as if unsure whether or not it was asking a question.

"And now, for her, we should defame our religion? When she understands nothing of it?"

"Forgive him," said Roya. She looked sideways at Sarah.

"Why did you come?" a man's voice demanded.

For a moment no one spoke, then Sarah realized, all at once, that he was speaking to her. She broke off a piece of bread and dipped it in yoghurt. It would be folly, she knew, to engage someone in such an aggressive frame of mind.

Parvin turned toward Sarah. Her face had an odd, hollowed-out look to it. She said, "She came to visit me."

Mahmoud held up two fingers in a dogmatic manner, his head and neck gone rigid. He started intoning in Farsi.

"The imam comes to Karbala with fewer than one hundred men," translated Roya, her tone official, impersonal, "to sacrifice himself to the army of Yazid."

Mahmoud floated his gaze over to Sarah.

"He is—how do you say it?—beheaded. He dies—for who? For mothers and for daughters. And now we are to spit at his face?"

Parvin, seething, replied in a low voice, in Farsi.

"He does not die for the little girl," said Roya.

Mahmoud spoke again. Roya said, "This week is to mourn the imam."

She waited for Parvin to finish speaking, then said, "Who will mourn the little girl?"

Then, once Mahmoud had spoken, she lifted her hand and flicked her fingers, unconsciously mimicking him, and said, "One has nothing to do with the other."

Roya led her to an upstairs study that smelled strongly of wood lacquer. The window had wooden shutters and, behind those, thick milk-colored drapes. A small writing desk fronted the view. A single bed against the wall. Roya went in and shuttled the curtains to either side, letting the sunlight strafe in.

"There is a bath," she said. For a moment Sarah was confused. Then Roya opened a semi-concealed, recessed door and showed Sarah into a bathroom as large as its adjoining room. The toilet, Sarah noticed, was Persian-style—a porcelain-lined hole with a hose adjacent. Through the walls Sarah heard the distinct sound of a BBC broadcast.

"You have satellite?" she asked.

Roya smiled at her almost maternally. Then she crossed her arms over the Chinese character on her chest and rocked back on her heels. Her face became pinched and brisk.

"Parvin says you come for the rally."

"Yes," Sarah said carefully.

She emitted a dry chuckle. "Parvin is excited about these things. Very easily. Always. Like the play."

The scene downstairs came back to mind. "Does that happen a lot?" Sarah asked. "Parvin and Mahmoud, I mean."

"Yes," said Roya, then, "No, not like that."

An impulse stirred within Sarah. "What do *you* think about the play?" When Roya didn't reply, she quickly pressed on: "You must be very happy to have Parvin back."

But Roya was thinking about something else. Finally she said, "Mahmoud does not talk about it." She stood, arms crossed, absolutely still. "In 1999 his brother was shot. In the square where the rally will be."

Sarah exhaled.

"And then his father, who is an important cleric here—how do you say it?—denied him. As his son. In the mosque."

At that, Roya pushed past Sarah back into the study, then hesitated by the desk. Her stance was guarded now, as though waiting to be dismissed. "Parvin likes it in America, yes?" She pronounced it *Amrika*. Without waiting for an answer, she said, "Parvin wanted to go, always, as a child." She leaned forward. Sarah realized she was being confidential. "I could have gone too, you know."

Late afternoon light streaked in, contoured Roya's face in sharp, ambiguous planes. All at once Sarah comprehended the woman in front of her. She was the one who'd stayed behind. She'd stayed, toiling the same unspoken trench of sacrifice so that her sister could escape.

"The play," said Roya, "it seems like punishment." She lingered on the word. "But who is it punishing?"

"Is it too late?" asked Sarah. "For you to leave?"

Roya stared at her for a moment, then her face dissolved into a slippery mess that had a smile in it. "I think about it," she said. "But why would I leave now?" She giggled into her fingers. "This is the most exciting time. If I leave now, what if I miss something?"

* * *

WHEN PARVIN WAS FOURTEEN, her family had long been marked as subversives by the revolutionary committees. Although they were religious—and had originally supported the revolution—her parents had been forced into hiding and her two older brothers into the front lines of the war.

Sarah started. She hadn't known about any brothers.

This was the war, Parvin went on, where thousands of boys cleared minefields by walking over them, clutching plastic keys to heaven. Where soldiers died in Iraqi chemical attacks because the beards they had grown to demonstrate their faith made it impossible for them to achieve proper seals with their gas masks. Parvin fell silent. She made no more mention of her brothers.

They were sitting in one of the villa's upstairs studies. Outside the window a busted streetlamp flashed, at long intervals, on and off. Sarah only noticed when the brightness was doused— the world steeped a grade darker.

Meanwhile, said Parvin, they were bombarded in Tehran not only by missiles but by announcements, victory marches, all extolling the glories of martyrdom. This was 1988. One day, a bomb razed their neighbors' apartment building. Her best friend lived there, and her cousins' family. She rushed over but already—even before the ambulances arrived—the wreckage had been blocked off by *basiji* in their red headbands. They barked out propaganda from their motorbikes. Parvin ran forward but was immediately knocked to the ground. Her ears were still ringing from the explosion. No one moved to help as one bike after another skidded inches from her head, spraying dirt and dust into her face. *No crying!* they shouted. *Death to Saddam!* they shouted. *Death to America!* It was in that moment, Parvin said, that she'd known she would have to get out of the country. The decision tormented her—her parents had already made it clear they could never leave their homeland. Her own loyalty, however, was used up. Or maybe it was greater than theirs. She didn't care where she went—to America, if those devils reviled it so much. All she knew was that she couldn't allow this place any further claim over her.

By the time Parvin finished her account, night had fallen and the broken streetlamp lit their room in long, freakish strobes. The wind had picked up and the dark world outside now seemed suggestive of peril: window boards banging against frames, cans scraping themselves jerkily, as though injured, across the roads. Looking up, it was unnerving to Sarah how fast the clouds seemed to move across the nimbus of the moon.

Parvin murmured, "I'm sorry about what happened at the meeting."

Sarah shook it off. She glared at Parvin. "Why didn't you tell me?"

"I didn't want to be defined by it. The exotic friend with the traumatic past." Parvin switched on a lamp. "You know how it is. Especially now."

"But your brothers."

Parvin averted her gaze.

"Your sister. I'm your friend. You could've told me."

A strange, abstracted pity sought its level within Sarah. For years she'd yearned to hear this story—this missing piece of Parvin's past—but now that she had, she felt no closer to her. She was confused. Hadn't she come here, in part, to make sense of Parvin's choices? And didn't this—the deaths of her brothers—now offer up that final sense?

"My sister?" Parvin looked blank, then started bemusedly to smile: "Roya? She's not—she was married to my elder brother." She broke off. "I've never really known her."

Outside, the wind squalled harder, skimming water up from

unseen surfaces and spraying it through the shutters. Parvin got up and closed the window. Sarah saw her face, as she did so, setting inwardly.

Parvin turned around. "They all talk about needing to be here," she said. "But I was here."

In a way, Sarah envied them their pasts—Parvin, Roya—joined even by atrocity and privation, a shared past of such moment that they'd been forced, in separate ways, to flee from it. Mahmoud, who could reach meaningfully back to mythic battles. What did Sarah have? A childhood dim and distant, a thing half chewed and incomplete as though first used up by someone else. Memories of her parents, their rubbed-out faces. Only Paul remained—his vividness constant, hurtful, taunting. He walked into a room and stood still. Her past had never offered her any real excuses.

"Anyway," said Parvin, "they're all hypocrites. They'd all get out if they had the guts."

Sarah hesitated. She thought of what Roya had said earlier. "Things are really that bad?"

"They've lost their nerve, is what it is. I'm so sick and tired of all this consultation. All this uprising by committee. All we do is hedge and prevaricate. The other side doesn't prevaricate. Ask that thirteen-year-old girl if they prevaricate."

She was speaking now as though to an interviewer—as though into a microphone or megaphone. Pacing the small study in consternation. Her two brothers, Sarah reminded herself, had vaporized on the western fields—but already that seemed too easy an explanation. She wanted a deeper sense. Parvin had left here young—returned of age, zealous and single-minded. All those prodigal years in Portland—the biggest part of her life—what had they meant to her? Had they been anything more than personal wilderness? And what, then, of Sarah?

"Look at what they do," Parvin said. "And we let them get away with it. We bend over backward—just to not offend their religious sensitivities. And the women"—she splayed open her fist in disgust—"all talking about equal rights, equal legal status, under sharia law. Under an Islamic state. All bullshit."

An image of Mahmoud came into Sarah's head: his two fingers pointing up vatically, like a mock gun, while he preached. She asked, "Do they know? The drama group?"

"Know what?"

"That you're not putting on their play."

Parvin considered her curiously. "If they want to put it on, who's going to stop them?" A gust of wind leaned against the house, creaking the walls in their joints. Parvin dipped her chin, then vigorously shook her head as though to cut short Sarah's protests. "So maybe they won't do it on the stage. Or as part of the official program."

"I just don't understand," Sarah burst out, "what it's meant to do."

Parvin stared at Sarah. Her mind shifting through its reactions.

Sarah said, "If the play's only going to antagonize people, religious people—"

"Remember the parade today?"

"During their most important religious holiday—"

"All those religious people, mourning together, right? Devout." Parvin squared round to face her. "Except—when you're in it, you realize it's more than that. I'll tell you what it is. It's sexual. That's how these things work here. All day, every day—it's don't do this, don't do that. Then—in God's name—step into one of these things and cop a feel." She strained, strenuously, intricately, for the words. "It's all a con," she said. "Step in—then step out and tighten your veils."

Sarah had been holding her breath. Now, as she let it out, she sensed that a mood in her head had cooled and hardened. "You know," she said, "what you're doing. All this. It doesn't mean anything to me." Her own calmness surprised her.

Parvin stopped, turned away from her. "Listen," she said. She took hold of her voice. "It's a shock at first, I know. But you'll see. Thursday—"

"I want to understand," Sarah continued, "I do. That's why I came here. But it doesn't make sense to me, not emotionally, not even in an intellectual way."

Parvin stood still for a while, then went over to the window and looked out. Wind, on the other side of the glass, absorbed the light, released it. From somewhere in the house rose the scent of burnt tea. Sarah waited, feeling the grief of a bygone situation, the deep-seated loneliness, well up into her like a drug. She'd made her choices years ago. They both had. How could they think to undo them now?

"Is this about Paul?" said Parvin.

Sarah didn't say anything.

Parvin thought for a moment, then said, "We can talk about it. Let's talk about it."

"Why does it have to be about Paul?"

Parvin's face contracted. "Isn't it?"

But there it was, in her voice—the habitual undertone, the unsaid charge that had tolled out between them ever since Parvin started the radio program. That Sarah's relationship with Paul wasn't worth talking about. That it had always been a luxury, ill-used and underappreciated, which Sarah had somehow snatched from the finite resources of other women—these women—and then squandered.

"Don't worry," Sarah said. "I won't make you talk about him."

It started raining. Standing at the window, her back to the room, Parvin said, "You must be tired. Roya prepared the guest room for you." She stayed standing there. Then she added, "I always thought Paul was fine. It was you who made things unbearable for yourself."

"I'm sorry," said Sarah, "that my problems—" she broke off,

her throat constricting—"that they were never as impressive as yours."

"God," said Parvin, a sneer in her voice, "you haven't changed at all." She started walking. At the door she spun around. "You know," she said, "this isn't all just make-believe for me." Her voice was unnaturally flat. "I just opened myself to you."

Sarah looked at her wretchedly, with the full force of accusation. "I know."

Parvin left. Sarah stayed and listened to the rain. She felt crushed, completely enervated. No matter where she turned—everything she touched, she ruined. Moments later—though it seemed too early to sleep—she crept out and closed the door behind her, cautiously, as though leaving a hospital ward. She went to find her bed.

ROYA WAS WRONG: it wasn't Paul who had broken her heart. Her heart had come already impaired. From the beginning she'd led a life of what seemed to be self-maintenance. She'd calibrated herself to be above average in all the average ways: running down the hours, the feasible commitments, the ready consolations of work and sleep. She'd built her life, elegantly, around convention—conventional aspiration, conventional success—and was continually astounded that no one saw through the artifice—no one recognized Sarah Middleton as all falsework and nothing within. Only Parvin had sensed this, she felt, and back in college had accepted Sarah into her friendship with as few questions as she wanted asked of her. It wasn't that they weren't intimate, or equal—more that Sarah, by nature, found it easiest to fall in with her, and had always been grateful for it.

Of course, Paul complicated everything. Parvin could never understand that for Sarah, being with him was, in a slanted way, like watching TV—one of the few things capable of dragging her, temporarily, to a deeper plane of living. He took her conventionality and gave it depth, luster, definition. How had that happened? Even now, her memories of him dulled everything else. Their last morning: the broad-branched maples catching and holding the last of the dew, running it down their boughs and bodies in streaming rills. How, underneath the canopy, the air was cold, below the frost point, and the cordgrass as she waded through it crackled and chinked like Christmas paper.

They broke up where, for Sarah, they'd truly begun. On their last trip to New Hampshire, in that held-breath space in a rare argument where they could be absolutely honest with each other, she'd asked—in a low voice as though to forestall any interest in his answer—whether he wanted to leave her.

He'd paused. Mulling it over, as if it were a trick question.

"Please tell me," she said. "You have to tell me. Do you?"

He said, "No." But his face had caved into a deep frown.

The next morning, ankle-deep in the wet grass, she'd thought over their life back in Portland—their shared apartment, their shared work—how it had seemed so tenable for so long. Years of her life. She turned to look at the blank-faced house and imagined him inside, asleep, buffered by his safe, solid childhood, his imperturbable parents—their mess of shared assumptions—and it occurred to her that maybe she had in fact simulated their entire relationship. Maybe she'd lived it on both sides. What did she really know about him?—about how he felt about her? The front door of the house opened and he came out swathed in one of his family bathrobes.

"Sarah?"

He crossed the back lawn in his slippers.

"It's freezing out here," he said. "Come on."

She watched him approach. The grass washed into a bright green that was full of light, that had yellow in it. Behind him, black clouds sprouting on the horizon, flying fast and low toward them, shaving the tops of trees. He stopped at the edge of the lawn. Then she saw it in his face. With a visceral hitch that was at least part relief, she thought of all the things that would happen now—the crushing logistics of moving out, parceling out property, navigating a shared workplace—all the wearying, recursive conversations she would be fated to have.

Paul took his bathrobe off and wrapped it around her. Underneath, he wore boxers and a T-shirt, and the sight of it tore her apart.

What had been real and what not? What must she hold onto, what release? Sarah sat on her bed, staring out into the dimly glowing night. Low gray boxlike buildings stretched away into brown slums and behind those, Mahmoud had told her, was the salt desert. Dasht-e Kavir. From out that expanse came music all night, parched, tattered—drums, always, but also fragments of a man's voice in harrowed mourning. Once Sarah heard the theme from *Titanic*.

In the beginning it had been terrifying. Her working life she'd spent assigning tasks to units of time; how, then, could she spend all her time *not* thinking about him? She quit her job, moved into her mother's house. She'd saved enough that money was never an issue. It had been far easier than she'd expected to leave work—but surviving a vacant day seemed impossible. She couldn't cast her life so far. It was a matter of hours—minutes, really, and through those minutes it had been Parvin who had talked her on, coaxed her to apprehensible distances. They'd pored over her pain together—Sarah, all the while, shirking the suspicion that her friend was now only ever present for her pain. What had been real? When had Sarah truly been happy? Here—now—in this dark villa—her life again revealed its fiber to her. Work: an overcast spread of clocked-in hours. Paul: streaks, dyed strands of memory, unraveling at every touch. To think about it now, the closest she'd ever come to real happiness had been by herself: swimming at the local indoor pool before work. She'd always liked the silence of new morning, the crisp smell of chlorine, the high stained windows that, during summer, filtered the light through like bottled honey. Sometimes, when she was first to arrive, the rectangle of unbroken water shone with the hardness and sheen of copper. She liked the companionship she shared with the other swimmers—all serious swimmers at that hour—the feeling of being alone, unrequired to commit any of the compromises required of human interaction, and yet a part of them; her mere presence the stamp of her belonging. Here she belonged. She liked standing on the blocks, goose-pimpled, second-guessing, and then the irretractable dive into cold water— the sheer switch of it against her skin—she was wet now, cold, her hair wet, and there was nothing to do but to swim herself warm. Lap after lap she would swim: pure sound and feeling; matching the rhythm of her strokes to the pace of her breathing, the ribbed circuit of air through her body. Conditioning herself into a kind of peace. Then, afterward—home.

SARAH WOKE FIRST THE NEXT MORNING. She ran the bath, turned the bathroom light on, then off again. The water reflecting the bone-dull sky. She slipped out of her underwear and into the cold water.

Beneath her, the house roused slowly into sound. She lay in the tub, studying the high, molded ceilings, taking in the scents of lacquer and rosewater. She'd made it through the night. Was Parvin awake? Sarah felt toward her now a mild, civilized remorse—as if all her antipathy had exhausted itself the previous night.

As she dressed, the sound of amplified stereo static, followed by a haunting ululation, piped through the street bullhorns. The call to prayer. She went to the wood-shuttered window, looked out through the web of large leaves. The sound touched a deep chord within her. For the first time, she strove to imagine the cleanness of belief that could pull all those foreheads to stone, unwaveringly, five times a day. What was the lie? That you could change your life? She looked out, watching the unknown city roll out before the new sun, its dazzling labyrinth of streets and walls, its villas and bazaars, the evil vizier cast down for good into the valley and the smog burned off to unveil magnificent Damavand—vast and near, seamed with snow and meltwater. It was a two-minute peace—she knew that—but she allowed it.

"I know, it still gets me too."

Sarah turned around and saw Parvin in the doorway. She wore, uncharacteristically, a long, fluid, green dress, and her mouth was pressed tight.

Sarah started to speak but Parvin held up her hand. She sat down on Sarah's bed. The call to prayer continued, the man's voice so elongated, so reedy, it sounded like an instrument.

"There's a word in Farsi," Parvin said, "*Khafeghan.* It means a feeling where you can't breathe. A kind of claustrophobia." Parvin lifted her face and stared straight ahead. "You hear it used a lot over here."

Sarah tried to repeat the word. "I think I understand," she added.

Parvin shifted on the mattress to face Sarah. "Listen," she said, "this is my work. This is what I do now." She made an effort to smile, and then she did. "It's enough that you're here."

"I can't believe it. That I'm here. You're here."

Parvin thought for a moment, then said, "I won't lie to you. Mahmoud thinks you shouldn't come tomorrow."

"What do you think?"

"There's something else," said Parvin. "One of our members isn't answering his cell phone." She jutted out her jaw, then closed her mouth again. "It's probably nothing, but you never know."

Sarah looked at Parvin, newly surprised by the green dress—gladdened, somehow, by how obliviously she wore it. A vestige of peace abided in Sarah. She wanted to share it with her friend but before she could figure out what to say, Parvin had already stood up and left the room.

ALL DAY THE PARTY CONVENED DOWNSTAIRS. Sarah was glad to keep to herself, perusing books in the study—mainly German books on art and architecture. She found the satellite television and sated herself on current events, most of which seemed irrelevant and repetitive. She watched clouds move across the mountains. Jet-lagged, she fell asleep.

Late in the afternoon Roya barged into her room. Sarah barely recognized her at first, fully arrayed, as she was, in robe and head scarf.

"Parvin is gone," she said. She looked at the cell phone in her hand. "Reza says she is going to the square."

"Is she okay?"

Roya shrugged, her expression indistinct. "He says she is meeting with the drama group. He went with her to help."

"Wait," said Sarah. "Where are you going?"

"I am going out." She puckered her lips, shot Sarah an astute look. "I think Mahmoud is driving to the square."

It was almost dark when they left. The motorway was clogged—cars like theirs—wide and metal and box-nosed. They turned down a one-way street straited on both sides by canals. Buses belched out charry exhaust. Sarah looked and spotted men with kerchiefs over their faces, women with rearranged scarves. A city of bandits. Suddenly a bus—going the wrong way—roared straight at them. She gasped, closed her eyes, then realized they were okay. The contra-flow lane, said Mahmoud, muttering his reassurances.

Neither of them wanted to talk about Parvin. They talked instead about the program for the rally. Sarah asked him about his father. He hesitated, then told her his father was a high-ranking cleric, one rank below ayatollah—here you decided for yourself when you were ayatollah—but his, Mahmoud's, own religion was more complex. He was born after the revolution. What did that mean? It meant he was supposed to feel a certain way.

He and his father no longer talked.

"I forgot you were a lawyer," he said wryly.

The Party stood for civil rights. That was all. It was not anti-Islam. Nor was it anti-America. After 9/11 they'd come out with the other thousands and did she know what they said? They said, *Death to terrorism!* They said, *Death to bin Laden!* They said, *America, condolences, condolences.*

Abruptly he turned to her. "Was Parvin like this when you knew her?"

"Like what?"

"Like she cares for nothing. For no one."

"What are you talking about?"

They rumbled across a low bridge. The water below soupy and junk-filled.

"She's trying to help," said Sarah. Without fully understanding why, she felt—in that moment—that before Mahmoud she would defend Parvin to the very end. She owed her that much.

"And you?"

She laughed uncertainly. "Don't ask me about politics," she said. "I'm just here for her. Moral support."

"Moral support," he repeated.

They parked the car and started walking. A drizzle came

down and made the concrete dark around them. At last they reached the edge of a large square. It shone with the changing light of a thousand candles. In the radiance Sarah could see that stalls had been set up in parallel rows and a stage erected at the far end. There was movement on the stage. Two large portraits of the black-bearded martyr bannered down on either side. Above the ground glow, trees had been hung with green lamps. According to Mahmoud, all the candles were to light the imam's passage after his death.

"Is this where . . ."

"Yes," he said. He pointed at the distant stage, then opened his hand and made a motion like a windshield wiper. "Tomorrow—there will be hundreds here."

"Where's Parvin?"

He frowned slightly. "Her phone is not on."

They wandered into the gridded space. It was crammed with people, mostly youth. Gas lanterns and feeble fluorescent tubes. In the half dark, fewer people stopped to notice her. The air smelled strongly of burning meat. Mahmoud behind her, she passed a cluster of stalls selling chains set in wooden handles. Then juice vendors and smoking grills. Her mouth watered; she stopped to buy kebabs and immediately a quick-witted boy accosted them, hawking popsicles. His eyes became large, almost insectoid, when he saw her face.

"I'm sorry," she murmured.

There was a stirring at the far end of the square. The sound of firecrackers and the sputtered brightening of smoke. They couldn't see anything through the crowd.

Mahmoud accepted a kebab from her but didn't eat it. They left the congested market stalls and walked into the green halo of a multi-lanterned tree. "You come to Iran—during Ashura—and do not want to talk politics?" He spoke loudly, over the square's hubbub, and his tone seemed to have risen in pitch. "Who comes to Iran if not for politics?"

She looked at him and realized he was joking. It accorded, she felt, with her beginning ease in this place, her sense of being slowly let in. She recalled what Roya had said about him being a hero. As though he'd read her mind, he turned away.

In front of them was the large stage. Actors mimed a battle scene with much shouting and clashing of wooden swords against shields. They were roundly ignored by the square's swarming youth. Parvin was nowhere in sight. Sarah sat with Mahmoud on a bench near the stage. On an opposite bench, a white-bearded old man bared his stained teeth at them. He was something sucked out from a dream. The tree behind him had flowers in it, a carpet of candles all around its trunk. As the night passed, people came and knelt and added candles in religious observance— shapes of women more fabric than human-form; men same-faced, retreating into their beard-shadows. Who were they? What were they to her? The more she looked, the less she saw of this city.

Mahmoud flung out his right arm. "You see them?" he asked. "Look."

They gathered, where he pointed, in fluid, makeshift groups. Teenagers, by the looks. Most of the girls wore high heels and flared jeans or calf-length capris. Their faces glossy and made-up. Their scarves not black but bright and diaphanous, pushed far back to expose their hair, and instead of the long, loose overgarment they wore figure-hugging trench coats that barely reached their knees. Even through her outward alertness Sarah felt self-conscious. She remembered the pilot's announcement on the plane, remembered feeling, curiously, the act of covering up as though she were stripping naked. But this. How could anyone arrest anyone at all when all this was in plain sight, was plainly permissible?

"They are not here for Ashura," spat Mahmoud. "They are here for Valentine's Day." Many of the girls in lazy possession of bouquets and teddy bears. Couples holding hands.

"You know what they call this? 'The Hussein Party.' " He didn't look at her. In the candlelight, his features seemed statuesque. He hadn't touched his kebab. She caught a sudden whiff of spice on the wind.

Firecrackers went off again, closer this time. She shifted in her seat. There ran a new restlessness through the youth. Cell phones, dozens of them, ring tones random as wind chimes.

They came from the southern edge of the park. Four cars—old sheet-metal heaps that could have been salvaged from American junkyards, one with a broken, million-glinting windshield—pulled up bumper to bumper and they spilled out, men with various beards, holding clubs and chains and walkie-talkies.

"It's them," hissed Mahmoud. He yanked her back down onto the bench. "They will see you."

One man swung a baton through the crowd of youth as though cutting through brush with a machete. They skittered apart. A girl screamed. Several of the men stood behind the others and spoke out through cupped hands, clearly and ecstatically. One came toward them. He paused in front of the stage and took in the show.

"Your scarf."

She pulled her scarf tight over her head, tucking in every strand of hair, leaving the front hanging, cowl-like, over her face.

More cries sounded out from the maze of stalls. The rows between them clearing fast. The men fanned deeper.

"You must stop looking at them," said Mahmoud. He moved closer to her on the bench. They were a couple now, close enough to be conventionally transgressive—but not too close. An older couple in this park of kids, with nothing to fear from these men.

Her breath caught when she saw a group of them dragging three shapes back to their cars. Then she saw. She actually felt her heart stop. The darkly stubbled face—it was Reza, seemingly unconscious. The other two were young men she didn't recognize. A strange girl stood rooted at the edge of the square and lifted her hands to either side of her nose and mouth.

"Stop looking," Mahmoud murmured. She let her face drop, inhaled sharply. Now the men were banging their clubs against steel poles. She felt each impact in the seat of her stomach. Warmth emanated from Mahmoud's body. The ground was wet, busy with candlelight, green shadows. The old man opposite started talking, roaring with laughter. Another man's voice joined in.

Mahmoud leaned in closer. "You are an American citizen," he said. "You will be safe."

"Did you see Parvin?"

"Listen to me," he whispered into her ear. "Listen to me. When Parvin first came back, she was taken."

Sarah's stomach, already riled, turned hot and sick.

"But she did not want to tell you. But she was safe. I tell you this because."

A man stopped in front of them. Bits of gravel and broken glass stuck to the rim of his soles: cheap, synthetic-leather shoes. You couldn't beat anyone with those shoes. The wooden club hanging beside them.

"*Salam.*"

"*Salam,*" Mahmoud said. Sarah kept her head bowed, the hard burl of cloth digging into her throat. The men conversed for some time. He sounded normal, in good cheer, this man with his wooden club. He told a joke and found it worth repeating again and again. Mahmoud laughed behind his words with terrible sunken sobs. Then the man fell silent—a short lull—and when he spoke again his tone had changed. He was speaking to her.

Mahmoud said something in Farsi. The strange man reacted animatedly, quarreling now with the exaggerated intonation she'd come to expect, through TV, from Middle Eastern men—

that windy, slightly petulant swing of voice. Mahmoud turned and murmured to her, but in Farsi. Those words—their lilting, curious energy—she was sure they held the key to her life. If she could just understand those words. The man reached down, elbowing Mahmoud aside, and lifted her chin.

Breath rushed into her windpipe; she started to cough, then stopped herself.

The man considered her. There was a dangerous looseness through his face—his wide-spaced eyes, his purple lips swelling out through his beard. She felt irrationally as though she already knew him, had encountered him already in some similar situation. Mahmoud so young, fresh-faced, next to him. The man said something to her. She was aware of his companions prowling the square behind him as he prodded the club into the damp ground, leaving a mesh of curved dents. She forced herself to smile—the effort tearing up her eyes—then she drooped her head again. The lamb kebab lurching up from her gut. She had to not vomit.

What choice did she have? She stood up. The man shouted aloud. Three other men rushed over, one snaking a steel-link chain behind him, another's trousers sodden at the ankles. The smell of gasoline strong off them.

Her heart pounded her skull. "I am an American citizen," she said. Her voice came out squeezed, for some reason English-accented.

They all fell silent. Then the first man laughed, a harsh, high-pitched sound. Mahmoud got to his feet, started talking, his speech gaining momentum. He took out his wallet and showed it to the man. Sarah kept her gaze trained on the ground. All four men started laughing, then at one point the man with the chain threw a question to Mahmoud. He replied. Behind them the clatter and thrum of car engines, distant human cries from the street. The square itself gone quiet. Finally the first man tossed back

Mahmoud's wallet and lifted up his club with a twirl, like a baseball player loosening his wrist, and tapped it against the sole of one shoe, then the other, and when his second shoe met the ground he'd already swiveled and walked away. The others followed him.

Sarah waited, blood surging in her ears. Not daring to look up. Finally, she did. The square was empty. The cars were gone. They were safe.

She turned to Mahmoud. "What did you say to them?"

His face was tight, sickly-looking.

"What did you say?"

"You saw who they took?"

She nodded.

"They said they took them as American sympathizers."

"But not me."

"Not you." He chuckled dryly. "I told them you were nothing. You are a foolish tourist I guide around our city."

She shuddered her head. She felt dizzy in the green-glowing landscape. Flags snapping in the wind.

"Who were they? What will happen to Reza?"

"I said I wanted to show you this beautiful square and it is too bad, with all these infidel youth."

She clutched his arm. "Where's Parvin?" she asked. She felt a desperate compulsion to keep asking.

Mahmoud chuckled again, an abrasive sound like he was hawking up phlegm. "You are an American woman. He was jealous of me, for being with you." They both sat down. She realized she was shaking, was chill with sweat. He took out his cell phone and dialed a number. She watched the fingers of his free hand as they twitched beside his legs, as though in some meaningful order, as though warming up some invisible instrument. He tried another number. Another. Finally he got through. His voice swerved to a different pitch and pace. She waited—all that time, waiting—time driven into the act of waiting for him while he talked. He hung up.

"Her phone is still off. No one has seen her."

She collapsed her face into her hands with a moan.

"No one knows who was taken with Reza." He cleared his throat. "I think it was a random arrest. But we must wait. We must go somewhere safe and wait."

"Who were they?"

His face went distant. "Ansar-e Hezbollah they call themselves. Friends of the Party of God."

"Then why did they let us go?" She swallowed; her throat was dry. "What did you say to them?"

He shrugged. She felt it through her arm and chest and legs.

"What did you say?"

He looked up at her with his dark eyes, then bowed his head. "You want to know what I said?" His jaw tensed. "It is not that I am religious or not."

"What?"

Now his voice was harsh. "I told them," he said, "I told them I was the son of my father." His expression glazed over for a moment, then he swung around to face her. "Now tell me the truth. Why did you come here?"

"What do you mean?"

He waited, his eyes coruscating in the candlelight. After a drawn-out silence she looked away.

"To escape," she said. And she laughed.

He laughed too, but bitterly. "Then you are the first American to escape to Iran."

"To escape from a man," she said. It surprised her to say it. To hear herself say it. A giddiness overcoming her and with it this urge to tell out her life, those problems so personal she could only tell them to a stranger. She looked at Mahmoud in the green-gold glow. His face drawn into the slightest suggestion of a smirk—as though it had forgotten itself in the middle of self-mockery. He'd invoked his father's name. He'd saved her from those men. He'd left her at odds with herself. There was sadness and then there was this, a field of candles, smoke-flowers in the wind.

"Parvin," he said, "she comes here to find a man." The mock-lines on his face deepening. "She says she wanted to meet me before she marries me."

"Marries you?"

"She will marry me to save me. So I can go to America if I want. If I choose."

He wasn't joking. He seemed amused by her silence.

"We are not all birds flying in the same direction. We are young—most of us are young." He rubbed his chin with the heel of his hand.

She forced herself to nod.

"Perhaps I will let myself be saved," he went on. "I, too, am young, and expect much from the world."

"How old are you?"

His pupils were gunmetal black. "I am twenty-three. I know what you think. You look at me and you do not see me as a man. I know."

"You're wrong."

And he was. At every turn he'd misunderstood her mind. She was thinking of Parvin; she was thinking of the man in front of her who was Parvin's betrothed, that it was yet another thing she didn't know about her best friend. She was thinking of Reza and of Zahra Kazemi and the man with fat purple lips. She was thinking of Paul. There was no incongruity at all—or maybe everything was incongruous. Maybe that was the condition of things. She was thinking of their drive here, how everything would seem like the grimy, industrial, urban standard—when suddenly she'd glimpse the yearning tapering of a spire, the delicate axis of an arch, and, for a moment, she'd remember to exist alongside the ghosts of this ancient city.

Mahmoud led her through the black streets. Many of the mourning candles now snuffed by the risen wind. Dogs roaming the alleyways. She followed him to a tall apartment building, one side of which had been whitewashed and painted over: a twenty-story portrait of a man with a gray beard and black turban. This one wearing glasses. The background was laid down in green and red, the whole wall unevenly illuminated by spotlights.

It was a different hotel. In a blocked-off alley behind them a group of men laughed raucously. A boy wearing a baseball cap urinated against the wall.

The man at the desk was angular and trim-bearded. He watched them unremittingly, not once looking away.

In the room Mahmoud went over and drew the curtains shut. "We will be safe here for now," he said.

"What will happen to Reza?" she asked again.

"I do not know." He started to say something else, then checked himself. "All we can do now is wait."

Again, her breath started coming short and fast. She gulped down some air. "But you think Parvin's okay?"

He sat beside her on the bed. "I think so," he said. Then in a smooth yet awkward gesture he wrapped his arms around her. She neither resisted nor relented.

For what seemed like hours they stayed in that room. Twice he answered his cell phone but learned nothing new. Sarah kept going to the window, lifting the curtains by their hems, looking out into the blinking night as though the act of looking might make her friend appear. Out there it seemed like any other place but underneath, she knew—she understood now—there was an alien body. A deep and adverse structure.

Seven thousand miles she'd come and she'd failed their friendship in every way. Parvin had confided in her—had made her mind and soul intelligible—and Sarah had pushed her away, pushed her into the teeth of some horrible proof. There was the thirteen-year-old girl, those small dark rooms and small bright rooms, there the woman with a girl's face, the man trussed by his wrists to a ceiling fan. A metal chair with a gas flame beneath it. Her heart smashing inside her ribs. Why had she come here? What had she wanted? She'd wanted purpose, sure, but every part of this turned-around place gave purpose to some action— leave, never leave, come back. She'd wanted to look past herself but now, when she did, she saw nothing at all that was different. She was alone. Parvin was alone.

Mahmoud was standing behind her. Then he was propping her up, sliding her closer to the bed. He laid her on her back and went away, returning with a glass of water.

"It is okay," he said. He handed her some hotel napkins. "Listen to me. She will be safe. Like last time."

"How do you know?"

"Try to rest," he answered.

She pushed herself back on the bed. The naked bulb glaring down from the ceiling. The sound of incessant traffic outside. She stilled herself, succumbed to the noise of her body—its angry clunk and shudder. After a while, Mahmoud leaned over her, looked at her closely before saying, "Wait here."

"Where are you going?" She was revolted, even before she spoke, by the desperation she expected in her voice. She closed her eyes, started shivering. She waited.

Hours passed, or maybe minutes, and he came back in and chain-locked the door behind him. He took off his jacket. Then he laid out on the desk two long pipes, a plastic-wrapped baggie, a candle.

"This will help," he said.

"What is it?"

He looked up at her curiously. "It is better than drunk," he said.

She knew, on some level—on the level that experienced this place as a series of unfolding stories—that there was amusement, irony, in this. She was receiving the all-Iranian experience. But two days had shattered that way of being here. What she'd thought about things no longer mattered. She was here, now.

Mahmoud fidgeted with his instruments. He struck a match, lit the candle. The pipe shifted in his mouth as he persuaded the white smoke in and out.

"Here," he said. It smelled like chocolate caramel. She watched his fingers, how he shaped the gummy resin until it was pea-shaped, worked it into the widened hollow at the end of the pipe. "Lie down like this," he said.

"Like this," she repeated.

The pipe's bum end was metal, black with an old burn, and he held it to the candle flame. A tindering sound. "Follow the smoke."

She did as he said and followed the smoke.

"Like that," he said. He was serious now, that little secret smile on his face. He didn't know her at all. He was kind. He taught her how to rotate the pipe. He prepared the other pipe. Then he gave it to her and she handed him the first and then, when they were done, they exchanged again, almost formally. His shirt tucked tight into his pants. He caught her eye and they both looked away. Much later, he talked, his words solvent with smoke. She talked too. At one point he stumbled up and turned off the light. At one point the streetlamp stopped working and after that there was only candlelight.

He put his hand between her legs. She saw it happening, the feeling arriving after the thinking about it—it was maybe mildly disagreeable, she decided. The candle flame reflected off his skin so that his cheekbones and forehead became patches of brilliant white, as though the light had burned clear through.

She closed her eyes. The floating night before her.

"How do you feel?"

He sounded far off, acoustic, calling to her as though from the bottom of a well. There was water in her now, light in her body, in her lungs. Words floating up in bubbles of air. She followed the smoke and breath by breath her body gave out its substance. She got up with the slow, easy motions of a swimmer.

She was at the window, looking out. The light-spilled streets like narrow banks, the metal stream rolling ceaselessly between them. Lights from cars, candles, distant streetlamps deranging themselves into an emptiness so bright it evaporated everything. Parvin was out there somewhere. Inside those lights. Parvin, her friend.

Mahmoud called for her from the bed.

You could never know. Streets. Women walking, wind whipping their clothes. Black chadors loose and flaring behind their bodies, shreds of shadow. Wind blowing against their faces, shaking the veils smooth as sheets on clotheslines. Lights. You could never know when the light would take on weight again and crush you. She pushed herself against the glass. She was alone, and there was time yet. From the tops of plane trees, black birds hurled themselves against the sky—thousands of them.

"Sarah!"

Her name carried, still, a remote comfort and she stopped for it.

The Boat

THE STORM CAME ON QUICKLY. The crosswind surged in, fil-tering through the apertures in the rotten wood, sounding like a chorus of low moans. The boat began to rock. Hugging a beam at the top of the hatch, Mai looked out and her breath stopped: the boat had heeled so steeply that all she saw was an enormous wall of black-green water bearing down; she shut her eyes, opened them again—now the gunwale had crested the water—the ocean completely vanished—and it was as though they were soaring through the air, the sky around them dark and inky and shifting.

A body collided into hers, slammed her against the side of the hatch door. The boat righted and she slipped again, skidding in jets of water down the companionway. The hatch banged shut. Other bodies—she was on top of them—thighs and ribs and arms and heads—jammed this way and that with each groaning tilt, writhing toward space as though impelling the boat to heave to, back into the wind. The rocking got worse. Light was failing fast now and inside the hold it had become uncannily dim.

Inches away from Mai's face, a cross-legged man tipped for-ward, coughed once into his hands, then keeled back onto his elbows. His face was expressionless. When the smell arrived she realized he had vomited. In the swaying half dark, people pitched forward and back, one by one, adding to the slosh of salt-water and urine in the bilge. People threw up in plastic bags, which they then passed on, hand to hand, until the parcel reached someone next to a scupper.

"Here."

Mai pinched the bag, tried to squeeze it out through the draining slit, but her fingers lost their hold as the boat bucked. The thin yellow juice sprayed into her lap.

On the steps below her, an infant started crying: short choking bursts.

Instantly she looked for Truong—there he was, knees drawn up to his chin, face as smooth and impassive as that of a ceramic toy soldier. Their eyes met. Nothing she could do. He was wedged between an older couple at the bottom of the steps. Where was Quyen? She shook off the automatic anxiety.

Finally the storm arrived in force. The remaining light drained out of the hold. Wind screamed through the cracks. She felt the panicked limbs, people clawing for direction, sudden slaps of ice-cold water, the banging and shapeless shouts from the deck above. The whole world reeled. Everywhere the stink of vomit. Her stomach forced up, squashed through her throat. So this was what it was like, she thought, the moment before death.

She closed her eyes, swallowed compulsively; tried to close out the crawling blackness, the howl of the wind. She tried to recall her father's stories—storms at sea, waves ten, fifteen meters high!—but they rang shallow against what she'd just seen: those dense roaring slabs of water, sky churning overhead like a puddle being mucked with a stick. She was crammed in by a boatload of human bodies, thinking of her father and becoming overwhelmed, slowly, with loneliness. As much loneliness as fear. Concentrate, she told herself. And she did—forcing herself to concentrate, if not—if she was unable to—on the thought of her family, then on the contact of flesh pressed against her on every side, the human warmth, feeling every square inch of skin against her body and through it the shared consciousness of—what? Death? Fear? Surrender? She stayed in that human cocoon, heaving and rolling, concentrating, until it was over.

She opened her eyes. A procession of people stepping over her, measuredly, as though hypnotized, up the companionway and onto the deck. She got up and followed them.

The night sky was starless. Only moonlight illuminated everything, emanating from a moon low and yellow and pocked, larger than she had ever seen it before. Its surface appeared to her as clear and as close as the ridges of a mountain from a valley. Pearly light bathed the stunned and salt-specked faces of the hundred people on deck, all of whom had expected to die but were instead granted this eery reprieve.

Nobody talked. Night, empty of sound, held every soul in thrall—the retching, the complaint of babies, the nervous breathings, now all muted. The world seemed alien, somehow beyond the reach of Mai's mind—to be beneath the giant moon, and have nothing but space, and silence, all around.

A fog rolled over the water.

Mai looked sternward and saw Quyen slumped, arms outstretched, collapsed to one knee. Her head lolled against her left shoulder. Her forearms were bleeding from rope burn—she must have been stranded on deck when the storm came in; someone had strapped her, spread-eagled, to a low horizontal spar, and saved her life.

Mai searched for Truong.

From below deck there now came a humming of prayer. Then someone gasped—Mai swung to find a face, then several, turning pale, hands to mouths beneath stupefied eyes.

"Do you hear?"

"What is it?"

"Be quiet! Be quiet!" an urgent voice commanded. "Listen."

But when the noise on the boat ceased, there still came from every direction the sound of people whispering, hundreds of people, thousands, the musical fall and rise of their native tongue. Barely intelligible. Sometimes right next to Mai's ear and she would whip around—but there would be nothing except the close, gray fog.

In a whisper, "It's nothing—the wind, that's all."

"Who's there?" someone demanded loudly, unsteadily, from the prow.

No answer, just the lapping of low murmurs.

On the foredeck, a man turned to his companion.

"Here?"

The second man nodded. Beneath the moonlight Mai recognized him. It was Anh Phuoc, the leader of the boat. He was, Quyen had told her, one of those mythic figures who'd already made his escape and yet returned, again and again, to help others.

He nodded and looked out into the haze.

And now she realized where they were—where they must be. Everyone had heard about these places. They had ventured into the fields of the dead, those plots of ocean where thousands had capsized with their scows and drowned. They stared into the fog. All drawn into a shared imagination, each in some space of unthinking as though they had leapt overboard, some madness possessing them, puncturing the glassy surface of the water and then plunged into black syrup, coming up into breath but panicked, disoriented, flailing in a viscid space without reference or light or sound.

"Try to sleep."

It was Quyen; she had untangled herself from her station and crawled forward. Mai turned to her, then looked away. There was a sort of death in her face.

"I saw Truong, down—" Mai began, then saw that he had appeared silently behind his mother. He stood close by Quyen without touching her. For a moment Mai was seized with a desire to take the boy up and press him hard against her chest, to keep him—his stillness, self-containment, whatever it was about him—close to her. But she, too, was contained, and didn't move. She began to smell incense from the hold. People praying to their ancestors. It lightened her head. A dim thought struggled, stabilized, in her mind—maybe the voices on the water were those of their ancestors. Maybe, she thought, they were answering their prayers. What did they know? What were they so desperate to communicate?

"It's over now."

She let herself pretend Quyen was speaking to her and not to Truong.

"The storm's over, Child. Try to sleep."

Mai submitted, and when she closed her eyes, knowing they were both beside her, she found the hum of the phantom voices almost lulling—almost like the wash, when she dozed off, of a monsoon starting, or a wedding, dim-sounding on distant midday streets. A sea wind bearing men's voices up from the wharf. At times she thought she almost recognized a voice. When her eyes opened a second later it was morning: the moon had disappeared and the cloud streaks were already blue-bruised against a sky the color of skin.

THE FIRST FIVE DAYS they'd traveled on flat seas. It had been hot, and Mai had faced the choice of being on deck and burnt by the sun or being below in the oven-heated hold. In the beginning people swam in the ocean, trailing ropes off the slow-moving junk, but afterward the salt on their bodies cooked their skin like crispy pork.

She spent as much time as she could bear out of the hold, which simmered the excrement of a hundred people. Their boat was especially crowded, Quyen had explained, because it carried two human loads: another boat organized by the same guide had at the last minute been confiscated by the Communists.

Each family kept mostly to itself. Mai was alone. She stayed close to Quyen and Quyen's six-year-old son, Truong. He was a skinny child with an unusually bony frame and a head too big for his body. His eyes, black and preternaturally calm, were too big for his head. He spoke in a watery voice—rarely—and, as far as Mai could tell, never smiled. He was like an old man crushed into the rude shape of a boy. It was strange, she thought, that such a child could have issued from Quyen—warm and mischievous Quyen.

When Mai first met him they'd been gliding—silently, under cover of night—through a port full of enemies. Even then his demeanor had been improbably blank. The war had that to answer for too, she'd thought—the stone-hard face of a child barely six years old. Only when the boat shifted and his body leaned into hers had she felt, astonishingly, his heartbeat through his trunk—an electric flurry racing through the concavities of his back, stomach and chest. His body furious with life. He was engaged in some inward working out, she realized, and in that instant she'd grasped that nothing—nothing—was more important than her trying to see whatever it was he was seeing behind his dark, flat eyes.

Two nights later, as Mai had been trying to sleep on deck, the song began. The faint voice drifted out of the hold with a familiar undertow. It was an old Vietnamese folk song:

> *I never thought to be a soldier's wife,*
> *You were not born to foreign lands preside;*
> *Why do the streams and hills our love divide?*
> *Why are we destined for this faithless life?*

In the shade of the hibiscus hedge her mother had once sung the same words to her during the years her father was away at war. The hibiscus flowers outside their kitchen in Phu Vinh, which bloomed only for a single day. And though dusk came, her mother would keep singing the soldier's wife's lament, her long black hair falling over Mai's face soft as a mosquito net, and Mai would trace the darkening red of the flowers through that curtain of hair.

Mai followed the song into the hold. She stopped at the bottom of the companionway steps; in the darkness she could just make out Quyen's form, lying on her side in front of Truong as though shielding him. Her voice was thin, attenuated in some way, stripped of vibrato. It didn't slide up to notes the way traditional singers' did. Mai stood on the dark steps and listened:

> *The path of wind and rain is yours to take,*
> *While mine does mourn an empty room and bed;*
> *We reach to touch each other, but instead . . .*

Her mother, who had waited each time her husband went to sea, again when he left to fight the Communists, and then—five years later—when he left once more, to report for reeducation camp. That was supposed to have been the last time. He was supposed to have been gone for ten days—the prescribed sentence for low-ranked soldiers. Mai remembered: on the eleventh day the streets were swept, washed, festooned with lanterns—women in their best and brightest outfits. The war had been lost, their husbands and fathers were coming home. Mai and Loc wore clothes their mother had borrowed. All through the afternoon they'd waited, through the night, too, the lanterns growing more and more dazzling, the congee and suckling pig cold, congealed. The next morning Mai's mother sent for word but received none. What could she—could any of them—do?

Overcome with feeling, Mai wanted to ask Quyen to stop singing—not to stop singing. Never to stop. How could she explain it all? Afterward, she had seen her mother caught on that cruel grade of time, growing old, aging more in months than she had in years—and yet she had given no comfort to her. She had been a daughter selfish with her own loss. From that day on, she never again heard her mother sing.

Squatting down, Mai dried her eyes with her sleeves. The song continued. With a shock, Mai realized Quyen's mouth was not moving. She was asleep. The singing cut off as Truong lifted, turned his head, staring at Mai with large obsidian eyes. Stunned, she said nothing. She looked back at his pale face, the slight, girlish curve beneath his nose to his lips. The intentness of his gaze. Then, slowly, she felt whatever turmoil broke and banked inside her becoming still. Watching her the whole time, Truong opened his mouth and took a deep breath:

> *You took my love southeast before I asked*
> *Whereto you went, and when you should return;*
> *Oh warring soul! through bitter years you learned*
> *To treat your sacred life like leaves of grass.*

Quyen stirred. Her eyelids still closed, she murmured, "Yes, you miss your father too. Don't you, my prince?"

He stopped singing. Shadows sifted in the darkness.

HERE WAS HOW IT BEGAN: her mother brought her through the dim kitchen into the yard. Her father had been released, three months prior, from reeducation camp, and immediately admitted into the hospital in Vinh Long. He had gone blind. The doctors were baffled because they could identify no physical abnormality, no root cause. His reeducation had blinded him. Mai, in the meantime, continued trundling every day from corner to corner, selling cut tobacco to supplement their family income. Her father's sickness was not unlike the war: something always happening elsewhere while she was forced on with her daily routine.

That day had been a slow one and she'd come home early. In the yard, beneath branches of mastic and white storax flowers, next to the deciduated hibiscus hedge, her mother had hooked her fingers under her waistband and handed her a damp bundle of money. The ink faded from the sweat of counting and recounting.

"Child can spend it however Child likes but try to keep, *nha?*"

Knowing her mother's usual frugality, Mai struggled to respond but her mother said nothing more, wiping her hands stiffly on her pajama pants and turning back into the house.

Two days later she told Mai to go visit her father at the hospital.

"Child is a good child," he told her after a long silence, his eyes fixed on some invisible locus in the air. He'd barely reacted when she came in and greeted him—it was only her second visit since he'd returned from reeducation camp. What had they done to him there? She remembered him being gaunt three months ago, when he'd first returned, but now his whole face was sunken— as though its foundation had finally disintegrated, leaving his features to their slow inward collapse. His eyes extruded from their deep-set sockets like black stones.

"How is Ba?"

"Ba is unwell," he said, rubbing his stubbled chin. He spoke to her as if to a servant. He didn't even look in her direction.

Mai hesitated. "Can Ba see?"

He didn't seem blind to her. She'd always imagined blindness to be a blacking out—but what if it wasn't? What if he *could* see—his eyes seemed outwardly unchanged—but had now chosen not to? What if his eyes were already looking elsewhere?

She said, "Ba will get better."

"Child is a big girl now. How old is Child now?"

"Sixteen."

"Heavens," he cried. Then jokingly, "So Child has a boyfriend, *ha?*"

Mai blushed and her father's hand searched for her head, patted it. Instinctively she twisted her cheek up into his rough palm. She'd come with so much to say—so much to ask—but he might as well have been deaf as blind. He laughed humorlessly. "At sixteen, Ba had to look after Ba's whole family."

Mai didn't reply. She felt insolent looking at his face when he didn't look back.

"Look after your mother," he said.

Look at me, she wanted to say. She considered moving into his fixed line of sight but didn't dare. Just once, she thought. Just look at me once, Ba, and I'll do anything you say.

"And obey her, *nha?*"

"Yes, Ba."

He gave a single nod, then smiled, but it was nothing more than a flexing of his lips.

"Obey your mother. Promise, *nha?*"

"Yes, Ba."

"Child." His voice lowered conspiratorially and, her breath quickening, Mai stooped down closer to him. He was going to talk to her. Once, that had been her whole life. He smelt like rusted pipes. "Stop it," he whispered. She held her breath, watching his eyes. They were still locked in midair. "Stop crying, Child."

She held herself still as he patted her head again.

"Good girl," he said.

The next day her mother put her on a bus to Rach Gia. It was a five-hour trip, she was told. Here was a plastic bag for motion sickness. In the market she would be picked up by an uncle she had never met. "Give this to him," her mother said, and pressed a fold of paper, torn from an exercise book, into her confused hands. Just before she got on the bus, her little brother, Loc, tugged at her shirt and asked if she minded if he used her bicycle.

"Use your own bicycle."

She boarded. Watched the two of them through the scuffed, stained window. Then, on the street, her mother raised one hand from her thigh in a hesitant motion, as though halfway hailing a cyclo.

"Ma?"

Mai pushed through the scree of indifferent bodies and rushed out to her mother. She stood there, breathing hard, sensing the larger finality in their parting. Her mother asked if she still had the money. Yes. Remember not to let anybody see it. Yes. Her mother smiled abstractedly, then brought her hand onto Mai's head and eased down, combing hair between her fingers.

"Child," she said softly, "remember, *nha?* Put your hat on when Child gets off."

Mai stammered, "Child hasn't said good-bye to Ba."

Her mother's hand followed the contours of her skull down into the inlet of her neck, a single motion. "Don't worry," she said. "Ma will say. For Child."

As the bus pulled out, a residue of memory surfaced in Mai's mind. Seeing her father off the first time—seven years ago, when he left for the war—her mother had clung fast to his elbow, her body turned completely into his, her face creased as though it were having trouble holding together a coherent emotion. But the second time—five years later, at the end of the war—her face had completely smoothed itself over. It had learned how to be expressionless.

Mai looked out of the back window—searching for her mother's face—but the street, like a wound, had closed over the space where it had been.

AFTER HEARING HIM SING, Mai caught herself, time and time again, searching for Truong. She was most at ease sitting in the shade of the hatch door, facing the prow, watching him with the other children. The only structure on the foredeck was the pilothouse and the children played in a small clearing behind it—a concession of territory from the adults teeming all around. Many of the children were twice Truong's age. He played with them laconically, indifferently, often leaving a game halfway through when he was bored, inevitably pulling a small group along—eager for him to dictate a new game.

Unlike the others he didn't constantly look around to find his family. He lived in a space of his own absorption. Quyen, too, seemed content to let him be. Hemmed in always by dozens of other sweaty, salt-gritted bodies, Mai watched him, stealing solace, marveling at how he could be in the sun all day and remain so pale.

It seemed impossible she'd known him only a few days.

According to Quyen, Truong's father—her husband—had already made his escape. She told Mai that he had arrived safely in Pulau Bidong, one of the larger Malaysian refugee camps, eight months ago. He was waiting for them there.

Why hadn't they traveled together?

"We are going to America," Quyen continued, passing over Mai's question. "My husband has already rejected one offer from Canada. He says he has made friends in the Red Crescent."

"Red Crescent?"

"Do you have any family there?"

After a while Quyen, misreading Mai's silence, continued, "You are probably going to Australia, no? Many people are going there now."

"No. I don't know."

"You don't know?" She pursed her lips in mock decision: "Then Mai will come with us."

"*Thoi,*" started Mai uncertainly.

"You must come. That one likes you," Quyen said, gesturing at Truong. "He talks about you all the time."

Mai flushed with pleasure, not fully understanding why—as she knew Quyen was lying. "He is very good," she said. "Very patient."

"Yes," Quyen replied. She reflected for a moment. "Like his father."

"And who has ever heard of a young boy who can sing like that? It's a miracle. He will make you rich one day."

"*Thoi,* don't joke."

She looked at her friend, surprised. "I am not joking."

Together they turned toward him. He stood skinny and erect, his clothes hanging from his limbs as though from a denuded tree's branches. His hands directing the ragtag crew to throw their sandals into a pile. Mai wondered briefly if it made Quyen proud—seeing all those children scrambling to obey her son. The game was one her brother used to play. Relaxing her mind, Mai could almost fool herself into thinking he was there, little Loc, springing away as the designated dragon swung around to protect his treasure hoard. He was about the same age as Truong. Her thoughts started to drift back to her last meeting with her father, at the hospital, when Quyen interrupted:

"That one was an accident."

Mai immediately blushed, said nothing.

"He slid out in the middle of the war."

How could she could joke about such a thing? Mai still

remembered her father's photo on the altar those five years, the incense and prayer, the hurt daily refreshing in her mother.

"You must miss him," said Mai. "Truong's father."

Quyen nodded.

"When were you married?"

"Nineteen seventy-two," Quyen answered, "in the middle of everything." For a moment her expression emptied out, making her seem younger. "I was your age then."

"Maybe more accidents will happen," Mai said, swallowing quickly through her words, "when you see him again. When we reach land."

Quyen snorted, then started laughing. Her face had recomposed itself now—was again knowing, shrewd, self-aware. She was pretty when she laughed. "Maybe," she said. She prodded Mai. "And what about you?"

But the mention of land—coming even from her own mouth—canceled out any joke for Mai. She had been trying not to think about it. From every quarter everyone now discussed, obsessively, their situation: they were on a broken-down junk, stranded in the Eastern Sea—here, or maybe here—an easy target for pirates—everyone knew about the pirates, had heard stories of boats being robbed and then rammed, of women being taken, used, dumped. On top of that they were starving, some of them beginning to get sick. No one, however, gave voice to the main fear: that they might not make it.

Mai pushed the dread down. Desperate to change the subject, she said the first thing that came to mind. "Wasn't it dangerous to escape," she asked, "with Truong so young?"

Her laughter subsiding, Quyen settled into a smile. "It was because of him," she said at last, "that I decided to escape." The smile hardened on her mouth.

They both turned toward him again. It had been three days. Watching him—letting in the thought of another day, and after that, another—Mai realized that Quyen's determination, as much as she tried to take part in it, felt increasingly superficial to her. She studied the boy's face. Above his awkward body it remained as stony and impassive as ever.

IN RACH GIA, IN THE MILLING MARKET, Mai had been met by a man with a skewed look who talked to a spot behind her shoulder. He called her name by the coriander-selling place. She was waiting for him, her hat on, next to a grease stand, petrols and oils and lubricants spread out like lunch condiments.

"Mai," she heard, "Mai, *ha?*" and, still sick from the lurching bus trip—it had been her first ride in an automobile—she was swept up by this man who hugged her, turning her this way and that.

"Child has the letter?" he grunted into her ear.

She was confused. He said it again, thrust her out at arm's length and glared straight at her for the first time. She tried hard not to cry.

"Heavens," he said, hastily letting go of her and stepping back. His face spread in an open, unnatural smile before he walked away. All at once Mai remembered her mother's instructions. The folded paper. She ran after him and pressed it into his hand. He read it, furtively, refolded it into a tiny square, and then he was Uncle again.

The first hiding place was behind a house by the river. Uncle told her to climb to the top of a plank bed and stay there, don't go anywhere. She lay with the corrugated aluminium roof just a few thumbs above her head, and in the middle of the day the heat was unbearable. The wooden boards beneath her became darkened and tender with her sweat.

A few days later Uncle came to get her—it was after the worst of the afternoon heat—and made her memorize a name and address in Rach Gia in case anyone asked her questions. She felt light-headed standing up.

"When Child reaches land," he told her, "write to Child's mother. She will say what to do next." She nodded dumbly. It was the first and final confirmation of her life's new plan: she was leaving on a boat. He looked at her and sighed. "She said nothing for Child's own protection." He gave her another abbreviated hug. "Does Child understand?" He wasn't, in all likelihood, her real uncle—she knew that now—but still, when he left, she felt in her stomach a deep-seated fluster. It was the last she saw of him.

The second hiding place was a boat anchored beneath a bridge on the Loc Thang river. Mai stayed down below deck for days and days, with sixty people maybe, among cargo sacks of sweet potatoes. No one talked; every sound in the dark was rat-made. She caught herself whimpering and covered her mouth. Once in a while the owner brought a few kilos of rice and they cooked it with potatoes over low kerosene flames and ate, salting their bit, chewing quietly. People coughed into their sleeves to muffle the sound. Parents fed their babies sleeping pills.

One night the owner appeared with another man who came in and tapped her on the shoulder. He tapped five other people as well. They all followed him out of the boat into the hot dark strange openness. A rower waited nearby and after some hesitation and muted dissent they climbed into his canoe, sitting one behind the other, Mai in the middle. The new man—the guide—instructed the rower to cross to the other side of the river. But he didn't, he kept on paddling downstream for what seemed to Mai like hours and hours. At one point she found herself falling asleep. She woke to the sound of wood tapping hollowly against wood. They were pushing into the midst of a dark cluster of houseboats. The rower stopped, secured a lanyard to one of the boats and leapt aboard. He lit a small lantern and began passing large drums reeking of diesel into the canoe. Moments later they moored against the riverbank. The rower crept onshore with a hoe and exhumed something long and gray from beneath a coconut grove.

"Detachable sail," someone whispered.

Mai turned around. The speaker was a young woman. She sounded as though she might have been pointing out bad produce at a market stall.

"It's a detachable sail," the woman repeated.

Mai began asking her what that was when the rower turned, silencing them both with a glare. A moment later Mai felt a cupped hand against her ear.

"My name is Chi Quyen." The woman used the word *Chi,* for "older sister." She reclined, smiling grimly but not unkindly, then leaned forward again, "Chi too is by herself."

Mai nodded. Shyly, she lifted a finger and crossed her lips.

For a long time they glided soundlessly, close to shore, and then they entered a thick bed of reeds. They stopped. The rower turned around, shook his heavy head and made the sign for no talking. It was dark. He struck a match and lit an incense stick and planted it in the front tip of the canoe. After a while Mai became confused. No one else seemed to be praying. When the stick burned down the guide asked the rower, in a low voice, to light another one. At least an hour passed. Occasionally Mai made out the rower's profile, hard and somber. She took the dark smell of sandalwood into her body.

The canoe swayed. "Maybe they're waiting," a new voice whispered gruffly. "Move out of the reeds so they can see the signal."

"Keep your head down!" the rower spat.

At that moment Mai realized the incense stick—its dim glow, its smoke, perhaps—was their signal.

Someone else said, "They won't wait."

"Move out of the reeds," the man repeated.

Mai felt a hot breath in her ear: "If they come, follow Chi, *nha?* Jump out and swim into the reeds. You can swim, no?"

"If who comes?"

"Fuck your mother, I said keep your head down!"

Someone behind her hissed and the canoe rocked wildly from side to side. The rower whirled around. Then, through the reeds, a light like a car beam flashed on and off. Fumbling, the rower lit a new incense stick, planted it at the canoe tip and paddled, swiftly and silently, back out. They saw it ahead, barely visible in the weird, weakly thrown light from the banks. An old fishing trawler, smaller than she'd imagined—maybe fifteen meters long—sitting low in the water. It inched forward with a diesel growl. A square pilothouse rose up from the foredeck, a large derrick-crane straddling its back deck, and the boat's midsection congested with short masts and cable rigs. Two big eyes painted on the bow. The canoe drew alongside and three men leaned over the gunwale above them and pulled them up, wrist by wrist. Everyone was aboard within a minute. Before being ushered down the hatch, Mai looked back and saw the canoe, abandoned in the boat's wake, rocking on the dark river.

Inside the hold, the stench was incredible, almost eye-watering. The smell of urine and human waste, sweat and vomit. The black space full of people, bodies upon bodies, eyes and eyes and eyes and if she'd thought the first boat was crowded, here she could hardly breathe, let alone move. Later she counted at least two hundred people, squashed into a space meant for fifteen. No place to sit, nor even put a foot down; she found a crossbeam near the hatchway and hooked her arm over it. Luckily it was next to a scupper where the air came through.

Quyen settled on the step below her, whispering to a young boy. She caught Mai's eye and smiled firmly.

The boat continued its creeping pace. People padded the engines with their clothes to reduce the noise.

"Quiet," an angry voice shushed downward. "We're near the gate."

But no one had been speaking. Through the scupper Mai peered into the night: their boat was gliding into a busy port. Pressed hard beneath her was the body of the boy Quyen had been talking to.

"Natural gate a hundred meters long," she heard suddenly. The water carried the low sound clearly. Then she realized the voice came from above deck, so subdued the person might have been talking to himself. "About ten meters wide. On the rising tide."

Then another voice under the wind, "Viet Cong . . . manned with two M30s—"

"Automatic, no?"

"Machine guns."

"What did Phuoc say about the permit?"

In the darkness, thought Mai, to feel against you the urgent flutter of a child's heart. The hopped-up fragility of it.

A tense sigh, "Even with the permit."

"Leave at night and they shoot. They shoot anything."

The speakers paused for a short while. Then a voice said, "We'll find out soon enough."

She settled forward against the young boy, not wanting to hear any more. Trying to block it all out: the voices, the smell. It was unnerving to think of all those other bodies in the darkness. Black shapes in the blackness, merging like shadows on the surface of oil. She crouched there, in the silence, beneath the hatchway. Spying on the bay through the scupper. Gradually, inevitably, the dark thoughts came. Here, in the dead of night, contorted inside the black underbelly of a junk—she was being drawn out into an endless waste. What did she know about the sea? She was the daughter of a fisherman and yet it terrified her. She watched as Quyen reached back and with a surprisingly practiced gesture pressed her palm against the boy's forehead. From above, watching the set of his grim face, Mai thought of her father. Their last meeting. His blindness. He'd taught her not to blame the war but how could she not?—all the power of his own sight seemed still intent on it.

Through the crack of the scupper the land lights, like mere tricks of her eyes, were extinguished one by one. Someone cut the engines.

She pulled the young boy's body closer to her; it squirmed like a restless animal's.

"Truong," a voice whispered sharply from beneath them.

She peered down. It was Quyen.

"Don't be a nuisance, Child." Quyen looked up at Mai, then said ruefully, "This is my little brat. Truong."

"Yours?" Mai frowned. "But—"

From the deepest part of the hold, several voices shushed them. In the silence that followed, even the tidal backwash seemed loud against the hull. Then a grind of something against the boat. Mai had never heard a sound so sudden and hideous.

"What is it?"

"A mine? I heard they put mines—"

The metal shrieked each minute movement of the boat.

"Heavens!"

"But boats pass here, must pass here every day—"

Fiercely: "Quiet!"

The sound sheared off—leaving behind a deep, capacious silence. Mai stiffening at every creak of the boat, every dash of water against its rotten sidewood. Then, without warning, the call and fade of a faraway voice. She crushed her cheek against the crown of the young boy's head and for the first time felt him respond—both of his small fists clamping her forearm. She shut her eyes and trained herself to his frenzied heartbeat, as though its pulse—its fine-knitting rhythm—carried the only possible thread of their escape. Long minutes passed. The boat glided on, pointed headfirst into the swell. Finally the fierce voice coughed:

"We're safe for now."

Murmurs rose up. The hatch was lifted. Under the sudden starlight Mai could see the whole of the boy's face, arching up to meet the fresh air.

"Child," said Quyen, "greet Chi. Properly."

He looked up at Mai—his eyes black and clear and unblinking. "*Chao* Chi," he said in his reed-thin voice.

All around them people's faces were untensing, bodies and voices stirring in restless relief. But Mai, clutching this strange young boy, found herself shivering in the warm night, relief only a sharp and unexpected condensation in her eyes.

ONCE THE STORM PASSED, six days out, everything changed.

Fishermen on the boat agreed that this storm had come on faster than any they'd ever experienced. It destroyed the caulking and much of the planking on the hull. The inboard was flooded, and soon afterward, both engines cut out completely.

What food had been left was spoiled. Water was short. Anh Phuoc, whose authority was never questioned, took charge of rationing the remaining supply, doling it out first to children, then the infirm, then everyone else. It amounted to a couple of wet mouthfuls a day.

The heat was unbearable. Before long the first body was cast overboard. Already a handful of people had been lost during the storm, but this was the first casualty witnessed by the entire boat. To the terrible drawn-out note of a woman's keening the bundle was tossed, a meek splash, into the water.

Like everyone else, Mai looked away.

After the storm it seemed to Mai that a film had been stripped from the world. Everything became more intense—the sun hotter, the light more vivid, the sea darker, every word a discordant affront to the new silence. The storm had forced people into their privacies: the presence of others now assailed each person's solitude in facing up to the experience of it. Children turned introverted, playing as though conducting conversations with themselves.

Even time took on a false depth: the six days before the storm stretched out, merged with memory, until it seemed as though everything that had ever happened had happened on the boat.

A man burned his clothes to let up smoke. He was quickly set upon, the fire smothered—the longer they drifted the more fearful they became of pirates. That night another bundle was thrown overboard. Minutes later they heard a thrashing in the water. It was too dark to see anything, yet, still, everyone averted their gaze.

Thirst set in. Some people trapped their own urine. Some, desperate for drinkable water, even allowed themselves the quick amnesia and prayed for another storm. It was fantastic to be surrounded by so much water and yet be dehydrated. Mai soon realized she wouldn't make it. The day following the storm she imitated some of the other youth, hauling up a bucket tied to the bowline. Under the noon sun the seawater was the color of amethyst.

She drank it. It was all right at first. It was bliss. Then her throat started scalding and she wanted to claw it out.

"You stupid girl," Quyen reproached her, demonstrating how to use her fingers to induce vomiting. She hugged her fiercely. "Heavens, you can't wait? We're almost there."

But what did Quyen know? Mai had heard—how could she possibly have not?—that other boats had successfully made the crossing in two days. She tried to sleep, to slide beneath the raw scour of pain in her throat. They'd been out seven days. How much longer? Her father was persistent in her thoughts now—all those weeks, even months, he'd spent on this same sea, in trawlers much like this one. He'd been here before her.

That afternoon, when she awoke, her muscles felt as though they had turned to liquid. She could feel her heart beating slurpily. She followed the weakening palpitations, counterpointing them to the creak and strain of the boat, the occasional luff of the sail. The sun brilliant but without heat. She was even thirstier than before.

"I'm not going to make it," she said. Saying it touched the panic, brought it alive.

"Don't speak," said Quyen. "Go back to sleep."

Mai struggled into a half-upright position. She made out a small group of children next to the bulwark, then pressed her imagination to find him again, little Loc, turning with a snarl as he growled, "Dragon!" She smiled, bit back tears. Behind him, her old school friend Huong was selling beef noodles in front of the damp stink-shaded fish market. Straight through the market she followed her daily route, picking up speed, past fabric stalls and coffee yards, the dusty soccer field where sons of fishermen and truck drivers broke off from the game to buy cigarettes, and then to the wharf, her main place of business, among the taut hard bodies crating boxes, the smell of fish sauce, the rattling talk of men and the gleaming blue backs of silver fish, ice pallets, copper weighing scales bright in the sun, the bustle of docking and undocking, loading and unloading—

A bare-chested man turned around and looked directly at her. "Ba?"

It filled her with joy to see him like that again: young and strong, his eyes clear and dead straight. He looked like he did in the altar photograph. It was her father before the war, before reeducation, hospitalization. Back when to be seen by him was to be hoisted onto his shoulders, gripped by the ankles. His hands tough, saltish with the smell of wet rope. She moved toward him, she was smiling, but he was stern.

"Child promised," he said.

During his long absences at sea she had lived incompletely, waiting for him to come back so they could tell to each other each moment of their time apart. He spoiled her, her mother said. Her mother was right and yet it changed nothing: still he went away and still, each time, Mai waited.

Her sudden, fervent anger startled her.

"Why send Child away? Child obeyed Ba." Her mind sparked off the words in terrific directions. "Child could have waited for Ba to get better." They had promised each other. He had left for ten days and returned, strange and newly blind, after two years. A thought connected with another: "It was Ba who left Child."

He stood there, tar-faced, empty-eyed, looking straight at her. She lifted her hands to her mouth, unable to believe what she had just said. The words still searing the length of her throat.

"Child is sorry," she whispered. "Ba and Ma sacrificed everything for Child. Child knows. Child is stupid."

He would leap off the boat and swing her into the crook of his arm, up onto his shoulders. Her mother fretting her hands dry on her silken pants, smiling nervously. I can't get it off me, he would say. His hands quivering on either side of Mai's rib cage—It's stuck, I can't get this little beetle off me!

She missed him with an ache that was worse, even, than the thirst had been. All she'd ever known to want was his return. So she would enjoy the gift of his returning, and not be stupid.

"Child is sorry."

He didn't respond.

"Child is sorry, Ba."

"Mai."

He was shaking her. She said again, "Child is sorry," then she felt fingers groping around in her mouth, a polluting smell and then her eyes refocused and she realized it was not her father she saw but Truong, standing gaunt over her.

"Thank heavens," came Quyen's murmur.

Looking at him she finally understood, with a deep internal tremor, what it was that had drawn her to the boy all this time. It was not, as she had first assumed, his age—his awkward build. Nothing at all to do with Loc. It was his face. The expression on his face was the same expression she had seen on her father's face, every day, since he'd returned from reeducation. It was a face dead of surprise.

She gasped as the pain flooded back into her body. She was awake again, cold.

"Mai's fever is gone," Quyen said. She smiled at Mai, a smile of bright industry—such a smile as Mai had never hoped to see again. Unexpectedly she was reminded of her mother, and, to her even greater surprise, she found herself breaking into tears.

"Good," whispered Quyen. "That's good."

Mai wiped her eyes, her mouth, with the hem of her shirt. "I'm thirsty," she said. She looked around for Truong but he seemed to have slipped away.

"You should be. You slept almost two days."

It was evening. She stood up, Quyen helping her. Her legs giving at first. Slowly she climbed up the hatch. On deck she shielded her eyes against the sunset. An incandescent red sky veered into the dark ocean. Rows and rows of the same sun-blotched, peeling faces looked out at nothing.

"Everyone's up here," Quyen whispered, "because down there are all the sick people."

"Sick people?"

Mai checked the deck, then searched it again with growing unease. He'd been standing over her. Keeping her voice even, she asked, "Where is Truong?"

"Truong? I don't know."

"But I saw him—when I woke up."

Quyen considered her carefully. "He was very worried about you, you know."

He wasn't in the clearing with the other children. Mai shuffled into the morass of arms and legs, heading for the pilothouse. Nobody made way for her. At that moment Truong emerged from the companionway. She almost cried out aloud when she saw him—gone was the pale, delicate-faced boy she'd remembered: now his lips were bloated, the skin of his cheeks brown, chapped in the pattern of bruised glass. An awful new wateriness in his gaze. He stood there warily as though summoned for punishment. Mai mustered her voice:

"Is Child well?"

"Yes. Are you better?"

"Truong, speak properly!" scolded Quyen.

"How is Chi Mai?"

"Well. Better." She leaned toward him, probing the viscosity of his eyes. His face's swollenness gave it a sleepy aspect.

"Ma said Chi Mai was very sick."

"Chi is better now."

"Tan and An were more sick than Chi," he said. "But Ma says they were lucky."

Mai smiled at Quyen; she hadn't heard him talk so much before. His voice came out scratchy but steady. He stood before them in a waiting stance: legs together, hands by his sides.

"Chi is glad for them."

"They died," he said. When Mai didn't respond he went on: "I saw the shark. All the uncles tried to catch it with that"—he pointed to a cable hanging off the derrick-crane—"but it was too fast."

"Truong!"

His eyes flicked to his mother. Then he said: "Fourteen people died while Chi Mai was sleeping."

"Child!"

He balled up his hands by his sides, then opened them again. "Chi Mai isn't sick anymore, *ha?*"

"That's right," Mai and Quyen said together.

It was difficult to reconcile him with his frail, wasting body. Seeing him, Mai's own body felt its full exhaustion. "Now . . . let's see . . ." She lifted one hand until it hovered between them, palm down. "Child wants to play slaps?"

His black eyes stared at her with something akin to pity.

"Pretend this is the shark," she exclaimed. Quyen glanced up at her. Immediately—horrified, shocked by herself—Mai pulled back her hand. "Chi is just joking."

Later that evening, a young teenage girl with chicken legs wandered over to the gunwale and in a motion like a bow that didn't stop, toppled gracefully over the side.

"Wait!" someone cried.

"Let her be," another person said. "If she wants to, let her be."

"Heavens, someone save her. Someone!" The first man stumbled to his feet, wild-eyed.

"You do it. Go on. Jump."

He stood like a scarecrow, frozen. Everyone watched him. He walked to the side and looked down at the shiny, dusk-reflecting water.

"I can't see her," he said.

"She must not have any family," Quyen whispered to Mai.

"She has the right idea," another low voice said. "Is there any better way to go?"

"*Thoi,*" Anh Phuoc said, coming over. "*Thoi,* that's enough."

REEDUCATION CAMP. For two years those two words had framed the entirety of her imaginative life. Her father, of course, hadn't talked about it when he returned—nor her mother. Now, for the first time, someone talked to her about it. Anh Phuoc had fought in the same regiment as her father—had been sentenced to a camp in the same district. No, he hadn't known him. By the time the Communists took Ban Me Thuot in March 1975, the Americans were long gone and the Southern regiments in tatters—soldiers deserting, taking cover as civilians, fleeing into the jungles. Escape on every man's mind. Soon they all learned there was no escaping the Communists: not in the country they now controlled. They were skilled, he said, at turning north against south, village against village. He fell quiet.

Mai waited. She watched him remembering. Nine days had passed and now she noticed how severely he had aged: his eyes gone saggy, his skin mottled with dark sun spots.

"In the camps," he said, "they do what they do best. They take a man—and then they turn him against things."

From the back deck a middle-aged woman started wading in their direction through the sprawl of bodies. She held the port gunwale with both hands for balance.

"Husbands against wives," he went on. "Children against parents. Your only chance is to denounce everyone, and everything, they tell you to."

The woman reached them. She made her complaint in a hoarse voice. She was owed water. She had tendered hers to another child who had collapsed, she said, and pointed aft. Anh Phuoc held Mai's eyes for a second, then followed the woman.

Her father wouldn't have denounced her—she was sure of that. Not in his own heart. But again she understood how necessary it was to stay on the surface of things. Because beneath the surface was either dread or delirium. As more and more bundles were thrown overboard she taught herself not to look—not to think of the bundles as human—she resisted the impulse to identify which families had been depleted. She seized distraction from the immediate things: the weather, the next swallow of water, the ever-forward draw of time.

"Mai!"

It was Anh Phuoc. She stood up, hauled herself on weak legs along the gunwale, toward the rear of the boat. Past the hatch she suddenly saw Truong—propped up against the rusty mast of the derrick-crane, his chin drooping onto his chest, arms bony and limp by his sides.

Mai leapt forward, swiping her elbows and knees from side to side to clear space. The surrounding people watched listlessly.

"Water!"

No one reacted. She looked around and spotted an army flask—grabbed it, swiveled the cap open, held it to his mouth. A thin trickle ran over his rubbery lips before the flask was snatched away. She looked up and saw a man's face, twisted in hate the moment he struck her, his knuckles hard as a bottle against her cheek. She fell over and covered Truong's body.

"She stole water."

"I'll pay it back," said Anh Phuoc roughly.

Truong started coughing. Mai sat back, her cheek burning, and mumbled apology in the direction of the man. He was picking the flask up from the ground. People glanced over, disturbed by the waste. There had been a minor outcry the previous evening when a woman—an actress, people said—had used the last of her ration to wash her face.

Truong squinted up at Mai. Everything about him: the dark sore of his face, his disproportioned, skeletal limbs, seemed to be ceding its sense of solidity. She touched his blistered cheek with her fingers—was reminded of the sting on her own cheek from the man's blow.

"Ma," he wheezed.

"It's alright," she said. "Ma is coming. Chi is here."

"Where's Quyen?" asked Anh Phuoc. He stood up quickly and walked off.

Truong said, "Child wanted to count the people."

He coughed again, the air scraping through his throat. Watching him, a helpless feeling welled up within Mai and started to coalesce at the front of her skull. "Child," she whispered.

Quyen arrived. She seemed to be moving within a slower state, her face drawn, hair tangled. She saw Truong and bent down to him. "Look," she murmured, "you hurt yourself."

"He fainted," said Mai.

"Why didn't Child stay with Ma?"

"I don't like it down there," he said.

"Oh, Mai," Quyen exclaimed, turning to her. "Are you all right?"

"He shouldn't be in the sun. He needs more water."

"It's too dark to count down there," Truong said. He brought up his arms, dangled them loosely over his knees. An old man's pose. Quyen squatted down and enfolded him, clinching him between her elbows, raking one hand through his hair and cupping his forehead with the other.

"I was so tired," said Quyen. "Thank you."

"He needs more water."

"Does Child know?" She was speaking to Truong. "Does Child know how lucky he is? To have Chi Mai look after him?"

Anh Phuoc leaned down close to both of them. "Come with me," he muttered. They followed him forward to the pilothouse, everyone watching as they passed. Once inside he closed the door. Carefully, he measured out a capful of water from a plastic carton and administered it into Truong's mouth.

The sight—even the smell—of the water roused an appalling ache in Mai's stomach, but she said nothing.

"Good boy," said Anh Phuoc.

Quyen's eyes followed the carton. "Is that all there is?"

Holding the tiller with one hand, he reached down and opened the cupboard beneath it. Three plastic white cartons.

"That's all," he said, "unless it rains."

"How long will it last?"

"Another day. Two at the most."

Her temple still aching, Mai looked out of the pilothouse windows. From up here she could see the full length and breadth of the boat: every inch of it clogged with rags and black-tufted heads and sunburned flesh. Up here would be the best place to count people. She wrenched her eyes away from the water carton and looked out instead at the sky. Not a cloud in sight. But the sky was full of deceit—it looked the same everywhere. She looked at the horizon, long and pale and eye-level all around them. Whatever direction she looked, it fell away into more water.

THE TENTH DAY DAWNED. Engines dead, the boat drifted on. Gray shadows strafing the water behind it. The detachable sail hoisted onto a short mast's yard and men taking turns, croaking directions to each other as they tried to steer the boat, as best they could, to the south.

Mai watched Truong with renewed intensity. Since Mai's recovery Quyen had kept to herself, remaining huddled, during the day as well as night, underneath the companionway stairs where they all slept. That morning Mai had found her sitting in the slatted light, staring vacantly into the dark hold. Squeezed between two old women.

"How is Truong?" Quyen asked her quietly.

Mai said, "I keep telling him to come down."

"He doesn't like it down here."

Mai nodded, not knowing what to say.

Quyen dropped her chin and closed her eyes. Mai looked her over. She didn't look sick.

"Is Chi alright?"

Quyen nodded almost impatiently. One of the women beside

her spat into her hands. When Quyen looked up her face was distant, drawn in unsparing lines.

"Look after him, *nha?* Please."

Above deck, each hour stretched out its hot minutes. Mai lay on her back under the derrick-crane, her head against someone's shin, limbs interwoven with her neighbors'. Truong wedged beside her. The crane cast a shadow that inched up their bodies. She threw her sleeve over her face to ward off the sweltering sun. At one point a wind blew in and the boat began to sway, lightly, in the water. She was riding her father's shoulders. Her mother watching them happily. Whenever he was home he brought with him some quality that filled her mother so there was enough left, sometimes, for her to be happy.

Truong started singing. Softly—to himself—so softly she wouldn't have heard him if her ear hadn't been inches from his mouth. She gradually shifted her arm down so she could hear better. He sang the ballad from the third night. She listened, hardly daring to breathe, watching the now-darkening sky knitting together the rigs and cables of the crane above them as though they were the branches of trees.

When he finished, the silence that surged in afterward was unbearable. Mai reached across her body and gently took hold of his arm.

"Who taught Child how to sing like that?"

He didn't answer.

THE NEXT MORNING, back below deck, she woke up to find a puddle of vomit next to his curled-up, sleeping body. It gleamed gray in the early light of dawn.

"The child has the sickness," a voice said without a second thought. It was one of the old women who had camped with them beneath the companionway stairs. The hatch was open and light flowed in like a mist, dimly illuminating the three other bodies entangled in their nook. The deeper recess of the hold remained black.

"No, he doesn't," said Mai.

"Poor child. He is not the last. Such a pity."

"Be quiet!" Mai covered her mouth, abashed, but no one reproached her. Several bodies stirred on the other side of the stairs.

Barely awake, Quyen rolled over to her son and propped herself up on an elbow. She brushed his cheek with her knuckles. For a second, in the half-light, Mai thought she saw an expression of horror move across her friend's face.

"Child is sorry," Mai murmured to the old woman.

Truong's eyes were glazed when he opened them. He looked like a burnt ghost. He leaned over, away from his mother, and dry-retched. There was nothing left in him to expel. Another of their neighbors, a man who smelled of stale tobacco, averted his legs casually.

"What it can do to you," the old woman said, her gums stained crimson from chewing betel leaves, "the ocean."

"Does Child's stomach hurt?" asked Mai.

"Yes."

"What it can steal from you and never give back. My husband, both my daughters."

"It's just a stomach-ache," said Quyen, then looked up as though daring the old woman—or anyone—to disagree. A gang of eyes, unmoving, inexpressive, watched them from the shadows.

That evening, Anh Phuoc ladled out the last rations of water. He shuffled wearily through the boat, repeating the same account to anyone who stopped him, intoning his interlocutors' names as though that were the only consolation left him to offer them. Weak moans and thick silences trailed him.

When Mai poured her ration into Truong's cup, Quyen frowned, and then flinched away. "Thank you," she said at last. For the first time she used the word for "younger sister."

"It's nothing. I already took a sip."

"Poor child," repeated the old woman, shaking her head.

Truong took some water in, then coughed some of it out. People looked over. In the dusk light his face was pallid and shiny.

He opened his mouth. "Ma," he said.

"I'm here," said Quyen.

"Ma."

Quyen bit her lips, wiped the sweat from Truong's brow with a corner of her shirt. Finally his eyes focused and he seemed to look straight at Mai.

"It's so hot," he said.

"*Thoi*," said Quyen, dabbing above his eyes, around his hairline.

"I want to go up."

"Sleep, my beloved. My little prince. Sleep."

Mai wanted desperately to say something to him—something useful, or comforting—but no words came. She got up to close the hatch door.

The old woman took out a betel leaf and inserted it into the slit of her toothless mouth.

HIS SICKNESS FOLLOWED the usual course. Muscle soreness and nausea in the early stages. That evening his blisters began to rise, some of them bleeding pus. He became too weak to swallow water.

In the middle of the night, Mai woke to find Truong half draped over her stomach. His weight on her so light as to be almost imperceptible, as though his body were already nothing more than bones and air. "Everything will be fine," she whispered into the darkness, her thoughts, still interlaced with dream, scattered remotely across space and gray sea. Back home she'd slept on the same mat as Loc. Her mother by the opposite wall. She reached down and touched Truong's brow.

He stirred awake.

"Is Child alright?"

"I want to go up."

The skin on his face was hot and moist. Mai lifted her eyes and noticed Quyen, mashed in the shadow of the companionway steps, staring at both of them.

"Take him," she said dully.

Mai found a spot for them by the pilothouse, surrounded by sleeping families. When dawn came, Truong's head slid with a slight thud onto the planking. Half asleep, Mai sought his shoulder, shook it. His body gave no response. She sat up and shook him again. His clothes stiff with dried sweat. Nothing.

"Truong," whispered Mai, feeling the worry build within her. She poked his cheek. It was still warm—thank heavens!—it was still warm. She checked his forehead: hotter than it had been last night. He was boiling up. His breath shallow and short. With agonizing effort she cradled his slight, inert body and bore him up the stairs into the pilothouse.

Anh Phuoc was slumped underneath the tiller, sleeping. Three infants were laid out side by side on the floor, swaddled in rags.

He woke up. "What is it?" He saw Truong in her arms. "Where's Quyen?"

She laid him down. Then she turned to find Quyen.

"Wait." Anh Phuoc got up, surveyed the boat through the windows, then retrieved a flask from behind the bank of gauges. He unscrewed the cap and poured a tiny trickle of water into a cup. "This was for them," he said, gesturing at the motionless babies. "How they've lasted twelve days I don't know." He screwed the flask cap back on and then, with tremendous care, handed her the cup. "But they won't make it either." He paused. "Let me find Quyen."

Truong wouldn't wake up. Mai dipped one finger into the cup, traced it along the inner line of his lips. Once it dried she dipped her finger again, ran it across his lips again. She did this over and over. One time she thought she saw his throat twitch. His face— the burnt, blistered skin, its spots and scabs—the deeper she looked, the more his features dissociated from one another until what she looked into, as she tended him, was not a face, but a brown and blasted landscape. Like a slow fire it drew the air from her lungs.

Commotion on deck. Someone shouting. She jolted awake, checked Truong—he was still unconscious, his fever holding. A weird tension suffusing the air. Another death? Mai opened the pilothouse door and asked a nearby woman what was happening.

"They saw whales," the woman said.

"Whales?"

"And then land birds."

It was as though she were sick again, her heart shocked out of its usual rhythm. "Land? They saw land?"

The woman shrugged.

All at once Quyen burst out of the hold, her hair disheveled and her eyes watery and red. She spotted Mai.

"Here!" Mai called out excitedly. "Chi Quyen, here!" She stood on tiptoes and scanned all the horizon she could see. Nothing. She looked again. "Someone said they saw land," she announced aloud. Realizing people were scowling at her, she turned toward Quyen. Too late she caught a new, rough aspect in her eyes. Quyen strode up into Mai's face.

"Where's my son?"

She pushed into the pilothouse. Mai stumbled back, tripping over the doorsill.

Inside, Quyen saw Truong and rushed toward him, lowering her head to his. She emitted a throaty cry and twisted around to face Mai.

"Stay away," she declared. "You've done enough!" Her voice was strained, on the verge of shrillness.

"Chi," gasped Mai.

"I've changed my mind," Quyen went on, the pitch of her words wavering. Her expression was wild, now—cunning. "He's my son! Not yours—mine!"

"*Thoi,*" a man's voice interjected.

Mai spun and saw Anh Phuoc in the doorway.

"What's the matter?"

Quyen glared at him. He waited for her to speak. Finally, her tone gone sullen, she said, "She took my son."

He sighed. "Mai was looking after him."

Quyen stared at him, incredulous, then started laughing. She clamped both hands over her mouth. Then, as though in embarrassment, she dipped her head, nuzzling Truong's chest like an animal. Mai watched it all. The thick dense knot back behind her temple. Quyen's body shuddered in tight bursts awhile, then, slowly, hitchingly, it began to calm. It seemed for a moment as though Quyen might never look up again. When she did, her face was utterly blanched of expression.

"Mai wouldn't hurt Truong," said Anh Phuoc tiredly. "She loves him."

Quyen threw him a spent smile. "I know." But she didn't look at Mai. Instead, she turned and again bent over the unconscious shape of her son. That was when she began to cry—silently at first, inside her body, but then, breath by breath, letting out her wail until the whole boat could hear.

* * *

HE WAS HER SHAME and yet she loved him. What did that make her? She had conceived him when she was young, and passed him off to her aunt in Da Lat to raise, and then she had gotten married. With the war and all its disturbances, she had never gone back to visit him. Worse, she had never told her husband.

"He would leave me," she told Mai. "He will."

But she couldn't abandon her only son—not to the Communists—not if she could find a way out of the country. Even if he didn't want to leave, and even if he didn't know her. Her aunt had balked, and Quyen had been forced to abduct him. She'd been wrong to have him—she knew that—but she'd been even more wrong to give him away. Surely, she thought, she was right to take him with her. Then, when she saw him weakening—then falling sick—she realized that perhaps he was being punished for her shame. Whether he lived or died— perhaps it wasn't for her to decide.

She begged Mai to forgive her.

Mai didn't say anything.

"He doesn't love his own mother," said Quyen.

"That's not true."

Quyen leaned down and unstuck his hair from his forehead, and parted it. They'd moved him back down into the hold, under the companionway stairs, for shade.

Quyen sniffed. "It's fair. What kind of mother watches that happen to her only son—and does nothing?"

"You were sick."

Quyen turned to her with a strange, shy expression, then lowered her gaze.

"I knew you would take care of him," she said.

"Of course."

"No." She looked down at her son's fevered face. "Forgive me. It was more than that. My thoughts were mad." She gave out a noise like a hollow chuckle. "I thought of asking you . . ." she said. "I was going to ask you to take him in—to pretend he was your son." She shook her head in wonderment. "He likes you so much. Yes. I thought—just until I could tell my husband the truth."

Mai remained quiet, her mind turbulent.

Quyen sniffed again. "*Thoi,*" she declared. "Enough!" Caressing her forearm—still scored with rope marks from the storm six days ago—she smiled into the air. "It's my fault."

"Chi."

"Whatever happens to him."

Mai stared down, unsteadily, at the marred, exposed field of Truong's face.

"You don't have to answer," Quyen continued in her bright voice. "Whatever happens, I deserve it."

HE ENTERED INTO THE WORST of it that afternoon, moving fitfully into and out of sleep. His breath short, irregular. Their neighbors kindly made some space for him to lie down. When some children came to visit, Quyen rebuffed them without even looking. Mai sat silently opposite them, next to the old betel-gummed woman, transfixed by her friend's intensity.

Then, at the end of the afternoon—after five long hours—Truong's small body suddenly unclenched and his breath eased. The lines on his forehead cleared. It seemed, unbelievably, that he had prevailed.

"It's over," Mai said joyfully. "Chi, the fever has broken."

Quyen cradled him in her lap, rocking him lightly. "Yes, yes, yes, yes," she sighed, "Sleep, my beloved."

His clothes were soaked with sweat. For a fleeting moment, as

Mai saw his face unfastened from its distress, the fantasy crossed her mind that he was dead. She shook it off. Quyen's hair fell over her son's face. They both appeared to her strangely now, as if at an increasing remove, as if she were trying to hold them in view through the stained, swaying window of a bus.

Truong hiccuped, opened his eyes and rasped, "Ma has some water?" With an almost inaudible moan Quyen hunched over and showered his brow with kisses. Outside the evening was falling, the last of the light sallow on his skin. After a while Truong gathered his breath again.

"Ma will sing to Child?"

"Sing for the poor child," said the old woman.

Quyen nodded. She started singing: a Southern lullaby Mai hadn't heard for years, her voice more tender than Mai had imagined it could be.

Truong shook his head weakly. "No—not that one." He made an effort to swallow. "My favorite song."

"Your favorite song," repeated Quyen. She bit her lip, frowning, then swung around mutely, strickenly, to Mai.

Mai reached out to stroke Truong's hair. She said, "But Child must sleep, *nha?*" She waited for him to completely shut his eyes. Quyen found her hand and held it. Mai cleared her throat, then, surprised to find her voice even lower, hoarser than Quyen's, she started singing:

> *I am the vigil moon that sheds you light*
> *My soul abides within the Thousand Peaks;*
> *Where drunk with wine and Long-Tuyen sword you seek*
> *And slaughter all the leopards of the night.*
>
> *And in the steps of Gioi Tu, seize Lau-Lan*
> *And quash the Man-Khe rivers into one.*
> *You wear the scarlet shadow of the sun:*
> *And yet your steed is whiter than my palm . . .*

Abruptly her voice broke off, then she swallowed, picked up the thread of melody again, and sang it through, her voice as hard as Quyen's face was tender, her voice resolute and unwavering, sang it through to the very end.

The old woman nodded to herself.

THE NEXT MORNING — the morning of their thirteenth day—a couple of the fishermen sighted land. A swell of excitement, like a weak current, ran through the boat. People looked at one another as though for the first time.

"We made it," someone quietly announced, returning from deck. He paused on the companionway, his head silhouetted against the sunlight. In the glare, Mai couldn't make out his face. He said, "We're safe now." The words deep in his throat.

Quyen and Truong were underneath the stairs. Mai had left them to themselves during the night. Now, with those others strong enough, Mai followed the man above deck. Outside, the dawn sun steeped through her, as though her body were made of paper. Dizziness overwhelmed her when she saw the half-empty deck—had they been so depleted? She thought, with an odd pang, of Truong, his incessant counting. Then she saw the prow, teeming with people, all peering ahead, attitudes stalled in their necks and shoulders. She made her way forward, then spotted, far ahead, the tiny breakers on the reefs, and behind those, the white sand like a bared smile. Birds hanging in midair over the water.

During the night she had come to her decision. Her thoughts starting always with Truong and ending always with her father, upright in his hospital bed, staring at some invisible situation in front of him. A street with its lights turned off. She came into morning feeling a bone-deep ache through her body. The boat would land—they would all land—Mai would write to her family, and wait for them, and then she would look after Truong as if he were her own child. The decision dissolved within her, rose up with the force of joy. She would tell Quyen. She would look after him, completely, unconditionally, and try not to think about the moment when Quyen might ask her to stop.

Nearly weightless in her body, Mai descended the companionway. When she reached the bottom she spun and searched behind the stairs. There they were. The hold awash with low talk.

"Chi Quyen."

She was about to call out again when she sensed something amiss. Quyen's back—folded over Truong's sleeping form—it was too stiff. The posture too awkward.

Mai moved closer. "Chi?" she asked.

Quyen's crouched torso expanded, took in air. Without turning around she said, "What will I do now?" Her voice brute, flat.

Mai squatted down. Her heart tripping faster and faster, up into her throat.

Quyen said, "He didn't."

She said, "All night. He wouldn't wake up."

She was wrong, thought Mai. What did she know, thought Mai. When she'd left last night, Truong had been recovering. He'd been fine. He'd been asking Mai, over and over, to sing to him. What could have happened?

Quyen shifted to one side. He was bundled up in a blanket. The bundle tapered at one end—where his legs must have been. Mai could see no part of him. How could this be the end of it? She wrung the heels of her hands into her eyes, as if the fault lay with them. Then she felt Quyen's face, cool with shock, next to her own, rough and wet and cool against her knuckles, speaking into her ear. At first she recoiled from Quyen's touch. What was she saying? She was asking Mai for help. She was asking Mai to help her carry him. It was time, she said. Time, which had distended every moment on the boat—until there had seemed to be no shape to it—seemed now to snap violently shut, crushing all things into this one task. They were standing—when had they gotten up?—then they were kneeling, facing each other over the length of him. Quyen circumspect in her movements, as though loath to take up any more space than her son now needed. She seemed not to see anything she looked at. Together, the two of them brought the bundle aft, through the shifting, silent crowd, past the derrick-crane, where a group of the strongest men waited. There, the wind turned a corner of the blanket over and revealed the small head, the ash beauty of his face, the new dark slickness of his skin. With a shudder Quyen fell to it and pressed and rubbed her lips against his cheek.

Anh Phuoc, standing with three other men, waited for Quyen to finish before touching her shoulder.

He said, to no one in particular, "We'll make land soon."

As though this were an order, Mai took Quyen's arm and led her the full span of the boat to the prow. Again, the crowd parted for them. They stood together in silence, the spray moistening their faces as they looked forward, focusing all their sight and thought on that blurry peninsula ahead, that impossible place, so that they would not be forced to behold the men at the back of the boat peeling the blanket off, swinging the small body once, twice, three times before letting go, tossing him as far behind the boat as possible so he would be out of sight when the sharks attacked.

Acknowledgments

For their patience, grace, enthusiasm and expertise, my deepest thanks to my editor, Robin Desser, and my agent, Eric Simonoff. Thanks also to Sarah Rothbard, Gabrielle Brooks, Sara Eagle, Paul Bogaards, Nicholas Latimer, and the rest of the superb team at Knopf.

For their invaluable early support, my thanks to Michael Ray, Brigid Hughes, Yiyun Li, Christina Thompson, Katherine Vaz, Hannah Tinti, and Bradford Morrow.

My heartfelt thanks to Ashley Capps, Leslie Jamison, David Sarno, Josh Rolnick, Fiona McFarlane, Salvatore Scibona, Danny Khalastchi, Chris Stuck, Ché Frye, Shiv Chandran, Priyanthi Milton, Meredith Rose, Marilynne Robinson, Ethan Canin, Lan Samantha Chang, James Alan McPherson, Margot Livesey, Chris Offutt, Adam Haslett, and Charles D'Ambrosio—friends, teachers, and readers all. Thanks also to Cecile Barendsma, Connie Brothers, Deb West, Maria Campbell, Josh Kendall, and Chris Lamb.

For their generous support, I am indebted to the Iowa Writers' Workshop, the Fine Arts Work Center in Provincetown, Phillips Exeter Academy, James Michener and the Copernicus Society of America, the MacDowell Colony, and the Corporation of Yaddo.

In memory of Frank Conroy.